SHERLOCK HOLMES

The Woman Who Wasn't

From the Journals of
John H. Watson, M.D.

Edited by
Kenton Hall

OAK TREE BOOKS

Published in 2024 by
Oak Tree Books
www.oaktreebooks.uk

Conceived and Edited by Kenton Hall
Artwork by Robert Hammond
Commissioning Editor Barnaby Eaton-Jones
Based on characters created by Sir Arthur Conan Doyle

Contents

The Woman Who Wasn't: Part One

It has been said of my friend, Sherlock Holmes—with varied intent—that he is a man of rare passions and even rarer pleasures.

The first count cannot be argued. I have commented, in previous accounts of our association, on the seemingly arbitrary nature of his expertise and obsessions and, I wager, it has passed into common knowledge via that route.

Of course, there *is* a rationale, and a strict one at that, behind their selection and attainment. I believe I have drawn ample attention to it—though my friend continues to mutter discontentedly about sensationalism—and I hope that it has gained respect even where it has not found understanding.

It is a lesson I have taken to heart myself. Indeed, whereas I might once have confessed myself bewildered at the need of any man to be able to distinguish one cigar maker from another on sight of the ash produced, or the hoofprint of a carriage horse from that of a pit pony, I now wonder at my own small-mindedness. Far too many guilty parties have been brought to justice—and, in turn, innocents rescued or avenged—on the basis of such arcane knowledge. There is method, in other words, and I'm no longer certain of the madness.

For all his gifts, however, there are areas of life into which Sherlock Holmes seldom strays and about which he is, by his own admission, as ignorant as those who decry his deductive powers as sham or sorcery.

1889 was a year that would see us both tested to our limits. Some of the adventures and misadventures of that period I have chronicled previously. Others remain sealed behind vows of privacy or decency and will remain so while their participants still live.

But then there are those stories that have simply awaited the correct alignment of the stars, in order to be revealed.

But I am getting ahead of myself.

The year in question, of course, followed a period of great change, both within the walls of Holmes' Baker Street rooms and without. I had not long married my beloved Mary and my time with my friend was, understandably, more limited than when we had shared a home. Nonetheless, as regular readers will be aware, he continued to take me into his confidence—as my practice and spousal responsibilities allowed—and our association never failed to enliven my existence.

But there is still much, as I have noted, that has remained hidden. It has taken fresh upheaval for me to draw a connection between a number of cases to which Sherlock Holmes applied himself during those twelve months and perceive a greater meaning. I have no doubt that Holmes himself would laugh tolerantly at the thought of my having been so blind; I cannot imagine but that he reached the same conclusions many years ago. If he acted on them, beyond the events to which I was witness, I remain none the wiser. He certainly did not speak of it.

But then, perhaps, my part in the drama has yet to be played out in its entirety. It may be that there is an entry in the casebook of Sherlock Holmes whose mysteries have not been entirely disentangled. If so, I am certain it lies somewhere between the lines presented here: the case of the "woman who wasn't" and those various adventures that touched, however tangentially, the hem of their garment.

In the early days of that year, quite apart from the practicalities that restricted me, I was little inclined towards mystery or crime. My attentions were divided between my new home with Mary and the expanding medical practice that made it possible.

Nonetheless, I did my best to visit Baker Street whenever time permitted. I still felt a sense of duty to my friend, both as a Boswell to his Johnson and, to be frank, as a concerned doctor to a favourite patient. I worried, to Mary's evident amusement, how well he would manage without me. She seemed to think this a rather patronising attitude to take towards a grown man with an international reputation. But then, I had not yet taken my new bride into my confidence regarding my friend's weakness for chemical stimulation when other occupations failed him.

We made a perhaps foolhardy attempt to include Holmes in our first Christmas celebrations as a wedded couple and he, to his credit, did make a singular appearance one evening towards the end of December, during which he offered sincere, if stilted, congratulations to the woman of the house, consumed a single glass of sherry and one of a pair of cigars produced from the pocket of his coat, before bidding us both goodnight and disappearing into the night, no doubt on the trail of some unfortunate criminal or the other.

The New Year came and went without word from my friend, though Mrs Hudson did me the good service of reporting on his moods and movements, to the degree that she was able. Holmes, for his part, must have tolerated my curiosity, for he was more than capable of veiling whatever parts of his life and work he wished to keep to himself. For the most part, I was relieved to hear, he was embroiled in a number of challenging cases and, thus, in good form.

I was surprised, therefore—though not unhappy—to receive a missive at my surgery one mid-January afternoon from one of the younger members of the Baker Street Irregulars, a good-natured, if bashful, boy of six or seven named Thomas. His surname, if he had ever possessed one, was lost to memory and the backstreets of London.

He handed the note to me with one hand while wiping his nose across the back of the other.

'From Mr Holmes?' I asked.

'Yes, sir.'

'Did he ask you to wait for a reply?'

'No, sir. Only he said I was to tell you to come at once.'

I smiled to myself. Some things would never alter.

'If it was convenient?'

Thomas blinked back at me.

'He didn't say nothing about that, sir.'

I laughed and resisted ruffling the boy's hair. I knew from experience that the children who formed Holmes' unofficial investigative force tended to resist any form of affection, however paternal. I would have been surprised, sadly, if they had any experience of it. Holmes, for all his supposed coldness, seemed to have struck the perfect balance in his dealings with them. Firm, respectful, pragmatic, even a little distant—with nothing more promised than a genuine 'well done' whenever it was earned. And, as a result, they'd run into hell for him, without a second's hesitation.

'No, I expect he didn't.'

I dug a coin from my waistcoat pocket and placed it in Thomas' hand.

'You may tell Mr Holmes that I will be with him presently.'

Thomas tried hard to keep his gaze from the shilling in his palm.

'Does that mean now, sir?'

'Yes, Thomas.'

Thomas gave the professional nod of a much older boy, which sent a pang of sadness through my heart, then turned sharply on his heel and ran back into the streets he called home.

***

'Holmes?' I said, as I entered the rooms we had once shared at 221B Baker Street.

Mrs Hudson had admitted me quite happily, full of New Year's wishes and excited questions about Mary and our new home. Holmes, she added, awaited me in our old, familiar sitting room. Indeed, according to that good lady, he had been keenly looking forward to my arrival.

There was, however, no immediate sign of him. Nor, for that matter, was there any of the expected detritus of abandoned experiments and half-eaten dinners that often accompanied his most distracted moments. In fact, the place looked as though it had been recently cleaned and then, for good measure, preserved in amber.

'Holmes?' I repeated. 'It's Watson.'

'Ah, my dear fellow!'

I jumped as Holmes appeared, like a jack-in-the-box, from behind one of the two chairs that faced one another in the centre of the room, from the furthest of which he had worked out the problems of paupers and princes.

My friend chuckled as I clutched the back of my own regular seat—in which I, for my part, had often napped, the afternoon edition spread neatly over my knees.

'It is fortunate,' I managed after an embarrassed moment of silence, 'that my heart is in good order.'

'Unlike your shoulder. The cold weather has been unkind to your old wound.'

I didn't bother to register my surprise. But I was determined to demonstrate that I was no longer entirely under his sway. Taking a quick survey of my immediate surroundings, I spotted an immediate solution.

'I grabbed the chair with the stronger of my two arms, despite it being further away.'

Holmes gave an appreciative nod and slung himself into his chair, one leg folding neatly over the other.

'Very good, Watson. We'll make a detective of you yet.'

I beamed, rather more than I meant to, and took my seat. Albeit with care.

'It was elementary, my dear Holmes.'

'Although, in fact, you informed of the fact when I visited you three weeks ago. I don't blame you for not remembering. A drop of sherry had been taken.' He smiled broadly. 'I surmised that as the weather has remained more or less constant in the interim that, alas, your pain must have followed suit.'

I laughed and shook my head, as much at my own continued ability to fall for my friend's verbal sleights of hand as anything else.

'This too shall pass,' I said.

'Just so,' replied Holmes. 'Now, you must be wondering why I sent for you.'

'Not overly. It wouldn't be the first time and I suspect it won't be the last. May I confidently deduce that there is a mystery afoot?'

'You may, Watson and without fear of contradiction. And a most compellingly knotty problem it is too. I shall need you at your best.'

'I shall endeavour not to disappoint.' I leant forward, feeling a tingle of the old excitement in my bones, despite my best efforts. 'What is the case?'

'Oh, I don't know that yet, my dear Watson. I've yet to hear the story in question. But what do you make of this?'

From the pocket of his smoking jacket, he produced a note—a folded piece of what appeared to be some antiquated parchment, two halves of a thick wax seal broken at its edges. The paper looked almost too frail to have supported such a weight.

Holmes handed it over gently.

'Tell me what you see.'

I knew better than to leap to a reading of the note's contents, so instead, holding it gingerly between forefingers and thumbs, I examined it from every angle.

'The paper is old. Ancient, one might even imagine.'

'One certainly might.'

I lifted it to my nose.

'It was perfumed at one time, but the scent has faded.'

'Oh, excellent.' Holmes clapped his hands together with glee.

'The seal is not that of royalty, but certainly from an aristocratic family.'

'You astound me, Watson.'

'There are slight burn marks along one of the edges, as if the paper was rescued from a fire.' I thought carefully. 'Perhaps the surviving part of a larger sheet.'

'I really will have to consider retiring, Watson. You surpass yourself. Now, I know you are impatient to read the note itself. Please do so.'

With great care, I unfolded the note and read the lines within. The line, that is, for there were only four words, neatly printed above the letter 'A'—its sender's initial, I presumed.

'I am not she,' I read aloud.

In confusion, I turned the note over in my hand, sure I must have missed something.

'Now what do you make of that?' asked Holmes.

'I don't know what to make of it, Holmes.'

'No, nor do I. And I find that immensely attractive.'

'But there is no indication of what the sender wants from you. Or even that they want anything at all.'

'Not so, Watson. The note was addressed to me. And, dear fellow, to you—' He handed over the far more modern envelope in which the note had been delivered. The address indeed read: To Mr Sherlock Holmes and Doctor John Watson, 221B Baker Street. There was no stamp, however, suggesting it had been delivered by hand. Suggestive of urgency? 'Clearly something awaits us to which our sender's protest of identity is key.'

'I am not she,' I repeated. 'Not who?'

'Well that, obviously, remains to be seen.'

'But when? Surely, we can't wait indefinitely for a case to arise to which this vague missive can be attached?'

'We needn't. The answer will be with us by 6 o'clock this evening.'

'How—?'

'Watson, you've come so far. Would you spoil one of my increasingly rare number of opportunities to surprise you?'

'Very well. I take it I should send word to Mary that I will not be home for dinner.'

Holmes inclined his head.

'Nor breakfast, to be on the safe side. We would not want Mrs Watson to pace the marital bedchamber with worry.'

'Would she have cause?'

Holmes' eyes darkened briefly.

'Very possibly.' He paused and I had the sense that the next sentence came at a price. 'I would understand if you have lost the taste for such dangers. Or if your newfound marital state precludes your partaking in them.'

'On the contrary,' I said reassuringly. 'If there are evils to be faced, I know my wife would rather a courageous husband than a milksop.'

'She has no fear of the latter, my dear Watson. I don't suppose you brought your revolver?'

I produced it from my pocket.

'Good man,' said Holmes. 'Let us hope it is only a precaution. Now, we have an hour or so to wait. I'm sure you have built up a new repertoire of medical misadventures with which to pass the time.'

I grinned.

'I'm sure I can oblige. If you promise not to snore.'

***

The sound of the knocker upon the door of 221B woke me with a start.

I was, at first, taken aback to find myself in pitch-blackness, and briefly concerned that I had slept longer than intended. But then I perceived Holmes, still in his chair, his fingers steepled beneath his nose and his eyes focused on the door with hawk-like intensity.

The curtains had been firmly drawn, which explained the darkness of the room, despite, I assumed, the relative youth of the evening.

'Holmes,' I whispered. He broke his statue-like pose just long enough to wave a finger sharply. I fell back into silence.

We heard the familiar sound of Mrs Hudson opening the front door, taking particulars and directing our guest—whomever they may be—towards Holmes' rooms.

It was followed by footfall—a quick, heavy tread, suggesting a large man, either in a temper or a hurry. These were, however, easy enough deductions to make, given that they might describe any number of Holmes' clients. I knew my friend would already be cataloguing an entire, astonishingly detailed life from those few steps, but I did not claim his gifts.

The door burst open, eschewing the courtesy of a knock, and we were graced for the first but, alas, not final time by Sir Harrison Frain. He was a tall man, though equally broad—the clear recipient of fine living and diminished activity. His chin was bare, though he sported a thick moustache and side whiskers in recompense. Even in the dim light, his aspect was cruel and self-satisfied.

He seemed astonished, at first, to find himself in the dark, but soon rallied.

'Holmes. Where are you, you devil?'

I glanced to where Holmes had been seated, but the chair was empty. For a man who had long proclaimed a preference for the sedentary life, he was swift enough when the mood was upon him. In fact, I believe his claim to idleness a pose, another of those steps he took to maintain a sense of wonder around his every thought and action.

There was the soft hiss of a match and a lamp on the mantelpiece began to glow. In its aura stood Holmes, a small smile of triumph on his lips.

'Sir Harrison Frain, I presume,' he said.

Frain swiftly repurposed his fear and surprise into rage.

'How do you know that, sir?'

'You have christened me a devil, sir,' was Holmes' reply. 'Was I wrong to imagine the suggestion of some familiarity?'

'You're a devil, all right,' said Frain, feeling himself on a sounder footing. 'And a bounder. Now, where is my daughter?'

Holmes and I exchanged a glance. Many men and women had entered this room, in various stages of distress. Angry, lonely, bereft and becalmed. None of them had suggested personal impropriety on Holmes' part. I struggled to repress a laugh.

Holmes, for his part, simply blinked.

'You have two daughters, Sir Harrison. One married and the other still at home. Which do you propose I have misappropriated?'

Sir Harrison growled and marched further into the lamplit room, bearing down on Holmes with all of his impressive girth. My friend did not move an inch, though I fancied I saw his meticulously trained muscles tighten against any eruption of violence.

'Ah, but you prove my suspicion. How else would you hold such intimate knowledge of my family?'

Holmes held up a hand. A stranger to Baker Street might have claimed sorcery, so instantaneously it stopped the furious father in his tracks.

'Your daughter's betrothal was reported in all of the papers, Sir Harrison. Some months ago. I know because the announcement of my friend Dr Watson's nuptials was printed in the same edition and he drew my attention to it on several occasions. I suspect he was ensuring that I would remember the date.'

Sir Harrison bristled.

'That's as may be. But what of my other daughter?'

'Your tone is that of a father who fears his child has been persuaded into misadventure. A daughter who had broken her wedding vows might incense a man, I'm sure. But you fear a loss of innocence. I deduced therefore the existence of a second, most likely younger, daughter. That she lives at home I draw from the fact that the letter I received from her earlier today bore your seal and was, therefore, most likely sent from your home at Allerton Hall. I confess your elder daughter *may* have been visiting, but I suspect not.'

'You had a letter from my daughter?'

'Sir Harrison, let us not argue over knowledge of which we both have possession. You know that she has written to me, or you would not be here. What was it? A discarded draft of the communiqué? Discovered in the grate?'

The look on the man's face confirmed the truth of Holmes' conclusion.

'And your first thought was that I,' Holmes covered a smirk with the back of his hand, 'was your daughter's lover and that she had flown to me behind your back. An elopement at midnight, or some other ludicrous notion.'

Sir Harrison glared briefly at my friend before the fight left him and his shoulders slumped, his height diminished by obvious sorrow. I left my chair and guided him into it.

There were tears in his eyes when he spoke again.

'You must forgive me, Mr Holmes. I am not a man given to emotional displays but my child is missing. Do you have children, sir?'

'I have not. Nor am I in the habit of seizing upon those of others.'

'Of course. That was foolish of me. You are not the man. I should have known that from the off. I have simply grown desperate.'

Holmes walked to the window and drew back the curtain. The evening had darkened, but it lifted the worse of the shadows.

'Watson. The lamps. If you would be so kind.'

I nodded and began the process of illuminating the room.

Holmes retook his seat, opposite the diminished knight of the realm and leant back.

'I think, Sir Harrison,' he said, 'that you owe us the tale of what has brought you here. Then perhaps we can shed light on more than simply the room.'

***

'I was not always such a shambling wretch as you see before you,' began Sir Harrison with surprising self-effacement. 'Indeed, I was, for many years, the proudest of fathers. My daughters were the lights of my life. Diverse in outlook and aspect but that is the wager placed when one has offspring.'

Holmes bade him continue. He had little interest in the man's thoughts on parenthood.

'Janet, my eldest, is, as you say, married. Her husband is a good man, possessed of a decent fortune, and I rejoiced at their union. Indeed, within the year, I hope to be blessed with a grandchild. I have never had any worries with Janet. She takes after her mother in that way. Loyal to a fault, careful, sensible.'

'Your other daughter does not aspire to these qualities.'

Sir Harrison sighed heavily.

'She does not, Mr Holmes. Nor, I suspect, are they amongst her gifts. Please do not mistake me, Anastasia hasn't an unkind bone in her body. And I believe she truly attempts to please. But she has a rebellious spirit. I fear she may have inherited that from me. As a young man, I was known to flirt with hazards. In business, indeed, it has often proved beneficial.'

'You are a banker, I believe.'

'I am.'

'So the journey between risk and security must be a familiar one for you.'

'You have put it plainly and well. And it far too well describes my daughter's approach to life. She has shown no inclination to marry, no drive to acquire the skills of a wife and mother. She would follow me into my business were she a man. She has an aptitude for it, has done from a child.'

'But something has occurred recently which worries you more than is usual.'

'Exactly that, Mr Holmes. Anastasia has taken to disappearing for days at a time and has been unwilling to give any explanation. That degree of insolence is beyond what I can stand. Still, at her mother's behest, I chose not to take immediate action but rather hired a man to watch her movements. I would prefer to make an accusation based on facts, rather than fear. I know my daughter and she is far more likely to answer the case if I can put it to her without doubt.'

Holmes had sniffed contemptuously at the thought of the sort of man hired for such work, but now nodded his understanding.

'The man has returned with his report.'

'Yes.'

'There is no sign of your daughter.'

'How did you know that?'

'Simplicity itself. Had the man discovered your daughter's whereabouts, you would have gone to her. Instead, you are here, following the only lead remaining to you. Her letter. This suggests that the man followed your daughter, but lost sight of her.'

Sir Harrison slammed his fist against the chair arm.

'Yes, dammit. The fool tracked her all across London, to a boarding house, only to claim that she vanished, all but before his very eyes.'

'But he did provide one piece of salient information, did he not?'

'Yes.'

'A man. At the same boarding house. Who appeared so soon after your daughter as to raise suspicions.'

Sir Harrison's head dropped in shame.

'Yes. Yet when I visited the boarding house, the only name on record was that of my daughter, albeit using her mother's maiden name.'

Holmes leaned forward, clicking his tongue in thought.

'And your daughter has failed to return since.'

'It is now two weeks hence. Her mother is in despair.' He hesitated briefly. 'As am I.'

'You were right to come to me, Sir Harrison,' he said finally. 'I will take the case. But I have one further question for you before we proceed.'

Sir Harrison's face had brightened when Holmes had pledged his assistance.

'Anything, sir. If it's a question of payment—'

Holmes waved a dismissive hand.

'No, Sir Harrison. What I wish to know is what you will do with your daughter once she is located.'

'I don't see how—'

'I will not place this young woman into the hands of a father who might mistreat her for her follies.'

The man looked stricken.

'I love my daughter, Mr Holmes. I simply want her safely returned. And out of the grasp of any adventurers of whom she may have fallen foul.'

Holmes clapped his hands together and sprang from his chair with such force that Sir Harrison flinched.

'Capital. Leave the matter with us, Sir Harrison. We will locate your wandering offspring.' Holmes turned to the mantel, produced his pipe and began to fill it with tobacco from the pouch hung there.

'Thank you, gentlemen.' Sir Harrison stood uneasily. He had neither expected the matter to be decided so swiftly nor ended so abruptly.

I walked him to the door, reassuring him—as I was so often called upon to do—that once Sherlock Holmes had put his mind to a problem, its solution was as good as hit upon.

I listened to the man's footsteps descend before turning back to my friend.

'Surely, Holmes,' I said, 'this case is beneath you. The girl's taken herself off with this mystery man. They've probably eloped by now and will return home to face her father when the money runs out.'

From within a cloud of tobacco smoke, Holmes looked at me slyly, then tutted.

'And yet you are widely accepted to be, of the two of us, the more romantic. Would you reduce everything to such brutal pragmatism? This is a case with unique features. It will require some thought.'

I knew from experience what that would entail. Several days scratching away at his violin or prostrate upon the chaise longue, dead to the world.

'Very well. I shall leave you to your contemplation in that case. I will, of course, return if and when you need me.'

Holmes nodded his assent.

'I suspect I will strike upon a course of action within the week. In the interim, perhaps you could do me a service?'

'Anything.'

'I know I have been dismissive of your accounts of our adventures in the past, but I wonder if you might consult your records on my behalf.'

'Of course,' I said. 'Is there anything in particular you hope I might find?'

'No, no,' he replied, moving to the window and gazing out over Baker Street. 'But pay particular attention to disappearances. Mysterious or otherwise. There is something about this case that strikes me as familiar.'

'Very well.'

I knew better than to wait for thanks, or for any further instructions, and so headed home, to Mary and a decent meal.

The next afternoon, having seen my patients for the day, I retired to my study and began to examine those cases that, for whatever reason, I had yet to put before the public. I had no idea what Holmes was looking for, so I cast my net widely.

The Adventure of the Stuffed Pekinese

H.E. Roulo

The first case on which I laid my hands was a peculiar one and my memories of it vague. According to my notes, it had taken place some two or three years previously, while in the midst of another much larger affair, involving the disappearance of the heir to one of the great Royal Houses of Europe. Indeed, with Holmes' instructions in mind, it was that case I had hoped to consult and for which I was searching when I came upon this manuscript. But as I read on, I became increasingly convinced that this manner of case might be precisely what Holmes had in mind.

Despite—or perhaps because of—the complexity of the puzzle at hand, I wrote at the time, Holmes had agreed to leave our apartments at 221B Baker Street to clear his head. The day being brisk, we made our way leisurely to the shop around the corner for tea and to obtain a copy of The Globe for later inspection. Holmes called the paper lad by name, and I imagined he might belong to that particular army of youths and wanderers sometimes employed by Holmes to collect information. I concluded that our task had likely been two-fold. Sadly, no additional information appeared with the paper, and we walked back to Holmes' rooms in contemplative silence.

I was therefore distracted when Mrs Hudson, met us at the door, rubbing her apron with anxious hands. The air smelled of sandalwood, musk, and lilacs. I wondered if she had received a bouquet but spied no flowers, only a small wooden crate by the entry table.

Holmes entered at his usual pace, his keen eyes surveying the room, clearly intending to deduce what had transpired before Mrs Hudson could speak. She followed a step behind, muttering.

'I suppose,' he said on the first stair, 'we've had a guest.'

'Just after you left,' agreed Mrs Hudson.

He paused on the second step. 'Will I find a room full of society ladies waiting, Mrs Hudson? You know I do not like crowds in my rooms.'

Indeed, he complained about anyone looking at his untidy collections and experiments. He did not have the patience to explain their natures. At the moment, several lizards hung suspended in clear jars along the mantle.

'Oh, hardly,' huffed Mrs Hudson. 'It was just one girl, and she's gone again.'

Our ascent halted as the entry door below burst open and a young man, dressed in an ill-fitting wool suit, appeared in the doorway. His thin, pale face was drawn with worry. He had a feeble moustache—much in vogue amongst young men to whom the growth of facial hair was a newfound skill—and I spied a black armband.

'You may as well come up,' said Holmes, hardly pausing to take him in. 'She's already left.'

The young man followed us up and Holmes stood at the windows, allowing the boy to pace back and forth. Mrs Hudson clasped her hands beneath her apron, frowning. She seemed uncomfortable to be part of our interview but, uncharacteristically, remained.

I moved away from the group to watch; I preferred for Holmes to do the questioning. A little space gave me room to follow the pieces of the drama.

'I'm sorry for the bother, sir. I've come about Katie, if you please, sir. Can you tell me where she has gone to?' said the eager young man.

Holmes ignored the enquiry, gathering enough from the question itself to ask in return: 'Your sister, who works in the department store around the corner? A young woman, dressed in black and, I assume, considered quite pretty?'

Mrs Hudson raised her eyebrows, and the young man rushed forward.

'You've seen 'er, then!' he cried.

'Oh, no,' Holmes waved a hand to dismiss the boy's assumptions and thereby erase any reassurance he had taken from them. The boy quivered. His disappointment was a familiar problem; Sherlock Holmes had never trained himself out of his misleading manner of speech because it allowed him to prove his deductions right or wrong in an instant.

'If you have not seen Katie, then how'd you know?'

'I smelled mingled expensive perfumes when I arrived home, only to discover they were from one woman. She being your sister narrowed things down considerably. Like yourself, she'll be in mourning. You're too young to have a wife, and your shoes say you walk all day. You're in a rush to find her, but not out of breath, so you didn't come far. Since you're a delivery boy or messenger, the nearest shop with a selection of fragrances is where your sister works. And if she's placed up-front at the cosmetic counter selling perfumes, she is thought to be attractive.'

I marvelled once more at Holmes' showmanship, but the brother was too concerned for his sister to do more than nod.

'That's Katie, all right. She's managed to get herself lost and always said we were to come to you if anything out of the ordinary happened. We reads about you in the paper—all the souls you've helped.'

The boy flopped into a chair, chastened. 'I do like Katie says, but it's me who has put her in harm's way. Can you help? We can't pay.'

'Oh, dear boy, Mr Holmes and Dr Watson are happy to help a boy in mourning find his missing sister,' tutted Mrs Hudson, casting squint our way as if to reinforce her assertion.

A quick glance told me her reason for concern. Holmes had turned aside wearing the bored expression of a man who had already reconciled his figures.

'What's your name?' I asked.

'Enoch Bryant.'

'Tell us your story,' I said, and sat across from the young man, hoping a show of interest from myself might offset my friend's apparent indifference. He, at least, stayed within earshot.

'Mr Holmes is right, sir. We work at the department store. Mum died when I was born. I had the cord wrapped around my throat three times, they say, though of course I can't remember. Katie was always good to me and kept me safe.

'After our dad died, money's tight. Katie got me a job as a delivery boy, but when there isn't anything to cart around, I work in the warehouse.'

'An honest living, lad. Nothing to be ashamed of. But today, something unusual happened,' I encouraged when Enoch stopped. He spoke slowly, and I saw his sister likely had to do more than the usual amount of mothering.

'Katie works the front counter, greets customers, sprays the ladies—sometimes manages an extra spritz for herself. Cheers us both up to come home to a nice smell. Except today a gentleman tried to take Katie's hand. Rattled her something awful. She complained of headache, and they sent her home. But I've been home, and she ain't there.'

'Could it be,' I put the question delicately, 'that her headache freed her for an assignation with someone? Perhaps this gentleman?'

Enoch sat up, eyes flashing.

'Katie ain't like that! And anyway, that's not what happened next, for sure. You see I—I needed her help, and I shouldn't have asked. I'm the new fellow, you see. Katie always said we shouldn't gamble, except the others explained that I had to try it once now that I'm working there. It's only companionable.'

No one responded. I found it unsurprising the men engaged in gambling during their free working hours, and Holmes was not one to criticize the vices of others. Mrs Hudson frowned but reserved comment. She shifted weight from foot to foot, drawing Mr Holmes' speculative eye.

'Well, I was down more than a bit from my pay packet, and I needed a chance to win it back. I had a delivery that needed running out this way, and I begged Katie to drop it off along the way.'

'What package?' I asked, hoping to speed the tale along for all our sakes.

'A small crate, the size of a large breadbox?' Holmes asked, his impatience growing. 'Your sister has left it here for safekeeping.'

Enoch shook his head so hard his narrow shoulders quivered too. 'Oh, no, just a sack of ingredients for the chemist's shop.'

'Well now, you saw the crate, then? And here I've been, wasting my time, being polite but waiting to tell you,' grumbled Mrs Hudson. 'The girl was in a hurry and when you weren't here, she dropped the case and rushed out the door in a whirlwind.'

'There was no message?' Without waiting for a response, Holmes strode out of the room and down the stairs toward the entry.

He returned a moment later with the case in his hands, still inspecting the construction. There were no labels or markings. From his easy handling, its weight must not be too terrible for its size. The top had been nailed shut. He scored the wood with his fingernail. Apparently finding it quite ordinary, he took no special care as he pried open the top of the box. His eyes brightened. The three of us angled for a look at the object inside that would be worthy of such rapt attention.

Slipping both hands within, Holmes lifted out the preserved remains of a small, hairy dog. He rested it on the table, studying the flat, ugly face. The muzzle was dark, as were the artificial eyes that jutted from its head in an appalling manner. Long, silky golden fur had been combed to the ground and more hair circled head and chest.

A red collar hid beneath the mane of fur with a tag resting on its barrel chest.

Holmes and I looked at Enoch but needed not ask a question. It was clear he had never seen anything like it.

'This is a Pekingese dog, stuffed and preserved via the art of taxidermy. The first Pekingese entered our country as gifts for Queen Victoria when the Forbidden City fell. See how it has been bred to resemble a lion?' Holmes studied the dead animal with more interest than he'd shown for the living boy or his sister.

'She said nothing before leaving, Mrs Hudson?' I enquired.

Our housekeeper's shoulder relaxed as if completing a burdensome duty.

'She asked for Mr Holmes and seemed disappointed to find him out. I said you'd both return shortly, but she couldn't wait. Said someone was in trouble, or lives were in danger—Oh, I've forgotten how it went. But she insisted she had to go immediately. I think stopping here was an impulse, and she hadn't thought out a message. She didn't seem to expect help.'

'No,' Holmes straightened. 'She is used to others relying on her. Her father wasn't much use, it's plain, and she's acted as mother since she was a girl. Now, there's someone else she means to help.'

'And you'll find her back?' Enoch asked.

'There's no address on the Pekingese or inside the box,' I said, sharing my disappointment.

Holmes pulled on his gloves. 'We'll head across the street.'

Enoch jumped to his feet and followed us down the stairs.

'I've just been to the chemist, a nasty piece of work with rheumy eyes and shaking hands. He wouldn't tell me a thing. I asked about my sister, but he said he had his own job to do without other people butting in and what business was it of mine? Since I could get us both into trouble, I didn't want to give my name. She's a bright girl, Katie, so I could imagine her worrying he'd complain to the shop that she weren't a real messenger, so I thought maybe she just dropped off the delivery and slipped away. That's all I tried to ask—if he'd gotten a package from our shop, but he was out of sorts, searching through cabinets and complaining how his runner was already out. I was worried and anxious and snapped at him. Next thing I know, he accused me of being a thief and drunkard, and cursed me with blindness. Said he'd known things were going missing, and maybe I was to blame. I swear, I don't know him. I never delivered there before, but I was already anxious over Katie and he scared me. I ran out to the street, and that's when I spied your address and seeing how Katie might have seen the same thing, well, I tried my luck once more for the day. I wouldn't like to go back there. I'm sorry Katie had to deal with him.'

Now that she'd seen the state of our rooms, Mrs Hudson wasted no time in getting out the dustpan. Fortunately, she had learned not to disturb the seemingly random piles of books and papers that had Holmes' interest.

'Keep an eye on the dog,' Holmes called.

I could not decide if his parting words were a joke or a warning.

Outside, the day was bright, and we crossed the road in no time. Holmes allowed young Enoch to lead, since he'd just come from the chemist's shop. I took a moment for a private word.

'Mr Holmes, what does the dead dog mean? Are you worried about the girl?'

'Although Mrs Hudson is not the best witness, Miss Katie Bryant seemed to think someone's life was in danger. A picture is beginning to form, but it is too early to share, except I recall the intriguing fact that this chemist's shop has in the back, yes, a taxidermist.'

Skipping the chemist's front door, Holmes strode around the side to a small door set off the alleyway. Four dirty steps descended to a store at the back with Norcott's Taxidermy on a placard above it. The three of us entered into a dimly lit room filled with antlers, skins, and the posed bodies of preserved animals. Gleaming black eyes sparkled at me from a wide-eyed, two-pronged deer head mounted beside the door. A solid oak block served as countertop and work surface. A rotund man in a canvas apron and reeking of strong chemicals came in from the back, wiping a strand of hair off his forehead with his wrist so it settled among half a dozen iron-coloured mates.

'What's this, then?' he asked without preamble. His deep voice held a grainy rasp and he coughed painfully.

Enoch tried to slip eagerly past Holmes, who glided in front of him.

'We're interested in a preserved animal.'

The man waved a hand impatiently at the shop walls. 'You see what we have.'

Enoch came to stand beside me. So nervous was he that he practically vibrated against my side. I recalled the vitality of my teenage years with regret and cast the boy a reassuring smile. Holmes might have a plan, and we must give him space to follow it.

'I didn't mean to cast Katie in harm's way. I know gambling is a sin, and on company hours, but I couldn't know she'd go missing,' said the boy. Perhaps my reassuring smile had been a touch too empathetic. Finding a sympathetic audience, he unloaded the burden he carried.

'If anything has happened to her, I won't forgive myself. When our father kept us locked out of the apartment for hours, and we had to wait for him to sober up enough to unbolt the door, Katie had read me stories of Mr Sherlock Holmes—and Dr Watson,' he added in a rush.

I smiled benignly, trying not to be too encouraging since I still wanted to hear Holmes' discussion. The taxidermist wiped off his hands while listening to Holmes, who had not yet brought up the sister to the ill-mannered and hurried clerk.

The man cleared his throat with a sharp bark and gestured behind us with a scowl. 'If you're not looking to buy, I have work to do and only two hands for it.'

'You should open a window, Mr Norcott. Chemicals aren't good for the lungs. I use something similar to preserve tissues in my own small experiments.'

He had apparently decided the man was the shop owner, for which it was named. The man offered no contrary argument.

Instead, Mr Norcott glanced at the windows above us at street level. 'We have vents in the back. My clerk is supposed to open them so I can do my work, but it's just another item on his list. Seems I must do his work and mine. I make barely anything as it is. I can't afford to have my health broken as well.'

'Some help is better than none, even if you have to share it,' observed Holmes.

'Too right,' agreed the man.

Enoch shifted beside me. His anxiety began to grate and I shared a growing concern over the long minutes it had been since Miss Bryant dropped the strange package off at our doorstep.

'It is convenient you live so close to where you work,' I remarked to distract the boy. I had investigated alongside Sherlock Holmes for long enough to know that indirect inquiries were often the most successful. Confront the belligerent shop owner, and we'd be thrown out as swiftly as Enoch had been booted from the chemist's shop.

The boy gave me a sidelong stare, mouth gaping.

Enjoying something of the feeling Holmes must frequently experience, I explained, 'Your sister was headed home, but you asked her to take the package. You must pass by here on the way to your apartments.'

'That's true enough. And a good thing because she doesn't like to pay for a cab.'

'No cab?' Holmes enquired, returning to our sides. 'That helps matters. Come, gentlemen, we are now in a race.'

'Are you done with the shopkeeper?' I asked in surprise, my eye flashing back across the countertop and, finding it empty, to the doorway beyond. I could just see into a storage space he evidently shared with the chemist's shop above. Animals, big and small, lined shelves on the wall while tidy jars, boxes, and bins were arrayed along the lower shelves where an elderly man might reach them. The shopkeeper stowed a bottle of alum beside a box of borax on the back wall. Smothering a hacking cough, he pushed a window open beside his bench.

Holmes made no allowances for the delay my curiosity caused. His movements were sharp and his step rapid, indicating some significant development I had missed by letting my attention wander.

We followed on his heels to the street, where Holmes flagged down a cab with a single wave of his arm. We gathered inside as Holmes gave an address I recognized as a once-refined neighbourhood that had seen better days. It was not far, although travel routes were limited by the choice of bridges.

'Well,' I asked, a bit disagreeable since I had missed a step in the process. 'What have you found out?'

'Very little, and a great deal more than I expected,' said Holmes. 'That was not the usual front desk clerk, but the man himself who does the work. A little admiration and a few questions, and he soon opened up about the tricks of the trade. I might go back in a day or two when this is all over. When I inquired about a Pekingese, he allowed that he had operated on one recently. A real front desk clerk would have been slower to open the books and give me a glimpse of the address to which we are now headed.'

'But how did Katie end up with the Pekingese?' Enoch asked.

'A mystery indeed,' said Holmes. 'Mr Norcott had not seen the girl. He was more concerned about his missing clerk.'

We sat in silence.

'How long would it take you to walk to this address?' Holmes enquired of Enoch, as if making polite conversation.

'Oh, that's easy. I've run it many times, though not to this particular house. It's half an hour, but with so many folks filling the streets it might take a little longer. I prefer morning deliveries when sidewalks are clear.'

'I expect your sister is slower on foot than you?'

Enoch agreed.

Holmes leaned his head back and closed his eyes, and we allowed a respectful silence for his thoughts to organise themselves.

The cab pulled up at the front of a large three-storey house with a dreary yard of sparse grass and an iron gate opening in a low brick fence that ran around the property, hiding much of the gardens. We got out, and Holmes passed through the open metal gate; we trailed behind. He studied the house, then waved in greeting. Only the red glow of the lit end of a cigarette allowed my eye to find a figure nearly hidden in a second-story window. Holmes took a keen look at the inner yard and moved to the front door. Beneath the window were the ends of cigarettes.

Before the first knock had sounded, a man pulled the door open.

Panting for breath, he stared feverishly at us. By age, he should have been a man in his prime. His clothes were refined but wrinkled; anxiety had left shadows beneath his eyes. He had a nervous habit of clicking the yellow-tinged nails together on his right hand. The house smelled musty and neglected. As a doctor, I wondered if he had been recently ill.

He opened and shut his mouth without speaking.

'Were you expecting us?' I prompted, surprised he had rushed to greet us so rapidly he couldn't breathe.

'What? Oh, no, of course not.' His eyes did not meet mine for more than a moment at a time. 'Only, I didn't want you to knock. My aunt is ill, and it disturbs her.'

'I am Sherlock Holmes and this is my esteemed companion, Doctor Watson. Perhaps he can be of assistance. Oh, and this young man is Enoch Bryant. Do you mind if we come in?'

Whether due to the assuredness of Holmes's manner or the convenience of a doctor, the man backed away and allowed us entry. Inside was as cheerless as out. The house had seen better days. Shades were drawn over the windows, and there were few ornaments on the sparse furniture. At odds with the empty dreariness was a large painting, surrounded by a gilded frame, of a family. A man in an older-style uniform stood beside a woman—plainly his wife—and a young girl in a white dress. More intriguing, the girl's arm rested on a Pekingese similar to the one currently residing in a box on Baker Street.

The man gestured for us to follow him up the sweeping staircase to the second floor, wherein lay the window through which I had seen him from the street below. He ushered us inside and closed the door with nearly palpable relief.

'We can talk here. My aunt has sensitive ears, and our speaking below might disturb her.'

'Your name?' Holmes inquired.

'Phineas Grimley.' The newly christened Mr Grimley seemed to regain possession of himself now that we were in his territory. He moved to the desk, which stood before the open window, and reached for a box then stopped himself. 'Now, see here. You've come to visit me. What is the meaning of this?'

'Were you expecting a delivery today, Mr Grimley?' asked Holmes.

Mr Grimley's eyes flickered to the driveway outside and back again, betraying himself. 'No, we allow no deliveries except perhaps from the chemist. Did you see someone?'

The nails on his right hand clicked against each other, setting my nerves on edge.

'We don't mind if you smoke,' said Holmes.

'I don't smoke,' Mr Grimley said curtly.

'My mistake. I see you have no ashtray in the room. Your aunt does not like it, I suppose.'

'It pains her lungs. I may smoke outside if I choose. Only it's blasted cold, don't you think?' Grimley shivered and drew his suit jacket around him to stare pensively down at the drive below. A large stickpin glittered in his lapel and new cufflinks glinted from the sleeves of his otherwise rumpled suit.

Enoch had paced the room, studied the smattering of books, and, perhaps thinking us a failure, asked, 'Did you see my sister? She's a pretty girl and might have come to this address.'

'No, we get no visitors. Indeed, I can't imagine why I let you in. Please be so kind as to leave.'

He made a show of ignoring us to check his pocket watch and adjust the time.

To my astonishment, Holmes swept up his hat with vigour.

'Agreed, I think we must. By my count, we will shortly see Miss Bryant,' said Holmes.

We moved toward the doorway and opened the portal, but Holmes turned at the last minute, catching Mr Grimley in the act of lighting a pre-rolled cigarette he had pulled from a box on his desk.

'The portrait in the entry is of your aunt and her family?' asked Holmes.

Grimley held still, his answer waylaid as his eyes widened with dismay and focused behind us. I turned and found a slender middle-aged woman with a cane. Although she was pale and her breathing shallow and rapid, she had dressed with precision in draped silks and bore a fur over one arm. A string of large white pearls encircled her neck and rings glittered on thin fingers.

'Phineas, who are these men?'

Holmes swept in a small circle, seeming to almost bow. 'I am Sherlock Holmes, and this is Dr Watson. Would you mind if he examined you? I fear I must head below, but I will retu—'

All at once, we heard a terrible scream from below. Enoch, who had lingered in the room, rushed to lean beside Phineas in the window.

'It's Katie! Why is she screaming? What's wrong?' Enoch's face was a picture of horror.

Through the window, I spied a woman standing in the drive, flailing at the air. I could see no attacker, but Holmes had me by the sleeve, dragging me with him toward the stairs. We raced down them, Holmes several paces before me.

I wondered what invisible force attacked the girl. Insects, perhaps, in a hive beneath the ground?

Holmes reached the foyer, grabbed a vase, and shoved it into my arms. He snatched up the tablecloth as well and flung it to me.

'Put out the fire on Miss Bryant!'

Holmes raced toward the corner of the house, chasing the retreating figure of a man.

Dutifully carrying the vase, I yanked out the tall gladiolus and floppy ranunculi to shove the tablecloth within and pulled it out, dripping. The screaming girl dropped to the ground, holding her arm away from her and slapping it with her free hand. Although my senses told me there was no light or flame—there was no fire—I trusted Holmes' deduction and flung the tablecloth from the vase onto the unfortunate girl, patting to smother the flames I could not see.

Steam puffed in hot white trails.

The girl sat up, sobbing and holding her arm. I knelt beside her. With a penknife, I opened her wool sleeve. The smells of perfume, alcohol, and smoke occasioned a small cough. I checked the slight burn on her forearm. The skin was red with a small cluster of blisters. Luckily, the unseasonably thick black fabric of her mourning dress had mostly protected her from the invisible force that had afflicted her.

'Katie!' cried Enoch, kneeling beside me to embrace his sister. 'I worried.'

Holmes returned with a small, dour-faced man in his grip. His shoulder bore a stripe of dirt and grass as if he'd been knocked to the ground during his failed escape. The knees of Holmes's pants were also smudged with mud, and I pictured him leaping after the attacker, landing on his knees as he dragged him to earth.

At the sight of Holmes' captive, Katie turned her face away and hid it in her brother's shoulder.

'Is Miss Bryant well enough to confront her attacker?' asked Holmes.

I rested on my heels. 'She has a minor burn. If there are basic supplies in the house, I can see to it myself.'

Phineas' aunt had by now reached the front door and stood in judgment of the strangers arrayed on her doorstep. 'You must come inside. I expect there is an explanation, and I am eager to hear it. You, Phineas, must attend.'

Halted in the act of slipping past her, Phineas hung his head. 'Yes, Aunt.'

We gathered in the front sitting room that Mr Grimley had rushed us past upon our first arrival. The room looked out upon the sparse front yard. We settled on several sofas placed in a u-shape before the absent fire. Enoch quickly gave himself the job of kindling one to fight the coldness of the house.

'I apologize for the state of the accommodations,' said the infirm woman without blushing.

'You have no servants,' observed Holmes, 'Not from lack of funds, but from a need to remain private, just as you do not accept deliveries. You are in hiding. This is not your home, but that of your nephew.'

The woman perched on an armchair, her ornate cane at her knee. 'Exactly so.'

While Holmes did his work, I engaged in soothing and bandaging the arm of Katie, for whom we had searched so assiduously. She remained docile, muttering words of gratitude so she did not interrupt proceedings. I sensed shock in her stillness and wondered what events had transpired in the afternoon she had been missing from her brother.

'Other than your arm, are you well?' I asked.

'I am and ever so grateful you've helped Enoch,' she said in an undertone.

On the far side of the room, away from any doorway, Holmes released the stranger from the yard. He stood with arms crossed, mouth pinched. His small eyes followed Holmes with hatred. He looked at no one else.

'I am Eudora Grimley,' said the lady. 'Who are these others?'

'This is Enoch Bryant and his sister, Katie, for whom we have been searching. On the other side of the room, we have Mr Mutter.'

Her eyes bored into Holmes without comment.

'You received threats of some kind, although nothing the police deemed sufficient for investigation. The threats were vague but unsettling. Your nephew offered to shelter you. This is plainly not your home—only a single portrait of you is hung in a precarious way, likely by your nephew. It's important to you, since it is the only decoration that you have brought. You are generous—if your nephew's new pocket watch and cufflinks are any indication. Although you were in hiding, you still required certain medications.'

Holmes did not point to her cane, nor mention the particulars of her conditions, but I had the sense he had already assessed them with a doctor's precision. For myself, I had done a cursory examination and found her to be congenitally weak, in need of her cane and likely requiring a pain reliever and medication for her lungs. Neither of us needed to state these facts explicitly.

'The clerk from the chemist shop was the only delivery you received, and it was through this individual that your nephew was able to receive illicit materials. Take, for example, the cigarettes he smokes, betrayed by his nervous habit and yellowed nails, even if I had not seen it for myself from the street below.'

Mr Grimley flinched and folded his hands behind his back.

Lady Grimley nodded. 'I am no fool, Mr Holmes. I am aware my nephew smokes despite my appeals. In attempting to hide his habit, it is, at least, contained and limited to his private rooms.'

At this pronouncement, Mr Grimley's face turned a light shade of red.

'Here, now, why am I being held?' shouted the man from the corner with sudden force.

Holmes turned to him as if he had been waiting for the man to speak. 'You are Mr Mutter, the clerk from the taxidermy shop.'

The lady followed his gaze and brought up a pair of pince-nez glasses hanging from a small chain. 'I'm afraid you are wrong, sir. He is the delivery boy for the druggist.'

Unperturbed by the correction, Holmes smiled. 'He is both. The shops share staff to keep down expenses. The missing clerk for the taxidermist and absent delivery boy for the chemist are one and the same. He is also a friend, or at least an accomplice, of your nephew.'

Mr Grimley's face turned a deeper shade of red.

'Now, see here! I've never been so insulted—'

'Sit, Phineas,' interrupted Lady Grimley. 'Let the man have his say. You have many bad habits but have taken me in when I most needed a friend. I will remember that.'

Mollified, Grimley sank unhappily onto a tufted ottoman and made a show of warming his hands while he regained his composure.

'The clerk is known to you from his deliveries. So, when Miss Bryant came by, he saw an opportunity. She does not look like a delivery boy, so if she came by the house, she might have a plausible story. Perhaps selling something. Or lost and needing directions.'

Miss Bryant raised her head. Her features were well-balanced and pretty, as Holmes had surmised.

'I was to say I was looking for work.'

The clerk in the corner seemed to deflate now that Miss Bryant had found her voice.

Holmes kept himself between the door and the pair he suspected. I, too, although seated, remained on my guard.

'He threatened,' my friend continued, 'to reveal you were making deliveries in place of your brother. However, you are an honest woman and argued with him enough that when you left with the package, he followed you. When he saw you enter 221B Baker Street, he knew he had been betrayed.'

Miss Bryant's eyes went wide. 'Followed! I didn't know what I carried, but I knew it was no good from his manner and threats. I couldn't bring it here, but I didn't know what mischief he might be up to, so I had to warn the house.'

'I don't see why you think I had anything to do with any of this.' Mr Grimley jumped to his feet again, his nails clacking nervously. 'I protected my aunt as best I could. I should not have let you inside, that was my failing, but you seemed respectable. And now you toss accusations at me as if I were a thief.'

'Not a thief,' said Holmes. 'A murderer, perhaps. Or simply a curse?'

Holmes's eyes studied the lady for a reaction.

Lady Grimley wavered on her seat. 'You already know my life has been threatened. How can you think it was my nephew?'

'Who else knew you well enough to seek a Pekingese from your childhood?'

'A gift!' blurted Mr Grimley.

'The threats to your aunt's life were specific enough for her to take them seriously. You offered her a haven, and she took you up on it. It wasn't the life you expected. She insisted on no servants or guests. However, she pays her way, and you've benefited by small luxuries.'

Holmes indicated his shining cufflinks, stickpin, and new pocket watch.

'But Lady Grimley has grown restless. She is not someone who lives in fear easily, having always been in ill health yet never having surrendered to it. The loneliness did not affect Lady Grimley alone. Disconsolate, you opened up to the only person available—the delivery man from the chemist. You must have thought it a clever plan, but Mr Mutter was really suggesting the most obvious thing.'

'Here, now!' argued Mr Mutter with considerable fire.

'Your bumbling attempt to get Miss Bryant to take the delivery in your place because you feared uncomfortable questions, demonstrates my point.

As does your inappropriate choice of methanol. And, if we needed further proof, when you saw the portrait of the girl holding the Pekingese from the doorway, you suggested the first thing that popped into your head, since you work in a taxidermy shop.'

Mr Mutter wiped his lips with the back of his hand.

'We weren't going to hurt her,' cried Mr Grimley.

Lady Grimley's stern expression faltered at her nephew's confirmation.

'No,' Holmes agreed. 'I am assured that murder was not the intention. Although it can be fatal, there are far better poisons than methanol available to someone in Mr Mutter's position. Arsenic or formaldehyde, for instance. Instead, he waited in the drive and splashed methanol on Miss Bryant— lending the scent of alcohol and making her far-fetched story seem even more unreliable. Methanol which, when lit by the errant end of a cigarette tossed out a window, burns invisibly. Thankfully, Miss Bryant's wool sleeve barely caught on fire before Dr Watson put it out.'

'The fire was an accident?' asked Miss Bryant.

'Indeed. The Pekingese was part of a plan to keep Lady Grimley isolated and provide Mr Grimley with a regular income for her protection. As Miss Bryant inadvertently learned, methanol has the property of burning cleanly, without excess colour or smoke. During the daytime the flames are so pale as to appear colourless.'

'So, how'd you know she was burning, Mr Holmes?' asked Enoch.

'When there was nothing to see, I recalled the chemist accused you of theft and threatened you with blindness. This is a known side-effect of methanol, which must have gone missing.

'It was bad luck, and nasty habit, that led Mr Grimley to defenestrate his cigarette. Although it was somewhat inevitable once Lady Grimley appeared since he had no ability to stand up for himself in his own home and demand the right to smoke in his rooms. Instead, he avoided confrontation by tossing his cigarette out the window. This same cowardice led him to perpetrate the fraud that her life was in danger. When she decided to face any real threat, perhaps finally declaring she would go to Scotland Yard and insist on an investigation, he and his accomplice set out to offer threats harder to admit to authorities. I take it you have no nefarious past or habits?'

Lady Grimly gave a small laugh.

'So, instead, he looked to your family. Your father?'

Her laughter stopped.

'He implicated your father in past wrongdoings, then. Your father and mother are both deceased, or you would have sought protection from them and not your nephew. The tenor of your sadness when I mention him suggests your father perished prematurely.'

Holmes turned to the room at large, musing aloud. 'Her nephew, Mr Grimly, chose stories from her youth, possibly told by her father—a world traveller and soldier, I would wager. He had enemies, as all conquerors do, and something of a romantic streak, to give his daughter a puppy from a foreign land.'

'My puppy?' Lady Grimly appeared startled at the change of topic. 'My father was a soldier in the Second Opium War. He helped lead the invasion of Beijing and the taking of the Old Summer Palace. An elderly family member had remained behind when the Emperor fled. My father found the unfortunate soul, who had taken her own life. She left behind five Pekingese. These animals could only be owned by members of the Imperial Palace and were prized. A pair were given to the Duchess of Wellington, and the other to the Duke and Duchess of Richmond and Gordon. The fifth, little Looty, was given to Queen Victoria. My father made special request for a puppy from among the first litters, and I was the happiest girl alive. My lungs have always been weak, and I spent most winters in bed, but Chancie was bred to stay in one place and guard apartments in the Forbidden City. You might notice how their front legs turn in. They're not meant for walking, but for guarding. Chancie loved to stay put with me. My father's fantastical stories were meant for a girl, but even then, I sensed he was sometimes disturbed by dreams. He died by accident, we were told, but it threw my mother into deep despair. Chancie disappeared at the same time, and she told me it was a sign of vengeance. I'm not given to flights of fancy, but in this house... I've been very much alone with my thoughts.'

'And your nephew knew enough to hint at unknown enemies and foreign curses. You likely felt attacked from all sides, with no one to turn to but him.'

The lady's eyes sought out her nephew, lips pursed tight in thought.

'Hardly anyone remembers Chancie, so to have a stuffed Pekingese that looks like him arrive on your doorstep, when no one knew you were here, might have felt like—'

'A threat,' she finished. 'As if my father's unseen enemies had become mine.'

Mr Grimley clicked his nails. 'I'd heard your stories so many times, the good and the bad. Ancient family history droning on and on. I knew how they discovered those dogs. They're hardly rare now, easy enough for Mr Mutter to procure one from an American ambassador after it had died. We thought to scare you a bit. To ensure you'd stay, Aunt. I wouldn't have hurt you.'

'Oh, Phineas,' said Lady Grimley in saddened tones.

'Monstrous!' said Miss Bryant.

'What Mr Grimley did was cruel, although not yet criminal,' observed Holmes.

'I will gather my things. I would prefer to put this all behind me. Your allowance, obviously, is at an end, Phineas. May you find no peace in the house you have made.' She put her hands on the arms of her chair and struggled to rise. Enoch appeared at her side to assist her. She looked at him with faint surprise, thanked him, and made her way out of the room with slow dignity.

'Mr Mutter, however, stole from his employer,' I said.

Mr Mutter's gaze skittered between us. 'They'll never have me back, anyways, since I ran off without a word to anyone. I didn't mean to harm the girl. Methanol was all I had, and it doesn't hurt you, just smells. No one would trust a girl that smells like alcohol.'

Holmes and I took turns delivering a scathing review of the two men's lack of character and their endangerment of Lady Grimley and, by extension, Miss Bryant. By the end, they couldn't look at us or each other, and when given the opportunity, Mr Mutter quickly departed down the back stairs.

Lady Grimley returned, and Enoch carried her bag. We gathered on the drive out front to say our goodbyes.

Phineas Grimley watched us from his pitch-dark office, the end of his cigarette a red glow. Even with his aunt gone, he confined himself to his rooms to smoke. I saw no bright future for the young man who had found it easier to torment a relative than find honest employment.

Lady Grimley turned resolutely from the house.

'Mr Holmes, I am grateful for your assistance. I underestimated my nephew's avarice. Or, at the very least, I assumed it would keep him loyal. Alone as we were, he could have done much worse. In his way, he wanted me to stay.'

'I wonder, would you like us to send the package on to you?'

'After my father's death, we were a chaotic house. It isn't surprising Chancie ran away—or was stolen away, since the breed was in high demand. I tried not to believe my mother's dark take on my father's accident.' She smiled. 'It would bring joy to glimpse a reminder of my childhood pet. Here is my card, please send the dog to my house. Perhaps you could use the young Mr Bryant. I would like an opportunity to thank him, and his sister, for their troubles. I also am aware of positions that might suit if there were interest.'

Lady Grimley arranged for a rare cab ride for Enoch and Katie Bryant, who seemed stunned at the day's events but happy with the outcome. They would see Lady Grimley the following day, and Miss Bryant would stop by Baker Street to have her small burn checked by me as frequently as needed.

Mr Holmes and I were pleased to ride back to our apartments with a sense of accomplishment for the short afternoon's activities.

The Woman Who Wasn't: Part Two

Setting the manuscript down, I leant back in my chair and pondered what I had read. Was this the manner of reminiscence Holmes had in mind? And if so, to what purpose? It did have several facets in common with our current case—a missing woman, family entanglements, the potential for incriminating information to come to light. But it would be hard to claim it as a mirror image.

Blast the man. Why could he never offer detailed instructions? There were times I believed that he was deliberately obtuse, using mystery as a way to guide his own thinking. At others, I suspected he took amusement from keeping me in the dark until he could display his intellectual wares in full.

Worse still, I knew that, as much as it frustrated me, I enjoyed the chase. I enjoyed the arrival at our eventual destination that much more keenly when it was preceded by a few yards of fumbling in the dark.

Mercifully, I would not be left waiting long for the action to resume.

***

Holmes appeared at my door three days later, shortly after I had dispensed with the last of the patients that comprised my morning surgery and returned home for my noon meal. Having spent the previous twenty minutes lancing, then dressing, a boil, I was more than usually pleased to see him.

Mary Jane, our maid, had shown him into the house—though knowing the girl, I was surprised she had managed such a simple task—and I found him waiting patiently on a chair by the front door, his coat still fastened, leaning on his walking stick, lost in thought. Mary Jane did not appear to have offered him refreshment, though that was more in keeping with her usual standard of work.

He looked up at me as I crossed the threshold.

31

'Good afternoon, Watson,' he said. 'I hope I am not inconveniencing you. I know how much you relish your luncheon.'

'Not at all, Holmes. I assume you have news in the case of Anastasia Frain.'

His expression was unreadable.

'Alas, not. And that is why I am here. None of my usual associates have turned up any sign of the young woman, which is either a cause for concern or further evidence of her determination to remain unfound.'

'If she were keen to remain at liberty, why would she draw attention to herself by writing to you?'

'To *us*, Watson,' he reminded me. 'If, indeed, it was she. But you have hit, precisely, on the first question that must be answered. What is that our client wants from us?'

'To find his daughter, surely.'

Holmes smiled softly.

'Oh, I do not consider Sir Harrison Frain to be our client. Far from it. He may well be one of our suspects. The author of that note is the one to whom we owe our professional allegiance. After all, they were the first to take us into their confidence.'

'But, dash it, Holmes. I don't understand why you are so taken with this case. Of course, if the young woman has found herself in trouble, I'm ready and willing to extricate her from it. But you seldom have such transparent motives.'

Holmes did his best to look shocked at this accusation and failed entirely.

'I shall not take that insinuation to heart, Watson. In principle, you are correct. If the case were as simple as you seem to believe, I would happily hand it over to Lestrade or Gregson. But that note continues to intrigue. "I am not she."'

'Well, we know that it came from Anastasia, or Sir Harrison wouldn't have found the discarded draft amongst her things.'

'We know that it likely originated from the *bedroom* of Anastasia Frain. And even of that, we cannot be sure. Did you discover anything of use amongst your scribblings?'

'Do you recall the affair of Enoch and Katie Bryant, and the stuffed Pekingese?'

Holmes cast his mind back.

'Ah yes.' His face lit with the pleasure of discovery. 'Oh, well done, Watson. I knew you would stumble upon something of use.'

I was, frankly, amazed.

'It has given you a clue?'

'Not in the slightest,' he replied. 'Though it has, perhaps, reassured me that my thoughts are running in the right direction.'

'How so?'

He demurred.

'Not quite yet, Watson. You know I disdain a tale told in fragments.'

'You tell no other kind,' I grumbled.

This time, he did look genuinely hurt.

'I shall put that down to your empty stomach,' he said. 'Which I shall now leave you to address.'

'You came all the way here just to tell me we're no further along?'

'It was on my route. I am following another avenue of investigation and it seemed prudent to liaise with you, regarding your research.'

'I can accompany you,' I said, perhaps too eagerly. 'I have a light load of patients this afternoon. I'm sure my locum could—'

Holmes shook his head.

'I will not presume upon you for the moment,' he said, his face darkening. 'But only because I fear I will have dire need of you come the conclusion of this enterprise.'

'Very well. I shall continue to look through my old casebooks.'

'Do, Watson. I know it may seem a scattershot request at present, but I really cannot stress how vital it may prove to be in the long run.'

'I shall take you at your word.' I felt a little gloomy at not being included in his immediate adventures, but my mood was slowly lifted by the growing scent of lamb stew from the kitchen—one of Cook's true masterpieces.

Holmes seemed to catch the shift in my attention and brightened.

'There you are, Watson. Satiation awaits.' He gave a small sniff of the air. 'Though I fear your cook may have overdone the potatoes. Never mind. A stew covers a multitude of sins.'

I laughed aloud.

'Are you sure you won't partake? Cook always makes more than is needed.' I patted my growing stomach by way of evidence.

'A kind thought, Watson, but no. Time is pressing and Mrs Hudson has already offered to leave something in the larder for my return. Should I appear already fed, there will be no peace at Baker Street.'

'You will let me know of any advancement?'

'And of any fresh crisis too, Watson. You have my word.'

And with that, he strode to the door and, like a wraith, disappeared into the midday bustle of London.

***

Later that evening, determined to contribute something more substantial than hints, I bid Mary goodnight and returned to my study.

Witnessing Holmes' response to our adventures in the taxidermy trade made me all the more determined to discover something that might contribute more directly to our understanding of the case at hand.

And, in lieu of further enlightenment from Holmes, I would follow my own train of thought.

This was, for better or worse, a matter of passion. When I combined that with Holmes' previous instruction to revisit cases involving mysterious disappearances, I knew precisely which papers I sought. A case that occurred only a month or two previously, not long after I left Baker Street for the marital home.

The Adventure of the Red Diamond

Elliot Thorpe

I hadn't yet stepped off the mat when Mrs Hudson pounced. She closed the door behind me and immediately set about taking my hat and coat. She was unusually anxious.

'Good Lord, Mrs Hudson,' I exclaimed, the warmth from the hallway flushing my cheeks. It was a bright, chilly morning and the snow had been settling steadily across the capital all night. 'Whatever is the matter?'

'Oh, Dr Watson,' she replied. 'I don't know what has come over him of late.'

'He has no case at present, I take it,' I said. 'That often leaves him ill at ease.'

'Do you think I don't know that, Dr Watson? But it's the noise! The last three nights he's been making such an awful racket.'

I heard nothing as I mounted the stairs towards the lodgings of my friend, Mr Sherlock Holmes, instead finding him sprawled over a chaise longue, apparently asleep. Mrs Hudson was a step behind, tutting as she peered around me. She continued muttering as she descended the stairs. I knew she was relieved I had arrived so promptly, even in this weather.

'Holmes?' I ventured.

He was still in his purple smoking jacket, the one he favoured when engaging in his terrible addictions. It was clear to me that he had been imbibing and was now paying the price.

The room was all a-clutter: newspapers strewn hither and thither, a pipe lying discarded upon the occasional table, all manner of test tubes and beakers tipped or cracked or both on his workbench. Under a book, a large cumbersome volume on the history of Ceylon, I found a plate of congealed, uneaten dinner. I set about tidying while allowing my friend to sleep off whatever he had taken.

'I gather by your actions you believe you have deduced the reasons for Mrs Hudson's dismay,' Holmes said suddenly.

'There is no doubt in my mind, whatsoever. Your damned ten-percent solution! Why you would dull a mind as sharp as yours—'

Holmes leapt to his feet, eyes wide and a twitch in one corner of his mouth.

'Then you will be relieved to discover I have been given cause to set all such pursuits aside for the moment.'

With his free hand he passed me a note, written in thick black scrawl.

'He has a heavy, rough hand,' I began, sensing Holmes' eagerness that I should understand the author of the note.

'He? It is unsigned.'

'But the paper is crinkled, torn. Little care has been taken to fold it. And that fact that it is unsigned tells me that whoever wrote it is assured enough that you will respond.'

'But I haven't responded! Hah!'

I read the contents. '"Holmes, I implore you to assist me in my plight. I shall come to your rooms in two days." Informal, direct, rather rude.'

'And no return address! How could I reply, my dear fellow? He has written it in haste, as though he had not the time to finish it. I do not think rudeness was in his mind.'

'When did this arrive?'

'Two days ago, hence why I sent for you this morning! I expect our strange guest imminently. Mrs Hudson!'

Holmes dashed around, throwing mess from the chairs and settee to the floor, as if that would help clear things up. Mrs Hudson arrived once more, tutting and scuttling behind him, ducking at least three times as Holmes waved his arms like a thing possessed while explaining to me that I was right. The letter had been written by a man. A gentleman at that, one who was more used to dictating, perhaps to a batman or secretary, judging by the laziness of the handwriting.

And then he sat down in his armchair, silent and glum, staring deeply into the flames crackling away in the grate.

'Can I get you something warm to drink, Dr Watson?' Mrs Hudson asked, knowing my friend would not offer.

I glanced at the decanted whiskey by Holmes' bureau. 'Thank you, I shall get my own.'

She nodded and departed. I sat in the armchair opposite Holmes. We could both feel the generosity of the fire.

***

Presently, after an hour or so of silence and following Holmes changing out of his jacket and into more formal wear, we heard the bell ring downstairs. My friend positioned himself by the mantelpiece, gazing into the middle distance.

I welcomed the visitor after Mrs Hudson had directed him to Holmes' door.

'I take it you are the gentleman who sent Mr Holmes the note?' I enquired. It had begun to snow quite heavily, judging by the powdery flakes upon the man's shoulders. He wore no hat, nor had any gloves. He seemed as if he had left from wherever he had come in a hurry.

'I am,' he replied. 'Will he help me?'

His look was desperate. I gestured towards Holmes who remained motionless. 'Holmes?'

'Will—will you help me?' The man was almost pleading, the melting snow from his receding hairline dripping down his large nose. When Holmes didn't move, the man dropped himself down onto the settee, with neither permission nor shame.

'I say,' I began. 'Won't you even take off your coat? It's sodden.'

'I do not expect you to be courteous. I do not expect you to be aware of your shortcomings,' said Holmes. 'Your brief and clumsy foray into literature,' he waved at the letter I was holding. 'tells me all that and more. But you have not introduced yourself. Pray tell us your name and what ails you.'

The man looked at Holmes as if he were mad. It seemed not to occur to him that he had been in anyway discourteous.

'Shall I tell you, then?' Holmes interjected as the man was about to open his mouth. 'You live some distance away. I'd say somewhere in the countryside judging by your boots. They are well-worn to fit you comfortably but not worn enough to indicate you work on the land. You arrived in London three days ago. One day before you decided to hand-deliver your note.'

'How do you know this?' the man asked.

'I saw you standing across the street. It is a habit of mine to know the faces and people who frequent Baker Street, particularly those who loiter with no apparent intent.' Holmes moved to open a silver cigarette case from his occasional table. He proffered its contents to our visitor and myself. We both declined. 'Of course, no one ever loiters without intent. You are anguished, about something or someone that has affected you deeply. A woman, perhaps.'

'That is—correct.'

'A fiancée?'

'How the devil—?'

I smiled inwardly at the man's confused expression. Holmes' eyes glittered with the opportunity to reveal his insight.

'You are neither beggar nor trader. You dress well, if somewhat untidily, which suggests the possibility that you normally take care of your appearance. Recently, circumstances have constrained your ability to maintain that pride. You stood outside my window every day since your arrival, considering whether or not to consult me. The ghastly manner in which you have composed your letter indicates there is still a reluctance, as if you subconsciously hope I will not take on your case.'

'If that's the case, Mr Holmes, then I will take my leave of you.'

'There is one thing I still do not know.'

The man frowned as he stood, clutching at his coat buttons. 'Mr Holmes?'

'Your name, sir. Your name!' Holmes gestured with an almost imperceptible motion of the wrist for the man to sit down.

'Slater, Mr Holmes. Oscar Slater.'

'Then, Mr Slater, how can we assist you?' Holmes was gracious then, nodding as Slater resumed his position on the settee, albeit with less irreverence than before.

I sat in one of the armchairs, listening keenly as the man began to tell us his tale of woe.

'My concern is a simple one, Mr Holmes.' He looked at me with suspicion.

'My dear friend Dr Watson can be trusted as equally as I,' Holmes assured him, and Slater continued.

'I am to be married to Miss Julia Kingsley. The date has been set and by this time next week she will be Mrs Oscar Slater.'

I offered our congratulations. Holmes glared at me for interrupting.

Slater continued. 'But I fear that this will not come to pass. She has been missing this last month.'

'Missing?' I enquired.

'Yes,' Slater nodded. I passed him a kerchief with which to mop the moisture from his head. Holmes and I both noticed he used it to dab his eyes, wishing no tears to be visible. 'I visit her weekly and have done since the spring, but I was turned away last month. Then I realised that she was not present.'

'Who turned you away?' asked Holmes.

'The housekeeper.'

'For what reason?'

'Mrs Gordon said that she had been unwell and had asked not to be disturbed, even by me.'

'And you accepted that?'

'Yes, doctor. I respect Julia greatly. If she asked to remain undisturbed, I would not go against her wishes.'

'Yet something told you all was not as it ought to be?'

Slater turned to my companion, who was staring out the window.

'Following the third visit on which I was declined an audience, I felt I had to insist on knowing what was wrong. Was she still ill? Had she been taken to her bed? I did not insist on seeing her. I insisted however on knowing the full extent of her condition. Even her sister refused to see me.'

'Perhaps she was caring for Miss Kingsley?'

Holmes breathed a response then stepped forward. 'What makes you suspect foul play?'

'Because my dearest Julia is the sweetest, most attentive and selfless young woman. It simply isn't possible that she is ignoring my enquiries regarding her welfare.'

Slater became a sorrowful individual then. I offered a clean kerchief.

'Will you find out the truth, sirs? Please?' He looked between us. 'Would you accompany me to Melfort Hall?'

I'd heard of the place but had never been there. It was in Sussex, on one of the lines that went down to the coast. Holmes' expression turned to hidden delight and he deftly offered his services on a formal basis. Slater seemed to sag where he sat in great relief.

'We shall leave on the morning train. Have you somewhere to stay tonight?' Holmes beckoned for the man to stand, waving to the door.

'Thank you, Mr Holmes. No. I have nowhere.'

'Dr Watson will see to it that you will have accommodation. Won't you, Watson?'

I was neither a hotelier nor an excursion agent but I nevertheless agreed to source somewhere for Mr Slater. 'Return here in an hour. I will have an address for you.'

'Excellent!' cried Holmes, clapping his hands together once. 'Then it is agreed. The first train of the day. Be punctual, Mr Slater.'

And with that, Holmes called for Mrs Hudson, who duly escorted Slater out into the street.

As my friend watched our visitor's departure from his window, I could not help but wonder what had piqued his curiosity so keenly. 'Surely, my dear Holmes, the domestic problems of a man and his fiancée are quite beneath your talents?'

'Normally I would agree with you. But there was something desperate about Oscar Slater. And crime enjoys no better hiding place than in the shadow of desperation.'

***

The train left Victoria Station punctually and Holmes, Slater and myself had a compartment to ourselves.

Slater seemed brighter than during our first meeting. Perhaps a good night's sleep at the Grosvenor had eased his burden. It's a pity I cannot recommend such an extravagance to my patients. He was clean shaven, his coat less crumpled than previously and he had bought himself a hat which sat by his side on the empty seat. Holmes, meanwhile, was sitting with his eyes closed. I knew he was not sleeping. Such was his way when sometimes he felt a silence could not be improved by conversation. Nevertheless, I was intrigued by the fellow and engaged with him as best I could.

'My family had a number of estates around here,' he was saying as, outside, the Surrey countryside replaced the bustling metropolis. The snow had melted overnight but there was a grey mist clinging to the fields as far as we could see through the fogging windows. 'Some were lost due to land rights following the Crimea, wills that weren't correctly fashioned, that sort of thing. Officers returning from the Black Sea were horrified to learn that their properties had been taken from under their noses. Three years fighting the bloody Kurds and that was the reward. I lost two uncles, not to the war, but to this. Did themselves in, in their despair.'

'But your own land remains secure?'

Slater leant back and looked down at his hands. 'I receive an allowance from my father. His property he has managed to retain.'

I had lost an older brother during the conflict in Crimea, so I was acutely cognizant of how it affects a family. The disputes over land ownership, however, I was not aware of, but Holmes gave a gentle snort at Slater's explanation, indicating his knowledge.

'And the Kingsley family?'

'They are unaffected. They only have Melfort Hall, but it is enough for Julia.'

Slater went on to describe how he had met her, that they had been courting for a considerable length of time and she had declined his proposal at least twice. But love knows no limit to its endurance, as the scriptures tell us, and she eventually agreed to take his hand in marriage. He was elusive in his response to my questions about her hesitancy.

I found him to be an agreeable fellow, a sea change from the brash, uncouth creature that presented himself to us in Baker Street.

As we pulled into Balham station, the gateway to the south, Holmes' eyes flicked open. 'It is highly improbable that you will be received warmly, if at all, when we get to Melfort Hall.'

'That's the case, I have no doubt, Mr Holmes,' Slater nodded. He reached into the pocket of his suit and retrieved a photograph. It was of a handsome woman, proud but with a saturnine expression. This seemed not to bother Slater, however, as he proudly showed us the sepia image of his beloved.

On the platform outside, luggage was loaded and unloaded, the snorting and wheezing of the great engine itself enveloping the station master and his boys in clouds of sooty smoke. Soon we were on our way again, the brooding metropolis of London falling even further away, the snow-laden marshes and heaths of Thornton and the Wandle commanding our appreciations.

The sliding door to the compartment moved to one side and the train's guard stood in the doorway. He said nothing to us, merely gesturing for our tickets, which we duly presented. I found him to be rather aloof and not at all what one would come to expect from the LB&SCR. He stepped forward and took Slater's ticket first, checking it then handing it back. The guard's bushy moustache and beard near bristled. His cap seemed to sit almost at his eyebrows. He turned to me next and then finally to Holmes. Task done, he departed as silently as he arrived.

'Have you any suggestions as to how we will be welcomed, Holmes?'

'My dear Watson, there are always suggestions. We will ask to see Miss Kingsley and gain an understanding as to the frosty reception we will no doubt receive.'

'Mr Holmes, they might be willing to accept you there. I feel it is me that is no longer welcome.'

'We will act as your—' Suddenly, Holmes grabbed my arm. 'Watson!'

'What the devil is the matter, Holmes?'

But my friend did not need to answer for before us Slater seemed to grow startled, clawing at his necktie as if it were too tight.

'What is it, man? Can you not breathe?'

He did not—could not—answer. I went to assist but Holmes, much to my shock, held me back. I could do nothing but watch the poor man gag and gasp, his whole body contorting and tightening. Froth appeared from his mouth and I knew then that this was no normal fit. He slumped lifeless to the carriage floor. The photograph of Miss Kingsley came to rest at his head.

'Carefully, Watson,' warned Holmes as he motioned for me to check Slater's pulse.

'He's dead!'

'Quite so.'

'Poison?'

'Possibly.'

'Shall we alert the guard? I'll pull the alarm.'

As I reached for the little chain above the door, Holmes stopped me. 'Really, Holmes. This is too much. You would not allow me to interject to help the poor devil and now I'm not to alert the guard?'

'If you pull that chain the train will stop. The murderer will be free to disembark.'

'Murderer? Good Lord! But we were here all the time!'

'Nevertheless, Mr Slater has indeed met his untimely end at the behest of a mysterious rogue.'

I was incredulous. 'How can we not be witness to such a tragedy when it befalls us right under our very noses? We have been alone in this compartment since we left Victoria.'

'Do not overlook our silent ticket inspector.'

'The guard! He was responsible?'

'Undoubtedly!'

'But how?'

Holmes stood, peering at the dead man's cuffs and collar. 'Something was passed between them. Did you not notice the delay in the guard releasing the ticket once he had handed it back to Slater?'

'I'm not sure.' In all honesty, the surprise of Slater's unexpected death made any recall a struggle.

'A sleight of hand?' Holmes stepped over Slater, head bobbing and twitching as he scanned the seat where the dead man had sat and the floor around where his body now lay. I noticed he did not get too close, which was unlike my inquisitive companion.

'What is it that's causing your hesitancy?'

'The guard passed something to him. A needle or a dart? Something poisoned that pricked the skin.'

'Wouldn't the effect have been immediate?'

'Slow toxins are commonplace and often necessary for those who require the chance to remove themselves from the scene. It is what I would have done.'

'Then perhaps we should be thankful that you put your keen mind to the study of detection not criminality!'

'Do you recall the cases of Dupin some years ago?'

'The French amateur sleuth involved with that murderous monkey in the morgue?'

'The same, Watson. Although it was an orangutan. An ape, not a monkey.'

'What of it? Surely, you're not saying the guard was an ape in disguise?'

Holmes' eyes widened and the corner of his mouth twitched. I could see he found amusement in my conclusion. 'I mention the Parisian because of his ratiocination. Think like the criminal and one is more likely to understand the mind of a criminal. Ha! Look here!'

Where Holmes was pointing gave me no indication of what he had seen.

'The sawdust, the flakes of wood—here, here and here.'

On closer inspection, I saw what he had found. 'They've come from our shoes, trodden in when we alighted.'

'They are clean. Not from the soles of our footwear. They were dropped here.'

'The door frame is made of wood. Shavings as the door to the corridor slides to and fro?'

'A logical deduction. But no.'

I sighed, finding equal fascination and frustration in Holmes' usual procrastination in explaining his thought processes. 'Then what, my dear Holmes?'

He stepped into the thin corridor, his sure footing barely troubled by the train crossing the points as we passed through Oxted into the Sussex countryside. He picked up a glass phial that had rolled around, coming to a rest in the crevasse where the door met the metal strip on the carriage's floor.

'By Jove, a test tube!' I observed.

'And within, more of the dust and shavings. And a scrap of what appears to be a leaf. There is no stopper, so whoever dropped the phial had already removed it.'

'The guard?'

Holmes nodded and returned to our compartment. 'Look at Slater's left cuff. That was the side of him nearest to the guard when he was seated.'

I did indeed look. There was a gentle smudge of the same sawdust on the hem of his coat sleeve.

'Slater did not collect that sawdust on his way down to the floor. It came from the test tube while he was still seated.'

'Left there by whatever fell from the test tube?'

'Ah! Watson! Yes! The dust, the shavings, the leaf. What do they indicate?'

'That something was kept alive in it? An insect?'

Holmes nodded gravely. 'An insect. One with a deadly bite, perhaps? We have a method. Now we need a motive.' He slipped the phial and the photograph into the folds of his Inverness cape.

'But the guard, though?'

'Likely not one at all. Let us leave Mr Slater to his mortal solace for the moment and notify this train's bona fide representative.'

We found the guard, six carriages down. It was obvious that the one who had inspected our tickets had not been genuine for this one towered above us and was growling with indignation that someone had been pretending to be a member of the train company.

But when we returned to our compartment, Slater's body had gone.

Uckfield Station was a lonely spot, the train line curving away out of sight down to Lewes, terminating at Brighton. Looking around, Holmes clapped his gloved hands together. Whipping his cane from under his arm, he marched out into the town itself, his coat flapping behind him like the wings of some flailing bird.

He insisted on walking, ignoring my complaints that the snow was thicker here than in London and that a cabby would be easier on the legs.

'This is not Baker Street, friend Watson! We could be here until dusk waiting for a suitable conveyance. We shall head to Melfort Hall on foot.'

The cold was, I must admit as I write this sometime later in my own warm lodgings, exhilarating. The sort of chill that pricks one's senses to an almost supernatural height. The gentle crunching of the snow under our feet was, with the occasional call of a rook or a cuckoo, all that we could hear. It was sublime in its simplicity. The main street up to the house was on a slight incline that became steeper as we neared its pinnacle. The slush underfoot made progress slow but that mattered little. No wonder Holmes had mentioned a few times his desire to retire one day to this astonishingly beautiful county and keep bees.

Melfort Hall came into view as we followed the road around, a line of majestic lime trees guiding us to the entrance which itself was rather sedate, especially for a grand country manor.

We spied some movement in the windows as we approached but on knocking at the door we were kept waiting for some time.

'The staff need to be more conscious of visitors,' I mused. Holmes waved me quiet as the door finally opened to reveal a butler. We introduced ourselves and were bade enter.

The large reception area was replete with all manner of stuffed animals from, I assumed, the African continent. There was an odd aroma in the air. Stuffy. Surprising seeing as the reception was as tall as it was wide.

'Yes, I noticed it as soon as we reached the doorway,' Holmes said, moving to a rearing lion. 'Look at this.' He was engrossed in staring into the glass baubles that had replaced the poor creature's eyeballs.

'Holmes—' I tapped my friend at the small of his back. He took a few moments to turn around to see a woman standing before us.

'You admire my father's collection?'

She was tall and elegant, proud. I frowned, sure I had seen her before.

'Taxidermy is an art that is quite beyond me. It is not that I do not appreciate the skill involved, far from it. No, the eyes are never quite captured. It takes one away from the magic of the thing.'

'It makes them soulless,' she agreed.

'Miss Kingsley?' Holmes asked, removing his hat and nodding once.

Of course! The woman from Slater's photograph! But she was not missing at all!

'I am, but perhaps not the one of whom you are thinking. I am Mathilda Kingsley.'

'Mathilda?' I asked.

'I am Julia's older sister. By twenty minutes.'

'Twins.' Holmes raised an eyebrow. 'I am Sherlock Holmes and this is John Watson.'

'Ah, Dr Watson. You are Mr Holmes' amanuensis.'

Medical life is full of dangers and pitfalls, and luck must play its part in a man's career—but to be thought of as a mere secretary was irksome in the least. Holmes detected my irritation so moved further forward into the reception area.

'Has news reached you of Mr Slater?'

'Indeed it has, Mr Holmes, although I am surprised you are on the case so swiftly.'

'We are not here for that.'

Holmes and I both noticed that Miss Kingsley did not seem overly perturbed about Slater's death.

'Then why are you here?'

'At Mr Slater's request, to locate your missing sister.'

'Julia?'

'You have another sister?' Holmes studied another stuffed beast, a chimpanzee, positioned on a plaster-of-Paris tree.

'No, just the one.'

'Then you must know that your identical twin is missing,' he reasoned. Then Holmes spun on his heels, an arm raised palm upwards. He gestured towards a closed door. 'Shall we?'

Miss Kingsley motioned to her butler to open the door to the Morning Room and we followed her in. She sat away from us, her back to the window so that her face was partly in shadow. Holmes made himself comfortable on the armchair by the door, facing inwards so that he had a full view of the layout before him. He indicated with a flick of his wrist that I was to sit as close to Miss Kingsley as was acceptable without appearing too invasive.

'Mr Slater was to be your brother-in-law, yes?'

The woman nodded once. 'That is correct, sir.'

'And you knew him well?' Holmes tapped the arm of the chair. 'He was a regular visitor to Melfort Hall?'

'Not as much as we would have liked.'

'What kept him away?'

'Let us say that he had other interests that commanded his attention.'

Miss Kingsley dabbed an eye with a kerchief. There was something peculiar about the action, as if it was for our benefit and not because she was distressed by that statement or indeed the fact that Slater was dead and her sister unwell.

I, however, maintained the stance that this was a lady suffering upset and acted accordingly. 'If you wish to continue this at a later time, Mr Holmes and I would gladly delay.'

'Tell me,' Holmes continued, completely ignoring my attempted subversion. 'What interests? Did he gamble? Drink to excess?'

'Women, Mr Holmes. My sister's fiancé was a cad and a womaniser.'

'Oliver Slater appeared to us to be an upstanding individual,' came Holmes' measured reply. He waited for a few moments, then: 'Come, Watson, we shall leave Miss Kingsley to her thoughts.'

We stood and went to leave. My colleague asked if we could return afresh in the morning. Miss Kingsley agreed and we left Melfort Hall to find lodgings nearby.

As I ate a cold supper and Holmes smoked at least four pipes, he asked me what was peculiar about our meeting with the elder sister.

'Why, nothing. She was, perhaps, a touch aloof. To hide her upset?'

'Ha! Watson! Have you learnt nothing during our time together? I stated Slater's fiancée was missing. She is not, from what Slater himself said.'

'Oh! Yes, of course. Julia Kingsley merely wouldn't have an audience with him.'

'Quite so. She did not correct me. Nor did she correct me when I purposely called him Oliver.'

I was embarrassed that I had not picked up on Holmes' deliberate mistakes. 'But why test the woman so? Of what can you possibly suspect her?'

'Her sister refuses to see Slater, Slater is dead, yet she seemed inconvenienced by our presence. I was testing her.'

'It seems you were right, my dear fellow.'

'Am I?'

'Well, yes.' I pushed the emptied plate away from me, my hunger appeased. 'She didn't even ask how Mr Slater met his end!'

'You have suggested, in your accounts of our cases, that I am not a man entirely at ease with women. I might usefully suggest that you have mistaken a lack of sentiment for a lack of knowledge, but if you are correct, I must read them as you would read one of your medical journals. I have merely established that her distress is carried within.'

'So you suspect her of nothing?'

'On the contrary. When we began this journey, we were to relieve Mr Slater of his worries concerning his fiancée. Now we are investigating his death and have heard the accusation that he was not an honourable man. Everyone is a suspect, including the sisters Kingsley.'

I couldn't shake the feeling that Slater was only murdered because he had sought us out. Holmes dismissed this with his usual pragmatism, reminding me that the guilty—whether of thievery or toying with the emotions of others—must always be looking over their shoulders.

***

The next morning presented us with a Miss Mathilda Kingsley in less control of her sorrow. We were with her in a different room, one that contained a grand piano upon which stood a selection of photographs. Towards the back were several of the sisters together (their similarity was truly striking), as well as sole portraits that took their places at the front of the display. Others were of older ladies and gentlemen, fathers, mothers, perhaps. There were none of Oscar Slater.

Miss Kingsley wept openly but gently into her kerchief, apologising for her manner.

'Think nothing of it,' I said. 'We understand this is a difficult time for all.'

'When did you last see Mr Slater?' Holmes asked her.

'Not for a while. The staff had strict instructions not to let him in.'

'Instructed by you?'

'Yes. I would not have that man darken our door, upsetting my poor sister so.'

'It was not, then, your sister who refused to see him?' Holmes paced the room. 'She was aware that he attempted to visit her, however?'

'Why would she be?'

The idea seemed ridiculous to her.

'Surely, she has the right to refuse her own visitors?' I interjected.

'I am the elder sister. I run this household. If I do not deem him worthy of her time, I will tell him so.'

'Regardless of your sister's feelings?'

Miss Kingsley curtly flattened the pleats of her dress. 'When Dr Watson visits you, are you no longer the master of your household? Would you not turn away those who might cause him harm? I see no benefit in these questions.'

'Miss Kingsley,' said I, trying to keep my voice even, 'there has been a murder!'

'It is nothing to do with me!'

'Then,' Holmes breathed, 'let us reach the same conclusion together.'

'There is no mystery here, Mr Holmes. My sister's fiancé was a scoundrel and his death most likely at the hand of some disgruntled lover. Or cuckolded husband, for he had no compunctions on that score. As far as I am concerned, she is rid of him. A mercy has been done.' She visibly shuddered at the idea of Slater's supposed dalliances.

'But surely a murder cannot go unpunished, no matter the motivation behind it? Do you mind?'

Miss Kingsley shook her head so Holmes lit a cigarette. She passed him an ashtray that was by her elbow on a side table.

'Perhaps if you were to tell us more about Mr Slater, then we can ascertain who might have known he was on the train,' I suggested.

'I did not keep a track of his movements. Those he foisted upon us were quite sufficient.'

'Then how do you know he was unfaithful to her?' Holmes looked at the end of his cigarette, watching the smoke curl up to the ceiling then dissipate surprisingly quickly.

Mathilda Kingsley hesitated, perhaps anticipating the reaction to her next statement.

'I saw it in his eyes.'

'On such proof, Miss Kingsley, we would all face the dock.'

'Mr Holmes, I do not doubt your skill—or your experience—but you are wrong.'

'I am? Did you ever confront him?'

'There was no need.'

'Because you had already tried and condemned him.'

'Perhaps so.'

'Whose animals are those? The ones in the entrance.'

'My late father's. He was a hunter in Africa. They are his trophies.'

'Who would have taken Mr Slater's body?' I was surprised at Holmes' question. It seemed quite clear to me that she knew nothing of Slater's murder. Even the sins she derided now appeared to be based on pure supposition. As she lowered her eyes to the hearth rug on which Holmes now stood, he pressed further. 'There is still some concern as to who murdered the man, but I believe you know the perpetrator, yes?'

'I—'

'Do you engage in your late father's hobby?'

'I said that I didn't,' came the reply.

'You said the art made the subjects soulless.'

'And I am assured of that.'

'Did you consider Mr Slater to be lacking in a soul?'

'I don't understand, Mr Holmes.'

My friend moved to the piano and stared intently at the photographs. 'By your assumption of his nature, you must conclude that he has no conscience, no soul, when it comes to matters of the heart—especially when it pertains to your sister. Where is she by the way? If you kept her from Mr Slater, why keep her from us?'

'She is unwell.'

'I can attend to her,' I ventured. 'I am a doctor, after all.'

'Indeed!' Holmes clucked his tongue. 'Dr Watson will see what ails your poor younger sister!'

'I—I forbid it!'

'Forbid? It is my duty to ensure the welfare of any who are sick or in pain. Do you deny her that, too?' I stood and went to move to the door. Miss Kingsley looked between us, an element of panic behind her eyes, if only for a fleeting moment.

'The family doctor is on hand. He will see to her.'

'You told a story to Slater that your sister was unwell. A story. Yet you endeavour to impress on us the same? Watson—' Holmes indicated I was to leave the room.

'Stop!' came Miss Kingsley's reply.

Holmes raised a hand, halting my progress to the door.

'I see no logic in your objection, unless of course your sister is perfectly well. Kept a prisoner, one begins to imagine.'

Miss Kingsley glared at Holmes. 'She will not take kindly to strangers. You must understand I only want to protect Julia from a life of servitude and unhappiness. Slater had no social standing to speak of. He only wanted to marry my sister for her wealth.'

'Mr Slater's family—'

The woman cut me short. 'Mr Slater has no family. He is a deceitful man. He approached you to bolster his innocence. He betrayed himself to you with lies.'

'I saw no evidence of any falsehood,' Holmes said. 'You speak great ill of him, yet—'

'Yet?' She looked up at my friend.

'Your voice trembles whenever you mention him. This is not the response of a woman protecting her sibling. This is a woman driven by a far more common human impulse.'

'Speak plainly, Mr Holmes.'

'Jealousy, Miss Kingsley.'

'Jealousy!' Miss Kingsley threw back her head and laughed. It seemed odd bearing in mind the mystery Holmes was beginning to unravel. 'You consider me to be some feeble woman, swooning in the presence of a man? That I should be jealous of my sister's lover! How dare you!'

'You mistake me, Miss Kingsley. You are not jealous of Slater. You are jealous of your sister.'

'You are grasping at straws, Mr Holmes! I ask you to leave Melfort Hall immediately and subject some more impressionable lady to your amateur sleuthing.'

I could see her comment made Holmes tense. It was imperceptible to anyone who wasn't a close confidant of his, but his left nostril twitched. Would we leave as she had so vehemently demanded? His expression cleared and I could read nothing further from him. Yet he stood quite still, locking eyes with Miss Kingsley, perhaps searching for any further weakness.

She was the first to break and rushed from the room.

'Good Lord, Holmes!'

'Yes. A performance worthy of Adelaide Neilson.'

'You believe her to be playing to the audience, as it were?'

Holmes moved in close to me. 'She had a line of dust on her left cheek, just below her eye. The same sawdust we found in the carriage. She is left-handed, judging from the manner in which she uses her kerchief, so she transferred the dust herself from her own fingers!'

50

'And what of her jealousy? How do we know Slater isn't what she claims him to be?'

'Last night, after you had retired for the evening, I went into the town. There's a members-only club, the Cinque Ports, that I correctly deduced would be a melting pot of gossip. It wasn't long before local talk turned to Oscar Slater. The evening press was running a story about a body found trackside not a few miles from Edenbridge. It was clear to me that it was Slater. I asked if anyone knew him. Everyone did. I did not announce that I knew he was already dead and that the body may very well have been his.'

'Do the locals share the same sentiment at Miss Kingsley?'

'No. He is highly respected. His father has been part of the Uckfield community for many years.'

'Many a rogue has been highborn.'

'True, but the Slaters are, by all accounts, financially comfortable.'

'Which suggests he is not the adventurer Miss Kingsley the elder suggests.'

'Completely. Hence my thoughts regarding jealousy.'

'But what, pray, could she be jealous of?'

'The younger sister attracting a noble bachelor? The elder feeling that she is soon unable to find such a future for herself?'

'They are twins! Surely minutes differ between them?'

'That may be so, but—'

The awful scream that assaulted our ears stopped us in mid-conversation. We looked at each other and raced in its direction.

We found the butler leaning over a crumpled figure in a room at the top of a flight of stairs. I drew my revolver—I rarely carried it but Holmes had suggested it on this occasion—and, now cocked, pointed it at the man's back.

'I say, step away now, if you please—'

The butler, aged and clearly distraught, struggled to right himself. 'It's Miss Kingsley! She's—'

'Wait!' cried Holmes. 'Stay where you are, Watson. You, sir, move back very slowly. That glass!'

'Glass, sir?' the butler asked, confused.

'On the table there. Hand it to me, slowly!'

The butler reached for the glass beaker and gingerly handed it to my friend who deftly hopped over the prone figure and placed the glass, bottom upwards, on the wooden floor, sliding it so that it was not over a join in the floorboards. Holmes visibly sighed with relief and stepped back.

'Lower your weapon, dear Watson. This butler did not kill poor Miss Kingsley.'

'Eh?' I was baffled but replaced the safety catch and slid my old army pistol back into my jacket pocket.

'*Latrodectus katipo.*'

Still none the wiser, I asked Holmes to explain further, but he motioned to the butler instead, who said:

'The spider, Dr Watson. Miss Kingsley and her sister, they were collectors.'

Then I realised what the room was that we had entered. There were no windows but on all four walls, with a gap just for the door, were cabinets, the glass fronts of each misted and murky. Within I could make out little plants and logs. They were display cabinets for all manner of insects and arachnids.

One such case was open; I peered into it. Holmes drew from his pocket the phial, pointing out that the leaf section it contained matched those in the cabinet, along with the scraps of wood shavings and chips. Other than that, the case was devoid of any living creature.

'It is under the beaker!' exclaimed Holmes. 'Look! The true mistress of this mysterious murder!'

And there it was. A spider, no bigger than a ha'penny, black with a scarlet diamond upon its back. It was sitting motionless, long legs rising up against the inside of its little prison.

'That thing killed Slater, and now Miss Kingsley?'

'Of that I am most certain, Watson.'

***

The local constabulary had asked us to stay on for a day or so while they went about their investigations. Holmes said nothing to them about Slater or the missing sister.

Now we sat again in his rooms in Baker Street, and I wondered if he would open up to me about his thoughts. He was prone to bouts of low mood and now was no different. I wondered if it was because this most peculiar case was still unsolved.

Eventually, as the afternoon turned to evening and the sound of the lamplighters going about their duties rose up to the tall sash windows, my friend finally spoke.

'The guard on the train who checked our tickets had the phial concealed in her sleeve.'

'Her?'

'Yes. Miss Mathilda Kingsley. Quite ingeniously disguised.'

'What on earth—?' I spluttered, my whisky going everywhere. 'How do you know?'

'She released the spider as she handed Slater's ticket back. The venom is quite capable of killing a man. And without antidote at present. The katipo spider, however, is normally docile until threatened. Slater's movements caused it to bite.'

'So that was why he collapsed without apparent reason.'

'The spider would have still been within his clothing. Once we had vacated the scene, it would not have been difficult for Kingsley to return, open the compartment's exterior door and push Slater's body out while the train was moving. She would have no doubt removed her disguise and continued the journey without any other passengers knowing or raising suspicion.'

'Why would it have not been Julia herself?'

'Because it was Julia whom we met at Melfort Hall.'

I was dumbfounded. 'Not Mathilda?'

'No. I realised as soon as she was bitten by the spider. You see, Julia loved Slater but was indeed barred from visits from him by Mathilda. As the elder sister, she was the head of the household and governed accordingly. That was well-known in the town, certainly by those who frequented the Cinque Ports. Mathilda, incensed by whatever it was she believed Slater to be, killed him to save her sister from what she was convinced would be a life of misery. Julia would never have killed him!'

'But why would Julia pretend to be her sister?'

'To protect her! She knew Mathilda had killed Slater. That would not have been easy for her, but they were still sisters and it was better to lose one than both.'

'And the spiders?'

'A collection inherited from their late father. Mathilda would have known which ones were deadly, as would have Julia.'

'Then why would Julia have been bitten?'

'She feared discovery. She was an unwilling accomplice to Slater's murder. The Edenbridge police will come to that conclusion when they have autopsied his body and traced the venom back to Melfort Hall. She went into the room, opened the katipo spider case and aggravated another of the beasts on purpose to force it to turn on her. I fear the unfortunate creatures will all be destroyed as a result.'

'The poor girl wanted only love. Was it jealousy?'

Silence returned to the room for a few moments; only the ticking of the clock and Holmes imbibing on his long clay pipe interrupted our contemplations.

'Holmes—'

'Watson?'

'If that was Julia we met and it was Mathilda who killed Julia's fiancé—?'

'Yes?'

'Then where is Mathilda?'

The Woman Who Wasn't: Part Three

The next morning, I made my way to Holmes' rooms at Baker Street with something of a spring in my step. It was not often that I had the opportunity to exhibit my own deductive powers for Mr Sherlock Holmes and I freely admit I found the idea immensely appealing.

Of course, I was not foolish enough to believe that he would be, in any way, demonstrative regarding my little triumph. At best, I expected a backhanded compliment of some sort. I was not "as literal-minded and unimaginative as my reputation suggested", perhaps. Something intended kindly but with a second, grander purpose—reminding all in earshot which of us was a consulting detective and which an ex-Army Doctor.

I paused on the doorstep, hand poised to knock. That had been an unkind thought. Infuriating as the man could be, I'd never had cause to doubt his loyalty. Even his affection, however lightly worn, was clear enough to me. So why such bitter contemplations?

I put some of it down to the inferior quality of the previous night's sleep. I had tossed and turned violently enough that Mary would have banished me to the guest bedroom had she not, in her words, feared for the furnishings.

Mrs Hudson appeared at the door in a matter of moments and the look on her face told me that she had slumbered no less poorly.

From up the stairs, Holmes' violin could be heard. It was not one of his more mellifluous airs, being more akin to the cries of an anguished feline.

'I presume Mr Holmes is in an ill humour,' I said, as Mrs Hudson took my coat and hat.

'You may presume what you like, Doctor Watson,' she said firmly. 'Though I would favour strange over ill. He took his breakfast as though he hadn't a care in the world. If he had burst into song, I wouldn't have been overly surprised. An hour later, he's scraping away at that blessed violin as though it had wronged him personally.'

I frowned. My friend's moods were mercurial, but seldom shifted fully pole-to-pole without some catalyst.

'Did he receive any message this morning?' I enquired.

'Nothing by post,' said Mrs Hudson. 'Though one of his street urchins did arrive shortly after breakfast.'

'That will be it,' I consoled her. 'Some frustration with a case, no doubt. I'll speak to him.'

'If it will stop that infernal noise,' said Mrs Hudson firmly, 'I don't mind if you whistle *There Grew a Little Flower* at him.'

***

As I entered the sitting room, Holmes allowed the violin to slip to his side.

'Ah, Watson,' he said, without turning. 'I take it that Mrs Hudson has reached her wits' end.'

'Her appreciation for the violin is certainly at a low ebb,' I conceded.

Holmes swivelled and graced me with a rueful grin.

'I tax the poor woman too much,' he said. 'I ought to be ashamed of myself.' He set the violin haphazardly on a nearby table and slumped into his chair. 'Although, it is to be noted, I am much provoked.'

'By Mrs Hudson?'

'No, that fine lady remains the picture of patience,' said Holmes. 'This case, however, tries me terribly. Every time I feel I am on the cusp of a vital discovery, it is torn away from me.'

'No closer to locating the errant Miss Frain, I take it,' I said, secretly pleased that he had not made too much headway in my absence.

'She grows further away by the moment.'

'Then be of good cheer, Holmes,' said I, seizing my moment.

Holmes' expression shifted almost imperceptibly to one of amused curiosity. He gestured towards the chair opposite and I slid into it.

'Your research has paid dividends, Watson?'

I suddenly felt a sense of insecurity creep over me.

'Well, Holmes, of course, it's not a solution, as such, but—'

'I will happily accept the smallest clue.'

'It may prove to be entirely inconsequential—' I cautioned.

'Let us take that risk together.'

His gaze was of such intensity that I found myself quite tongue-tied.

'The Adventure of the Red Diamond!' I managed finally.

Holmes pursed his lips.

'My dear Watson, forgive me. I haven't the slightest idea to what you are referring. I take it this is the fantastical title you have given to one of our cases.'

'The Kingsley sisters.'

'Ah,' said Holmes. 'Julia and Mathilda. Yes, that was an unfortunate affair.' He leapt from his chair to the mantel and began to fill his pipe. 'And one, if I remember correctly, in which the murderer escaped justice, aided and abetted by her loving, if misguided twin.'

'There are two Frain sisters,' I offered, my confidence slipping away even as I spoke.

Smoke drifted upwards from his pipe's bowl as Holmes considered this.

'Ah. You believe that the elder Miss Frain—or, more correctly, Mrs Manson—may have knowledge of her sister's whereabouts.'

'It's possible, is it not? Why, she might even be concealing her!'

Holmes gave a whoop of exultation.

'Congratulations, Watson!'

I felt colour rise to my cheeks.

'You think there's something in it, Holmes?'

'I'm afraid not, Watson.'

'Then why—'

'Well, you continue to surprise me, old fellow. That is precisely the line of enquiry I was pursuing until just this morning.'

'I see,' I said, somewhat crestfallen.

'Buck up, Watson. It was an excellent piece of reasoning. You should be proud of it. Unfortunately, my own investigations have ruled out the possibility.'

'Ah. The message you received from the Irregulars.'

'Quite so. Or rather, that was the final nail in the coffin. You see, I was *en route* to the home of Mr and Mrs Manson myself when I saw you yesterday. I disguised myself—rather convincingly, if I do say so myself—as a labourer in search of honest work. My intention was to inveigle myself onto the grounds. But I found neither Mr nor Mrs Manson at home. The solitary servant on staff informed me that they had decamped to London, on some business matter of Mr Manson's, days before.'

'Suspicious timing, with her sister missing.'

'Not necessarily, Watson. Although, yes, I wondered if she was shielding her sibling by remaining on the move. Perhaps even plotting an elopement with Sir Harrison's mystery man. It certainly wouldn't be the first time, as you so rightly noted, that siblings had conspired together. That was when I put the Irregulars on the case, but they turned up nothing of Miss Frain. Indeed, from the report I received, I believe that Mrs Manson may be taking the opportunity afforded by her husband's business to mount her own search.'

I couldn't help but feel disappointment at this turn of events. I had been so sure that I had stumbled on, if not the answer, then, at least, a set of pertinent questions. I said as much to Holmes.

'Do not be disheartened, Watson. We have closed down an avenue of enquiry. That is a discovery in its own right.'

'Perhaps you should take your own advice, Holmes,' I replied, with a nod to the abandoned violin.

Holmes smiled thinly.

'Wise as ever, Watson. You are, of course, quite right. We have eliminated Mrs Manson from our list of suspects. Why, if we can only do the same for the remaining five million inhabitants of London, the case is closed.'

I chuckled.

'Have I said something amusing, Watson?'

'Not at all, Holmes, you have simply reassured me. It is only when you on the verge of a breakthrough that you allow yourself to become so hyperbolic.'

Holmes gave a reluctant bark of laughter in return.

'You know me far too well,' he conceded, tapping at his temple with one long, bony finger. 'There is *something* stirring. But I cannot christen it as yet.'

'Much like our mystery man.'

'You strike at the heart of the matter. He appears to have disappeared even more completely than Anastasia Frain.'

'Then that is where we ought to focus our energies.'

'Indeed, Watson. And I'm sure, given a few more hours of quiet contemplation, I will hit upon where to begin.'

I looked once more at the violin and thought of poor Mrs Hudson's nerves. I feared she would be in for another difficult night.

'Leave me to my misery, Watson,' he said, grasping the instrument and tucking it once more beneath his chin. 'I shall call on you in the morning, refreshed and revitalised.'

'Very well,' I said, standing to leave.

Holmes turned back to the window and raised his bow.

'Feel free to continue your studies,' he said, as I made my way towards the stairs. 'Who knows what you may discover?'

***

I returned to my papers that evening with less enthusiasm than previously. I was becoming increasingly convinced that Holmes was simply trying to keep me occupied while he went about his own investigations.

But I soon lit upon an unusual, recent case that drew me back in. It seemed to have been written in haste, rendering my medical scrawl even more difficult to decipher than usual.

'The Mystery of Flower & Dean,' I read aloud.

The Mystery of Flower & Dean

Penny Jones

'Dangerous.' The word was muttered under Holmes's breath, but to whom it was directed remained uncertain.

I was about to enquire further when the peace of the room was shattered by the chiming of the front doorbell. From below came the sound of Mrs Hudson's slow and measured tread, swiftly followed by the clip of heels as the new arrival made their way along the hallway, past Mrs Hudson's door and towards the stairs that led up to Holmes's rooms.

'A woman?' I deduced. 'That or a small man, wearing new shoes.'

'A *woman*, Watson. A most dangerous woman.'

I turned to ask Holmes what he meant by this—he was currently in his favourite chair, by the fire with his back to the window so that the late afternoon light would fall upon his newspaper. It also meant that I would have to leave the comfort of the fire to light the lamps when the shadows finally crept too deeply across my own pages. Was his comment about the dangerous woman linked to his earlier statement? If so, then how had he known that there was anyone out there? Male or female, dangerous or not? I had not chance to form the words, however, before my musings were broken by the rap of Mrs Hudson's knuckles on the door. This was followed by her steps as she made her way back down the narrow stairs. Holmes remained seated behind his paper, seemingly unaffected, and after a few moments, propriety drew me up from my seat to discover what manner of monstrous woman lurked in his hallway.

As I opened the door to greet her, the woman stood back, as close to the stairs as she could without tumbling back down them, the shadowy landing hiding her features. Her clothes were bright, almost garish, in the fashion of the day. Her demeanour, however, was not that of high society; her bearing was meek, withdrawn, as if she wished to hide herself from the scrutiny of others, rather than attract their attention.

'How can we help you?'

The words had barely left my throat before the onslaught of words erupted from this woman's mouth, flustered and hysterical, but with clear intent. I stepped forward, my hand outstretched as to calm her before she fainted, but instead of soothing her, it seemed to aggravate her further. She pulled away, lurching dangerously towards the steep flight of stairs behind her. The sudden pain that showed upon her face, as she clipped her elbow on the newel post, alone reminded her of her precarious position. Although for a moment as she lifted her eyes up towards mine, her gaze that of a deer startled by a hunt, she seemed to consider allowing herself to fall. To let gravity take her, break her fragile bones and snap her neck against the steps and walls and the tiled floor of the hallway far below, rather than step forward into Holmes's rooms.

Panic seized me as I debated whether I should step back and allow her to pass, or forward, grabbing at her to prevent her plummet down the long steep stairs. Before I could make the decision, she made it for me and rocking on her ankles, stepped towards me, as if that had always been her intention. By the time she had stripped off her gloves and moved past me into Holmes's sitting room, any sign of fear had been replaced with a calm, confident manner. As she approached the fire, she extended her hand and waited for Holmes to rise and introduce himself.

***

The tale of the disappearance was one all too common in England at that time.

Holmes sat listening, as I transcribed Mrs White's complaint to paper. Her childhood friend, Lucy, was missing; she'd been due to come down to London to visit but when Mrs White went to Covent Garden to meet her, there was no sign of the coach, or of the young woman.

'It was a week ago.'

'A week?' Holmes countered.

'Yes.' Mrs White counted off the days on her fingers 'One week ago exactly.'

'And why have you come to me now? A week is little time for the police to have finished their investigation.'

The woman dabbed at her eyes with her handkerchief, the letters A.S. carefully embroidered on the white material. 'The police. I haven't been to the police. I came straight here.'

'Understandable.' Holmes muttered under his breath. 'But then why wait so long to come and inform me of your friend's disappearance?'

Mrs White took a long breath to calm herself. 'I only just heard back from her family today. I wrote to them in case Lucy hadn't been able to make the coach down from York. But they said that she got on the coach; they waved her off themselves.' She dabbed at her eyes once more her words faltering as her composure broke 'I—I came straight here.'

'I can see you're distressed Mrs White. I have just one more question for you, before I take on your case. What was the exact date and time that you had arranged to meet Lucy from the coach?'

'It was last Thursday, the 17th, at five o'clock in the evening.'

***

I had barely set foot back in Holmes's rooms before the questions started. Each one designed, ostensibly to test my powers of observation, though in truth I knew I was little more than a sounding board for Holmes—his mind running through the myriad misfortunes that could have befallen a young woman in our often cruel city.

'Was she crying when you saw her out, Watson?'

'Yes.' I thought back to the woman who hurried in front of me down the stairs, her handkerchief held to her eyes. Once again, I worried that she would stumble and fall, her eyesight obscured by the material and her tears as she sobbed.

'Was her handkerchief wet?'

'Yes. No—I don't know. I couldn't see it.' I thought back to the woman's departure, her flight down the stairs, only briefly broken whilst I unlocked the front door, her handkerchief clasped in her hand as she constantly dabbed at her eyes, the motion obscuring both face and cloth. 'Now I'm not even sure if she was crying. Wailing certainly, but thinking about it, I only deduced that she was crying from that and her incessant dabbing at her eyes. But for the brief moment I saw her face as she bid me goodbye, her eyes were dry, and her countenance although worried, showed little sign of the distress that I would have expected.'

'Good. And did you get a close look at the handkerchief?'

'No, as I said she had it clasped in her hand, only the corner peeking out.'

'Did you catch glimpse of it when she first removed it from her pocket?'

'Yes. It was—a handkerchief.'

'But what made it different, to say yours or mine?'

'It was monogrammed, but that's not unusual. I believe they are quite often given as gifts.'

'Especially as wedding gifts?'

'I suppose so.' Holmes watched as I tried to figure out where this line of questioning was leading.

'And would it be usual do you think for a married woman to use those monogrammed handkerchiefs?'

'Yes. I don't see why not. Mary has a set gifted us by my Godfather of which she is particularly fond.'

'And for a married woman to still use those handkerchiefs embroidered with the initials of her maiden name?'

'I—I'm not sure. I suppose it would be odd. I'm not sure if I would be altogether happy for Mary to cling to those vestiges of her past life. Though I expect it would depend on circumstance.'

'Ah! That brings me on to my next question. How would you describe the circumstances of our recent client?'

'Well I would say she was quite well-to-do.' Holmes watched me, pausing, a common trick I saw him use often with clients—when he was waiting for them to trip themselves up in their own story. 'I mean she was wearing the latest fashions, they must have cost a pretty penny.' Holmes nodded, but not in agreement, it was a habit I had noticed of late. He seemed to use often with both myself and Mrs Hudson. Fatherly in manner, it was condescending in intent. 'Well I suppose she could have borrowed the money for the clothes. Do you think that's the reason behind the disappearance, money? Could it be for a ransom, do you believe she was in on it? Were they both in on it, a hoax maybe?'

Holmes didn't answer, just checked his pocket watch and bolted to his feet 'We'll have to hurry if we're to catch the five o'clock coach.'

***

Covent Garden, although still busy, wasn't packed to the rafters, having reached that odd lull that came over it once the costermongers and barrow boys had sold their wares and left for the day. The young flower girls and their posies had yet to be replaced by the older, more knowing flower sellers and their poses. The latter came in at night with the theatre crowd.

Posters for the Grand Circus covered those depicting the gruesome Whitechapel murders, their gaiety lending a thin veneer of normality to the fear that had gripped London since the previous year. Holmes stood back as he watched the coaches arrive and leave, each one drawing a crowd, as friends and families reunited, many peeling off to celebrate their reunions in one of the area's many taverns.

The five o'clock coach was early; its inhabitants disembarked and any travelling cases were swiftly stacked upon the pavement before the coachman departed, mere minutes past the hour.

'Holmes. Didn't you wish to go speak to the driver?'

I watched as the coach drove past, but Holmes did not even glance its way, let alone raise a hand to stop it leaving. I watched as the final travellers and their companions dispersed, noticing that Holmes appeared distracted, his eyes flickering this way and that as the piazza began to fill with the evening theatre crowd—in their fine clothes and finer moods—as they carefully stepped across the cobbled thoroughfares, slick with the detritus of the day's market.

'Do you see that woman, Watson?'

I followed Holmes' gaze, the streets now rapidly filling as the day darkened and the night crowd came to take its place within Covent Garden.

'Which woman, Holmes? There are many of them out there.' I squinted across in the dimming light.

'The one over by the pillar, by the apple market.'

I squinted. I could barely tell that the figure was anything more than shadows formed by crates and burlap, let alone whether it was a woman or not. 'I can see a figure, though not much more. Why?'

'Oh no reason.' Holmes stepped into the growing crowd and edged his way through towards the exit furthest from the apple market and the shadowy figure. 'Now your Mary, how would she like to assist us in our inquiries?'

I thought to myself that she would probably be as little enamoured with assisting Holmes in his inquiries, as I would be for her to do so. To assist my friend was often indistinguishable from peering down the barrel of a loaded gun. But once Holmes has an idea in his head, and a process to follow, he is a stubborn man, so I just nodded, replied 'I'm sure she would be delighted' and hoped that my wife's forgiving nature and passion for justice would save me some hard words.

***

Mary was not, as I'd expected, entirely enthralled by the prospect of facing danger on Holmes' behalf. Or rather, I suspect, she knew she would find it more difficult to picture me safe, the next time I ventured out at my friend's side. Still, she—we—owed our current happiness to Holmes' efforts, so there was a shared duty.

'I am quite sure,' I said, over breakfast, hoping to stem the concern written upon her brow, 'that is some small matter, too delicate for the rough manner of Mr Sherlock Holmes.'

'I'm sure you're right, John.'

***

'A prostitute.' I stared in horror at Holmes.

'Well not a prostitute as such, Watson,' he replied dryly. 'More correctly, a potential one.'

'You ask too much, Holmes.'

'Watson, my dear fellow. The good lady Mary won't be portraying herself as a prostitute. She need simply disembark from the coach and appear lost. Nothing could be simpler' He chuckled to himself. 'From the expression on your face, it appears to run in the family.'

'But what if the woman approaches her?'

'Well, that's exactly what I'm hoping for. Then we can follow and discover which rooms or lodging house she frequents.'

'But how will she escape?'

'Don't worry about that, when the time is right, we will intercede. Now I can hear the cab arriving, why don't we go straight down? Then we'll have plenty of time to meet with the coach.'

Grudgingly, I followed Holmes down the stairs. Mary must have realised from my face that there was something wrong; she embraced me and patted my hand in the manner she employed when she wished to calm me. Then she strode off down the street after Holmes, towards Regents Park—where she would leave us and take the last leg of the journey by coach towards Covent Garden.

'You wish me to do what?' The pigeons scattered, and even the shopkeepers in their windows turned towards the shrill enquiry that echoed briefly down the street before Mary's conversation with Holmes became muted and intent. She flushed red with anger towards Holmes and I expect myself as well.

Then they stopped. Stood stock still in the middle of the street. I slowed my pace in the hope that their conversation might have ended before I caught up with them and, at least, in that regard, my prayers were answered—by the time we grew level, they stood in silence, Mary glowered at Holmes, whilst he, oblivious, checked his pocket watch and waited for me to catch them up.

'The coach stop is just over there.' Holmes gestured towards the corner of Regents Park. 'Now make sure you catch the four o'clock carriage. That will get you in to Covent Garden at five—giving us plenty of time to set ourselves in place. If the coach driver queries why you are travelling by coach for such a short distance, then play simple. Tell them that you're new to London and have become lost, that you're to meet someone there at five on the dot. Keep your answers short, play the bashful maid, and don't be lulled into conversation with anyone. Especially the coachman, for he might be complicit.'

Mary's only reply was a curt nod to Holmes, and a perfunctory kiss on my cheek before she turned away and headed towards the park. Holmes hurried us across the road back towards Baker Street where he had a cab waiting to ferry us across London to Covent Garden.

***

'See, she's there again.'

I peered over Holmes shoulder and sure enough the patch of shadows, now formed the obvious shape of a woman in the afternoon sun.

'But Holmes,' I protested. 'Won't she recognise us from yesterday? It might spook her. Then Mary will have gone through all this for nothing.'

'See how she lurks in the shadows of the apple market.' Holmes indicated the market with the stem of his pipe. 'The setting sun, casting her in shadow.' I nodded. 'She has placed herself there very deliberately, Watson, thinking that she cannot be seen, though still giving her the perfect view of the coach stop opposite. See how intent she is on watching the coaches come and go. She hasn't considered that what the winter sun obscures for others may also be concealing vital information from her. The dazzling brightness of the low winter's rays may pool the shadows around her figure, but they also blind her if she so much as glances in our direction. Indeed, she is blind to everything except the coaches and the ladies who alight from them. Mary is perfectly safe.'

Holmes raised his hand to halt any further discussion, as through the archway of Covent Garden trundled the five o'clock coach, the driver ignoring the bustling crowds of the piazza as he drove the horses towards the station. A crowd of people gathered, waiting, excited to be reunited with loved ones. Jostling each other as they waited impatiently for the coach driver to unload the cases, and to assist those within to navigate the narrow wooden step he placed to the side of the coach. I couldn't see Mary within the crowd that rushed forward, hands grabbing at cases that may or may not have belonged to them, arms embracing without embarrassment or ceremony those that stepped out of the coach and onto the slick, filthy cobbles below.

'Holmes, should Mary have had some luggage with her?' I watched as the crowds dissipated, familial groups chattering away animatedly, couples content in their silence as they waltzed away arm-in-arm. 'I mean if she was supposed to be travelling a long distance, wouldn't she have some kind of travelling case?'

Holmes once again held up his hand.

'It is of no worry. See.'

I watched as the woman peeled herself away from the shadows and headed over to the coach. Only the driver and Mary remained; a feeling of pride came over me as I watched my wife play the part that Holmes had given her, tears springing to her eyes as she gesticulated wildly at the crowds. I watched as the woman placed a hand on Mary's shoulder and although Mary remained stoic and straight at her touch, I shrank back as if I'd been struck. My wife wiped away the last of her tears as she nodded and stood demurely to one side as the woman went to speak to the driver. It was obvious from our vantage point that something was passed from woman to man in that moment. 'What do you think that was, Holmes?'

'If my suspicions are correct then I expect it was his payment.'

'My God, Holmes are you saying she is paying him to ferry women to her?'

'No. I expect she is simply buying his silence. Though we shall find out more once Mary has left.'

'Left?' I watched as Mary headed out through the evening crowds of Covent Garden and towards Temple. Holmes stayed my departure with a hand against my chest.

'Observe, Watson. I told you Mary is perfectly safe.'

I watched as a gaggle of children ran off grubby and barefoot, winding their way through the crowds, each one passing the job of keeping the two women within eyesight to another as if they were playing a simple game of tag.

'We have work to attend to here. We must go and speak to the driver.'

I stood quiet, fury building in me, as I listened to the driver telling Holmes that there had been no one named Eliza Shaw—the pseudonym that Holmes had instructed Mary to use—or, indeed, anyone of her description on the coach that day. How he managed to keep a straight face, as he queried if Holmes was sure she was due on the five o'clock coach, was as astounding as my ability to refrain from setting about him with my stick.

The coach driver had not long loaded back up and left the piazza once more, before myself and Holmes were accosted by one of his Irregulars. Holmes smiled at the boy who gave us the name of a lodging house in Spitalfields on Flower and Dean Street. The name of the street turned my blood cold—a den of vice and carnality, the street was one best avoided in ordinary times. Since neither Scotland Yard nor Holmes had managed to apprehend the Whitechapel Murderer, the whole area was shunned by all but the most depraved or destitute. Whatever the reason that woman had taken Mary there, it would not be for safety and succour.

***

It was dark by the time Holmes and myself had made our way across to Spitalfields, and although I was accustomed to seeing the destitute in their hundreds huddled in the corners of Covent Garden and Trafalgar Square, here it seemed like hell had been split open and its denizens loosed on the streets of London. It was not possible to move but one foot before being accosted by both men and women attempting to sell you their wares—or themselves—in return for a penny towards their night's bed or, sadly likely, bottle.

Children who should have been safely tucked up in beds or sat before hearths learning their words or stitching their clothes, were instead rampant, playing barefoot with nothing more than rags to keep the biting cold away.

Holmes didn't bat an eyelid as he passed coin after coin to the children he saw, heedless that the pack that soon flanked us along Flower and Dean were most likely to pass it to parents who would use it to buy liquor to dim the pain of living in such slums. To say that the lodging house that Holmes led us to was the worst on the street would be untrue, though from the crumbling frontage and stinking drains, I would have been hard pressed to say it was one of the better ones, if such a domain actually existed here. Although the door was open, leading onto a darkened hallway and a kitchen full of those making the most of the burning stove, Holmes's propriety still instilled in him the need to knock upon the jamb before entering.

The boisterous laughter and chatter of the kitchen's inhabitants died down as Holmes stepped in. Obviously wary of the newcomer, they weighed up whether the well-to-do gentleman was there for good or for ill. Either deciding that Holmes was there as a patron, or that their lot couldn't be much worse, the group turned back towards the warmth of the fire and the carousing we had interrupted. They were, obviously, keeping an eye upon us, however, as they turned, interested once more, as Holmes drew a coin from his pocket.

It could only have been a matter of minutes before the landlady of the house made her way into the kitchen, but already Holmes had integrated himself into those clustered round a scarred table by the stove. A fan of cards was in his hands; he placed unlit matches down alongside the burnt and used matches that his opponents were betting with. He stood and removed his hat as the landlady stepped in. Excusing himself from the game, he left his matches upon the table which his opponents quickly divvied up amongst themselves, disappearing into pockets as they continued their game with the charred stumps they had betted with before.

Holmes indicated to the woman that he wished to speak to her in the hallway, and soon she was leading us both towards the top of the house, where she stated the best rooms were kept. As we passed the other floors I saw rows of hard single beds, accompanied by a smell strong enough to turn a man's stomach. But the beds were still full, the thin blankets draped across their fully clothed inhabitants. Their meagre belongings hugged in their arms, so as not to be stolen or trampled on as the other inhabitants made their way through the narrow gaps between the beds. Upon the next floor, flimsy partitions hid the beds from my view, but still there was little privacy, with at least eight beds crammed into a room that would have originally been intended to house but one couple; the sounds of coitus mingled with the squalls of infants and the chatter of families as each went about their nightly routines. Finally we made our way to the last floor, the attic. The rooms there were small and sparse, designed to house maids, but now held a very different kind of servant.

'Only the best here, sirs.' The woman removed from her pockets a bunch of keys, tipping a knowing wink at me. 'My girls rival any of those at Brompton Square, but at a fraction of the price.' In that moment, it was all I could do to not just knock her flat, woman or not. 'We have a new one in today, unblemished, if you know what I mean. Though you will have to pay extra of course.'

'Of course.' Holmes replied. 'Only the best for my friend here.'

I felt my face flush in anger. Thankfully, the woman must have thought it embarrassment as she unlocked the door at the end of the hall.

Sat hunched on the bed was my Mary, I wanted to gather her up in my arms, so forlorn she looked, her dress ripped, and her head bowed. A broken doll, cast away, but behind her delicate porcelain features, I recognised simmering anger. I only hoped that her anger was for the madam or Holmes, rather than myself. As I stepped forward into the room, the woman followed close behind.

'Now you be a good girl. There's a fine gentleman here for you—' The woman paused as if debating whether the girl was good enough for me, or I for her. 'You will be a good girl for him, won't you? Because if he's not to your liking, there are others, plenty of others, and I can't vouch for their characters as I can for this fine discerning gent here—'

Her words were cut short, as Holmes struck her from behind, and I rushed forward to Mary, flustered as I tried to check her for injuries—both physical and mental. She pushed me away, her words brisk, as she informed me that other than a twinge in her shoulder, where she had been dragged up the stairs, she was unharmed.

Swiftly, we trussed the woman, gagging her with strips ripped from the bed's filthy sheets. Once we were sure she would be unable to raise an alarm, Holmes made his way to each of the adjoining rooms, knocking upon each door. Most of the rooms had but a solitary occupant; though one contained two—one of whom was Mrs White. Though, from the speed of his departure, we had our doubts whether the gentleman with her would answer to the name of Mr White. Mrs White lay in a state of undress, but Holmes paid no attention as he made his way in, pressing his hand against her mouth to still any potential screams. Once Mrs White had been suitably subdued, Holmes and I continued our search of the rooms. None of the ladies admitted to the name Lucy, if and when they spoke at all. And even with the threat of the police, neither the landlady nor Mrs White would reveal who she was, or whether she had ever resided within their sordid dwelling on Flower and Dean.

The women, or at least those that hadn't fled by the time that Lestrade arrived, were escorted to the lock hospital for examination and treatment. 'At least we managed to save someone today.' Holmes looked at me in the same way I might have looked upon a child, there was pity in his face, though even that was preferable to the unreadable expression on Mary's.

'I mean, we may not have found Lucy, but at least those poor wretches are out of here and safe.' Mary and Holmes turned away and slowly made their way down the stairs, as the destitute of the street made their way in, in search of a free bed, knowing that, at least for tonight, the landlady would not be there to turf them out if they could not produce the required fourpence. Carefully, I stepped over the bodies that were already huddling in the corridors—too late for the beds that had been snapped up in moments once Lestrade had led the landlady—Mrs Tallow—and Mrs White out and into the waiting cab for their onward journey to Scotland Yard.

***

I left earlier than was usual the next morning. Mary was still out of sorts following her ordeal the night before. Although I had offered her something to help her sleep and a sympathetic ear, she had refused both. Instead, she insisted I made my way to bed alone, whilst she sipped at her tea by the fire. Had she been angry—justifiably—with what Holmes and I had put her through, I might have weathered it more easily. But she had retreated into some other emotion, one she seemed neither willing nor able to share.

When I awoke, I woke alone, the bed beside me cold. And though I attempted to be quiet in my ablutions, Mary was awake once more—or still—when I made my way downstairs. She stood to put the kettle on to boil, but her gait was unsteady and her face as pale as a ghost's. I removed the kettle from her grip and placed it back down upon the stove. At my insistence and my promise that I would grab some breakfast on my way to Holmes, I finally managed to persuade Mary to take herself up to bed and made my way across town to Baker Street.

Holmes was already up and reading through his correspondence when I arrived at his rooms, though his expression was dour and there was a fug that spoke of several hours of dedicated tobacco smoking.

I opened the window to air the room.

'Do you think there really was a Lucy? I mean why would Mrs White request your consultation when she was involved in such dealings?'

'I am sure of the fact that there is or was a Lucy.' Holmes drew deeply on his pipe, his brow furrowed more in dismay than in thought, though I had rarely seen him exhibit such emotion in relation to anything, let alone his cases. 'I believe that the story that Mrs White told us was truthful in all but outcome. That street and that house in particular are renowned for their vice. I think that Mrs White had got herself into some kind of debt, and her way of repaying her employer was by way of her childhood friend.'

'My God. Do you think that she realised? I mean is that why she wasn't there on the coach when Mrs White went to collect her?'

'Unfortunately Watson, I believe that this is where Mrs White's story departs from the truth. I expect that Lucy *was* met by Mrs White and was taken to Mrs Tallow's house on Flower and Dean. For whatever reason, Mrs Tallow decided that the risk of their venture being discovered was worth an attempt to get Lucy back.'

'Well Holmes, we must find her.'

'How Watson? We have a name, and but a Christian one at that, and although there is little reason to believe that Mrs White would have given us a pseudonym for her friend, we cannot rule it out. Whatever the motive for it, it would appear that Lucy's disappearance has been complete enough for Mrs Tallow to risk the loss of her business and imprisonment, rather than allow Lucy to fall victim to the streets or the Lock. I fear like many of the city's destitute we may never find out what befell Lucy.'

The Woman Who Wasn't: Part Four

'Holmes,' I cried as I stumbled to the end of the alleyway, 'where are you, man?' My revolver felt heavy in my hand, as yet unfired.

I glanced left and right. There was neither sign of my friend nor any indication that he or our quarry had passed this way. Londoners, young and old, went about their various occupations, seemingly undisturbed.

Although, I conceded, the ability to blind oneself to the untoward was likely essential in this part of the city. One's life might depend upon it.

Whereas the life of Sherlock Holmes might now hang on my actions, or lack thereof.

I shut my eyes tightly and attempted to block out the interminable melee of sounds.

There!

Masked by the declarations of market stall owners, the howls of hungry babes and the guttural laughter of stumbling inebriates, my friend's voice called out.

'Watson! This way!'

***

I readily admit, the reminder of young Lucy's unknown fate—and the lengths to which my sainted wife had gone in our attempt to prevent it—had lit a fresh fire in my heart. Anastasia Frain could not be allowed to slip away so completely. It could not be borne.

It would seem that Sherlock Holmes felt similarly. He threw himself into the Frain case with all of the considerable energy at his disposal. For days at a time, he would disappear, only to return looking defeated, with another tale of a trail gone cold.

One might have expected Sir Harrison to have lost patience with our progress, but he remained insistent that we continue our work. He had, he maintained, utter faith that his daughter would be located and soon.

If only I could have shared his conviction. The longer Miss Frain remained at large in the capital, the easier it would be for her to vanish entirely. If, indeed, she had remained in London. And, the more sobering thought, still lived.

It therefore felt like the hand of providence when one of Holmes' urchins arrived with news of, if not Miss Frain herself, the mysterious fellow identified by Sir Harrison's man and whom I still presumed to be our missing woman's lover. Or, as I pondered in my more disconsolate moments, her killer.

He had been spotted in one of the less salubrious boroughs of the metropolis.

I was not at Baker Street when the news arrived, but Holmes arrived soon after in a cab and pressed me into immediate service, a call to action I made no effort to resist.

Within an hour, we had reached the lodgings at which the man had last been seen.

'We must proceed softly,' said my friend as we approached the house. 'If we spook our horse, he will gallop.'

I nodded, glad of the service weapon in my coat pocket. Although if any harm had come to the young woman we sought, I worried about how I might employ it.

As if reading my thoughts, Holmes turned to me.

'Your passion does you credit, Watson,' he said. 'But, at present, we are woefully short of knowledge. I would take it as a great personal kindness if you were to allow me to rectify that before indulging your chivalry.'

I nodded, red-faced.

'You can count on me, Holmes.'

'Of that,' he said, 'I have no doubt.'

***

The woman who answered our knock was tall and thin, though my medical eye told me the latter was due more to malnutrition than nature.

'Yes?' she barked. 'What do you want?'

If Sherlock Holmes was taken aback by the brusque enquiry, he did not show it. Indeed, he replied in kind.

'You have a new lodger.'

The woman fixed him with a gaze of steel.

'Often has new lodgers. Being a lodging house.'

'A young man,' insisted Holmes. 'Slight. Likely comes and goes at all hours.'

I wondered briefly at the relevance of this last piece of information, assuming it must have originated with the Irregulars.

'No idea who you mean,' the woman replied, far too quickly and began to shut the door in our faces. But Holmes had wedged his cane in the opening before she had finished her denials.

'This is a matter of the greatest importance,' he said firmly.

'That's as may be,' said the woman, her fear manifesting as anger, 'but this is my house and you've no business interfering with how I's runs it.'

'If you are protecting a murderer,' said Holmes. 'Then I assure you it is quite literally my business.'

'I don't know nothing about no murderer.'

There was a rustle from a window above us. Without breaking eye contact with the proprietress, Holmes shouted an order.

'Watson! Follow that man!'

My eyes flew to the figure clambering from the top floor of the house and towards the rooftop.

'You've been most helpful,' purred Holmes, retrieving his cane from the door and wheeling to face me. He gestured for me to head left, then bolted in the opposite direction himself. His goal was clear. The short run of roofs was broken by a narrow alleyway and he intended for us to surround the fleeing man at the point he would be forced to come to ground.

***

When I finally caught up to Holmes, there was no sign of the young man. My friend leaned thoughtfully against a nearby wall, tapping rhythmically at the ground with his cane. I came to a stop, breathing heavily.

"We've lost him!" I cried. It seemed almost too much to bear. To be so close and to have our hopes dashed again.

But Holmes was smiling.

'On the contrary, Watson. He may have slipped our grasp now, but I assure you it is for the final time.'

Then he held up a small square of silk for my inspection. It was a handkerchief, in the corner of which the letter 'A' had been painstakingly embroidered. The material was smudged with dirt and blackened by what appeared to be soot.

It also seemed to have reassured Holmes almost entirely, a feeling I did not share.

'But, dash it, Holmes. All that tells us is that we are right to pursue him. It gives us no clue whatsoever about his whereabouts. Or those of Miss Frain.'

'Ah, Watson. You see, but you do not observe.'

I was in no humour for my friend's assessment of my deductive skills. But I was too weary to argue the point.

'Pray, enlighten me, Holmes.'

A look of mischief stole over his features.

'Not quite yet, I think,' he said. Then taking in my thunderous expression, he continued: 'I am not being wilfully obtuse, my dear fellow. I believe our mystery is within reach of being solved, but there are still some small matters to clear up before I can put the case before you in its entirety.'

'Very well,' I muttered, knowing there was little to be gained in pursuing the matter further. 'What must we do now?'

'If you would oblige me,' said Holmes, stepping into the road and waving his cane towards an approaching cab, 'There is a particular record of our adventures that I would like to consult.'

The Eyes of the Fae

Kara Dennison

On this particular day, Holmes had summoned me to Baker Street "with urgency" but had not deigned to elaborate further. I explained to Holmes' messenger, with all due respect, that I was on my way to make a house call that very afternoon. My patient, Henrietta Francis, had been assigned to bed rest one week prior, by myself, and my hope had been to reassess her case and perhaps restore some small degree of freedom.

The lad sent to fetch me simply replied that he had been warned of my likely response, and was told to insist on my presence, nonetheless. I am still unsure what compelled me to follow the boy rather than shutting the door in his face, save perhaps for the fact that it was a young boy and not Holmes himself. Regardless, I soon found myself in the familiar sitting room, in my usual chair, opposite which Holmes sat alone, perusing the day's newspaper.

'Have you seen the reviews for this new play in Brighton?' he asked, with a casual tone that didn't at all fit the exigency with which he'd summoned me. 'Fascinating work they're doing with effects. Far more interesting than what I saw last Sunday. You should have been there; it was terrible.'

'I do hope you haven't pulled me away from my work to ask me about the theatre.' There was every possibility he had—a summons from Holmes could be a matter of life and death, or a matter of the previous evening's entertainments—the more garish the better, in Holmes's eyes—but on this day in particular, I was uninterested in such trivialities.

'Not at all,' he assured me, and folded the newspaper up tidily. 'I respect the time and effort your work takes. In fact, it is those very skills of which I have need.'

As I was about to question this assessment, the door opened yet again. I was shocked to see a familiar face; and it was equally shocked to see me, judging by its expression. As Holmes's and my respective practices have grown, it is not uncommon to see people I have met during my office hours within Holmes's rooms, or vice-versa. It was not, therefore, the familiarity that shocked, but the person in particular. For the woman who entered was the same Henrietta Francis I was meant to be visiting that very day. The same Henrietta Francis, moreover, whom I had deemed in desperate need of bed rest until further notice.

'Doctor Watson,' the poor woman stammered, and it was clear she took no pleasure in operating outside my orders. It was also clear that she remained unwell—perhaps even less well than I had left her. Her face was pale, her eyes bleary with exhaustion. I could tell at a glance she hadn't slept in some time.

I rushed to the poor woman's side, offering my arm in support. She looked at it suspiciously at first, as though fearful that accepting my aid might open her up to some sort of attack.

'I assure you,' Holmes spoke up, 'Dr Watson will not judge you for your presence here. I requested he be on hand, as your problem is related to your indisposition.'

'Is that true?' Mrs Francis asked.

I very nearly told her that we were similarly in the dark as to Holmes's intentions but realised this might only distress her further. Instead, I nodded wordlessly and walked her to the chair I had just vacated. Her hands were shaking, though whether from nervousness or continued weakness it was difficult to tell. Reluctantly, I had to admit that if Mrs Francis's condition were this advanced, I preferred to be on hand.

'I am sorry,' she continued. 'If this weren't of the utmost importance, I wouldn't have come. But you see, it's Silas.' And here she steadied herself before she attempted to speak again. 'He's been taken.'

Holmes's face registered no reaction, but I could not contain my shock. 'But Mrs Francis, surely that's a case for the police!' I had met her son on a previous visit: six years old, towheaded, pleasant enough in the company of strangers but with darting eyes constantly seeking out the next available opportunity for mischief. During my last call, I had been asked to assess young Silas, though no reason for special concern was given. He was, as I had told his mother then, exactly as a healthy young lad of his age ought to be. She seemed unsatisfied by my assessment, but thanked me, nonetheless. Now he had apparently been taken—kidnapped—yet she hadn't rushed to action?

'I have instructed her,' Holmes said calmly, 'not to involve them for the time being.'

'Why in God's name would you do that?'

Holmes held out a hand to Mrs Francis. 'I believe she should explain in more detail. I know the basic facts, enough to give her my initial advice earlier today, but it is time to hear the whole story.'

She hesitated, suddenly unsure of herself. In particular, she eyed me, as though my presence made all the difference.

'Please, Mrs Francis.'

She composed herself and said, 'I believe he has been taken away by the fae folk.'

***

Henrietta told her story slowly, riddled with tearful pauses and moments spent regaining her composure. Too, she told it largely out of order, recalling incidents here and there that she considered essential to the greater picture. For ease of telling, I've untangled her narrative and laid it out chronologically as best I can.

As a child, Henrietta lived with her parents in a small cottage in the north, far from any cities. She did not mention what it was her father did for a living, only that she had a comfortable life and freedom to roam the fields near her home. While walking one night she met a girl her own age named Beatrice. Henrietta described her in loving detail, as one might a favourite doll: pale skin, long black hair, a mole just below the left corner of her mouth, and—what Henrietta remembered most vividly—haunting grey eyes.

The two would meet in the fields and play together until dark, telling stories and playing pretend, but never asking questions about each other. Henrietta finally broached the topic one day, pointing out her home in the distance. Beatrice, however, claimed her home could not be seen, nor could her family.

'Are they invisible?' Henrietta had asked. Initially hesitant, Beatrice said yes, that was exactly it. Her home and her family were invisible to most people, but Henrietta was special. Beatrice was, she said after further prying, a faery, hidden from the world but happy to have a friend at last. Then she pressed Henrietta to make a promise with her: keep her secret, and always remain her friend. She had no human friends, after all. Henrietta agreed, and the two carried on their secret friendship.

But the day came when Henrietta's father took a job in London, the family set to follow him there. Henrietta assumed Beatrice would be excited—

perhaps she could accompany them!—but the girl began crying. Of course, she couldn't come to London. She couldn't be seen among so many people. Hadn't they promised never to leave each other?

Henrietta tried to explain that the matter was out of her hands, as were so many things for a child. But Beatrice stood firm, irate at the breach of promise. Henrietta remembered Beatrice's last words to her then clearly: 'Since I'm losing the one thing that makes me happy, I shall come back one day and make sure you lose whatever makes you most happy.'

In time, the wounds of this childish encounter healed. Henrietta ultimately filed Beatrice away in her mind as an imaginary friend: a magical, temperamental fae child dreamed up in the absence of children her own age and, perhaps, as a way to blame her own mischief on someone else. It was the only sensible explanation.

She acclimated to life in London, eventually marrying a promising young businessman, Archibald Francis. Silas came not long after, and the three made a happy family for a handful of years. When the boy was about three years old, Archibald informed the family one evening that he might need to begin taking slightly longer business trips than usual. Both Henrietta and Silas were saddened at first, but Archibald promised it wouldn't be for long, and they'd hardly miss him. Neither of these things turned out to be true.

The trips lasted weeks at a time and involved little correspondence. Henrietta once asked what kept Archibald so silent when he was away. He never answered, but cheerfully offered, instead, gifts of jewellery to Henrietta and toys and books to his son. The boy imagined his father must be doing something very secret and very important and would come up with wilder and more elaborate stories during each trip. A secret agent one month, a brilliant scientist performing wondrous experiments the next. Henrietta never corrected him; if anything, the child's flights of fancy eased her own mind while her husband was far away and silent.

It was one of those long trips that took Archibald's life, not a week before Silas's sixth birthday. The poor man had been murdered by a would-be robber, who was never identified or brought to justice. The news was wired to Henrietta via Matthews, an apparent associate of Archibald's, who had been with him only the night before.

The contents of Archibald's will were sparse. Henrietta and Silas kept the small set of rooms in which they lived, but it appeared the late patriarch had no further money or assets to impart. This surprised the young window, considering how well she and Silas had lived and how much Archibald had worked, but she was not ungrateful to maintain a roof over her head. Her parents assisted where they could, and it was suggested that Henrietta and Silas move back into the family home at a later date. This, for the time being, had not been pursued.

It was Henrietta's mother's idea to find a nursery maid. Henrietta resisted; she had so little in this world now, she was happy to carve out a little life for herself and Silas and not share it with anyone else. But her mother insisted, and days later sent her well-thought-out selection to Henrietta's door: black hair, fair skin, a mole just under the corner of her mouth, and deep grey eyes. Her name? Beatrice Spenser.

***

'The same Beatrice?' I asked, taken aback. 'But you dreamed her up her as a child, didn't you?'

'That is what I had come to believe. But it was Beatrice, I'm sure of it. I would know those eyes anywhere.' Mrs Francis looked troubled, as though not quite believing her own statement. 'At first, she didn't appear to recognise me. I suppose I must have changed over the years, even if she hadn't.'

Holmes looked on impassively, but I saw the glint of interest in his eye. 'You say "at first." Can I take that to mean she eventually did acknowledge you?'

Mrs Francis nodded. 'Yes, eventually. But not for some time. I conducted an interview with her on her first day, even though Mother had already hired her and approved of her references. I told myself it was for Silas's sake. But really, it was for mine. I had to prove to myself that this wasn't the Beatrice of my childhood. And, at first, I felt I had. Her background seemed perfectly normal… though she was somehow—' Our guest searched for a word.

'Uncanny?' Holmes offered.

'It sounds such a petty observation, but she did seem to always be looking off somewhere else. Never at me, never at Silas. Detached from her surroundings. But not unintelligent. I wanted a reason, any reason, to send her away. I searched in vain for anything I could tell Mother that would convince her of the woman's unsuitability. But I'll admit, I feel I also wanted reasons not to. Having my fears disproven would have allowed me to feel safer. As it was, I could only watch and wonder. And I couldn't bring myself to send Beatrice away—Mother would take it as an insult. She was only trying to help us in whatever way she could.

'Things went well for the first few weeks. We had no place for Beatrice to stay, not in our little house, but she claimed she was near enough that she didn't mind. And she must have been—she always arrived before I awoke and left after both Silas and I had gone to bed. And she never asked for full weekends off—only Sunday afternoons, and only for a few hours. She was always very attentive and patient, even when I broke or misplaced things.'

I could not recall Mrs Francis ever being clumsy or forgetful. It was possible she had become so temporarily during her illness, but to state it so—as if this were a known habit—struck me as odd.

Clearly, it struck Holmes, too. 'Is this a problem you have regularly?'

Mrs Francis nodded hesitantly. 'Apparently so, though I was never told until recently. Beatrice was the first to notice. I would idly wander off with things and drop or misplace them. One night I ripped several pages out of a book. I must have been distracted and fidgeting, but fortunately Beatrice found the missing pages under my bed.'

I looked at her hands as she spoke. They were folded and still in her lap. I recalled that, during my house call, she had been similarly calm.

'And young Silas?' Holmes asked. 'How did he take to Beatrice?'

'Extremely well. He enjoyed her company very much.' Mrs Francis paused. 'Actually, I began to worry he was happier in her presence than in mine. I said as much to Beatrice a week ago, though I attempted to do so offhandedly. 'We can't have him running off with you and abandoning me,' I said.'

'And what did she say?' I asked, suspecting I knew the answer.

'She looked at me with those haunted grey eyes of hers. And she said, very calmly: "Then you should not have abandoned me."'

She paused again, looking at her hands. 'I suppose I should have called the police then. My mother dropped in on her way to the station the next day— to visit friends for the next few weeks—and I told her what happened. But Beatrice denied it. She was pleasant and calm and said I must have imagined it. Mother believed her. So did I, after a time. A part of me believed I must be going mad, another was convinced Beatrice was enchanting Silas and plotting to take him from me.'

A week ago, she had said. This would align with her attack of nerves and my visit. At the time, she had claimed it was grief playing on her mind and nothing else.

'Silas spoke with me less and less, and eventually pretended not to know me. I was hoping to speak with you again, Dr Watson, when you visited today. But this morning—he was gone. Vanished. None of his things had been taken. There was no sign he had slept in his bed. And his bedroom window was open.'

'And your mother?' Holmes asked.

'Still away. I've not been able to contact her yet. I'm still trying, but I'm beginning to wonder—' She looked at Holmes, then at me, desperately. 'What if it's true? What if Beatrice really has come back to take revenge on me?'

Holmes smiled—an odd thing to do, for most, in the circumstances. But the reactions of Sherlock Holmes often ran counter to those of ordinary men. 'Whoever or whatever she may be, Mrs Francis, I promise we will bring your son back to you.'

Rather than send her home, I asked Mrs Hudson to allow our guest to lie down in another room. She was distraught, besides still being ill. Once she'd had some time to rest, we could send for a cab. In the meanwhile, Holmes made ample use of my presence.

'Well?' he asked, leaning back in his chair. 'You're her physician. Would you vouch for her wits?'

I nodded. 'She's clearly and understandably tired. But she speaks clearly and sanely. Even the moments when she doubts her own memory make that apparent.' Then, realising I should speak more plainly: 'Yes, I would vouch for her wits.'

'As I suspected.'

'Though perhaps you'll tell me why you've told this poor woman not to alert the police? This Beatrice character could be miles away by now with Silas!'

Holmes steepled his fingers, pressing them to his lips. 'No one in Mrs Francis's neighbourhood has seen anyone of Beatrice Spenser's description enter or leave her building.'

'I beg your pardon?'

'I was quite thorough. Neighbours, lamplighters, coachmen. In fact, next to no one comes or goes from that particular building in the first place.' He leaned forward. 'Come to that, you did make that house call. Did you happen to catch a glimpse of our fae visitor?'

I thought back—and no, I had not. In fact, until today, I hadn't known there was a nursery maid of any description. 'No. She must have been elsewhere at the time. I only saw Mrs Francis and Silas.'

Holmes nodded. 'A recent widow, living alone and visibly ill, has her child spirited away by a woman matching the description of her, by her own admission, imaginary childhood friend. With no proof that this woman exists, save for a relative who is conveniently inaccessible. And, it seems, highly suggestible?'

'This is why you instructed her not to involve the police?'

'For the time being, at any rate. I'm not sure who or what our Beatrice is just yet. But just in case she's as clever as she seems, I should like a look around the Francis household before anyone else is called in. I have some suspicions.'

'What sort?'

'Nothing I am yet prepared to divulge. You are most welcome to accompany me, however.'

**

As I mentioned, I had been to the home of Mrs Henrietta Francis once prior. That was on the occasion of my house call, and I saw only her front hallway and the sitting room in which we met. Mrs Francis and her son lived on the upper level (the only thing above their heads being the building's attic storage space) with a rather unsocial landlord and his yowling cat just below. Mr Francis had had plans to move them to a larger house, but such dreams were now never to be realised.

The Francis home also contained a kitchen and dining room, a bath, a bedroom for Mrs Francis and her late husband, and a room that served as both bedroom and playroom for young Silas. Nothing had been touched since Mrs Francis's flight to Holmes's office this morning, meaning the house would be in the same state as when the poor woman had discovered her son's disappearance.

'I instructed her not to touch anything,' Holmes told me as he let us in with Mrs Francis's key. The terrified mother was even now with Mrs Hudson. My associate had still not divulged to me what he expected to find, only that he thought it best to not have the lady of the house present when he found it. Beyond this, he refused to elaborate any further.

The foyer was tidy, albeit with a scant layer of dust. The dining room was similar. The kitchen showed the first signs of activity, likely as Mrs Francis had had to prepare her own meals and take them to bed. I had prescribed her a simple diet, with the assumption that a cook or maid could bring her meals to her in bed. It hadn't occurred to me that she might not have such a luxury available to her. As Holmes picked his way across the room, I couldn't help but feel a tinge of guilt at my carelessness.

'Whatever it is you believe you've done,' Holmes said sharply, his head in a cupboard, 'I do hope you'll divest yourself of those emotions shortly. Please recall you are not the criminal in this narrative.'

What I had done to betray my feelings, and how he could sense them from his position, I had no idea. Nonetheless, I did my best to take his advice to heart.

The kitchen yielded nothing of interest, at least as far as Holmes was concerned, and he moved on to the small bath. It was as tidy as it could be expected to be: not especially ornate, but functional. A small hand towel tucked beneath the wash basin caught Holmes's attention. He turned it over in his hands, looking with interest at the corners. There were small, dark smudges on them, as one might expect to see on any cloth used regularly for cleaning appliances.

'Perhaps an issue with the pipes?' I suggested. Holmes gave no answer, and we moved on to the bedrooms.

First, that of young Silas. Just as Mrs Francis had described, his window was open. Holmes put his head out, looking to the street below, then upward at the sky.

'What do you see?' I asked.

Holmes pulled his head back in. 'Nothing. No sign of a ladder or rope or any other sort of means of egress. I believe the open window may be a ruse. Either that, or our Beatrice truly has sprouted faery wings and flown off into the night.'

I looked around the rest of the room. Silas's bed was indeed unslept in. More than that, the room was neat as a pin: all playthings put away, all clothes neatly folded away in their various proper places.

'Nothing at all seems out of sorts,' I noted.

'Perhaps not.' Holmes directed his attention to the small chest of drawers in the corner. He pulled each drawer open and shut with a speed which, I believed, could not have offered him any information of value. Once he had been through them all, though, he went back to one drawer in particular, eyeing its contents. 'Our Beatrice isn't the tidiest of nursery maids, is she?'

I looked at the contents of the drawer, but for the life of me couldn't see what it was that Holmes had spotted. 'What is it I'm looking for?'

Holmes pointed to the tidily folded stacks of shirts, drawing my attention to one sleeve slightly askew and resting on the next stack. 'Perhaps she was putting shirts away in a hurry, but it appears to me as though she's pulled something from the bottom of this stack.'

'She may have taken a change of clothes for Silas.'

'Then why not take the first things visible?'

I recalled that Mrs Francis said nothing of Silas's had been taken that she could see. 'Perhaps to make it less apparent that things are missing?'

'Then she was careless.' Holmes moved swiftly on to Mrs Francis's room. 'What is there to see there?' I asked.

'Nothing, I hope. Nevertheless, we must exhaust all possibilities.'

Holmes picked over the entirety of the room, sorting through dresser drawers with a sort of detached abandon that I knew I could not muster. There appeared to be nothing of interest in the room, at least to my eyes. It was the room of a sick woman in distress: bedclothes askew, the second unoccupied bed a home for hastily discarded items of clothing and accessories. Nothing at all I did not expect to see.

Holmes disappeared briefly from my sight; a moment later he reappeared, sitting up behind Mrs Francis's unmade bed. 'It would appear we have a problem.'

Holmes was rarely given to shows of emotion. However, I had learned to recognise this specific tightness of expression, this particular softening of the voice, as a sign that he was perturbed. Something had slipped outside the bounds of his defined universe, and his brain (impressive as it might be) was wrestling to come to terms with it.

Slowly, he held up a child's shirt, ripped through and smeared with what appeared to be a great deal of blood.

I could not contain my feeling of disappointment when I saw it. It was what I had most feared: that Mrs Francis herself had a gruesome hand in this whole affair. But it didn't sit right with me. I would swear on my life that she had spoken genuinely to us earlier. How could this be?

Holmes turned his perturbed expression toward me. 'It seems you have not noticed yet, Watson.'

'How can I not notice when you're holding it right there in front of me?'

'Not that.' Holmes waved the shirt gently. 'The scent of blood.'

I paused, inhaling deeply. 'I smell nothing.'

'Precisely. Nothing. No blood, but also no cleaning agents—the latter of which would necessitate Mrs Francis's ability to handle such a degree of cleaning. Which, as we know, she cannot.' Now Holmes held the shirt to his face. 'Not even the blood smells of blood. Isn't that interesting?'

Now, that could not be. I moved to Holmes's side to see the shirt for myself. To look at it, it certainly seemed to be soaked in very real blood—blood which, at my best guess, would have been there since approximately that morning. But there was no odour in the air, no sickly smell from the clothing.

'It's marvellous,' Holmes said with quiet fascination. 'I shall have to bring it back with me.' He then folded the shirt up, blood-side inward, and stowed it away in a pocket of his jacket fearlessly.

'Should we not give that to the police?' It sickened me to think it, much less to say it; but the proof was there, and I could not bring myself to argue with it. Holmes, however, had no difficulty ignoring my question entirely.

***

Mrs Francis had no desire to go home that day, which was understandable. Did she have a friend who might stay with her for a few nights, I asked, or someone to whose house she might go? She admitted she did not—she had only Silas and her mother, and now one was far away and the other might be gone forever.

My dear Mary, being as kind a soul as ever she is, agreed that she should have our guest room. I spoke only minimally of her case; though, knowing that Holmes was in some way involved, she shrewdly allowed our guest to lead any conversations that might arise. That would ensure that no one tripped over any painful topics.

I spent the afternoon with Holmes, visiting every landlord within walking distance of the Francis home. Our search ended much as we both expected it would. No one had rented out rooms to a Beatrice Spenser, nor to anyone matching her description. I began to grow concerned, both for Mrs Francis and for young Silas.

'Perhaps I was wrong,' I admitted to Holmes when we returned to Baker Street. 'I would swear on my life that Mrs Francis spoke nothing but truth and had her wits fully about her. But it appears this Beatrice simply does not exist.'

'It does begin to look that way,' Holmes agreed, and turned his attention back to the blood-covered shirt he had retrieved from the grieving widow's bedroom.

A few unpleasant possibilities had begun to fill my mind—all feasible, all tragic. Unfortunately, all either incriminated Mrs Francis, or made assumptions that would have rendered her a menace. As possible as they all seemed—as likely as they all felt—I could not resolve any of them with my assessment of her. But Holmes interrupted my thoughts.

'Which do you believe to be more likely, Watson: that your medical judgment has failed you, or that our Beatrice Spenser has found a way to disappear into thin air?'

Put so plainly, there seemed to be no other option. 'The former, I fear.'

'Is that so? I beg to differ.'

'I'm afraid I don't understand.'

Holmes would not hear of it. 'I don't keep you in my company because your judgment is occasionally correct. I associate with you because I trust your observations on such things implicitly. I would sooner swear in court that the fae folk have made off with young Silas than I would that your medical acumen could have failed you.'

I told Holmes that I hardly believed fae folk were involved.

'I agree,' Holmes said. 'In which case we must no longer focus on who or what Beatrice Spenser is—or, indeed, if she exists—and instead, begin to piece apart how it is that a human being has erased herself from existence for the past few weeks and made off with a woman's child. I believe that search begins here.'

Holmes placed a hand on the blood-covered shirt. More specifically, he placed his hand on the bloodstain itself, his hand covered in red as he lifted it away. 'Once again, I will need your medical knowledge.' And he held his hand out to me.

My stomach remained unturned by the sight. Not because I was familiar enough with the sight of blood that it didn't upset me (though this is also true), but because on closer inspection I realised that I was not, in fact, looking at blood. While it looked real enough on the shirt, it should not have come away so easily on Holmes's hand after this long.

'What is that?' I asked.

'An excellent question. We have both surmised that this is not real blood. However, it is excellently rendered, provided you remain a certain distance from it.' He tasted a bit of the red on his hand. 'Glycerine. And the colour, I assume, is carmine. There are likely other ingredients, but it would take me some time to ascertain their nature. Impressive, though, is it not? Almost indistinguishable from the real thing. How fortunate that we found it before anyone else.'

Almost indistinguishable, I pointed out, but not entirely. Scotland Yard would likely have debunked the false evidence as quickly as we had.

'That is true,' Holmes mused. 'Which would mean it was never meant for them. Perhaps it was simply to cause confusion. Even though the odd clue would be found to be falsified, she would have time to slip from the authorities' grasp.'

I wasn't completely certain that she had not already slipped. 'It will have been nearly a day tonight. If she can come and go from Mrs Francis's home for weeks and never be seen, how much headway might she make in a single day?'

A fair enough point, Holmes acceded, but one with which he was not overly concerned. And with that, he waved me off; he had several things to attend to that night, none of which he was inclined to outline for me. He would summon me when there was more upon which we might act. For the time being, I was to remain silent on the points we had discussed and continue to observe Mrs Francis's health while at home.

I did both, as requested. Our houseguest was weary and fitful, and retired early. Mary noted that Mrs Francis had spoken of the current case of her own accord. However, she had offered no information beyond what I already knew.

'She believes she is mad,' Mary confided to me in a whisper after Mrs Francis had gone to bed. 'She went over the story again and again, reciting every point of it out loud. But the more she repeated it, the more she disbelieved it. As though she were seeking out contradictions in her own memory. I fear she wants to believe this is somehow her fault—that she imagined this Beatrice, and that whatever happened to her son, happened at her own hands.'

'Why would she want such a thing?' I asked, baffled.

'Perhaps because it would mean she had an answer, any answer, and no longer had to wonder.'

It seemed an unpleasant way of thinking (far better to wait for us to finish our investigation, surely!) but it was also not my son who had disappeared.

***

The note was simple, to the point, and completely illogical—and came with three tickets to a play.

'Meet me this evening at the Seaside Rose after the performance. I believe we will have our answers then. Bring Mrs Francis.'

I had no desire to see a play of any sort, much less a play that required more than a few minutes' travel to be attended. I showed both the note and the tickets to Mary.

'I can only assume that Holmes will be appearing in the play,' she said primly, 'and deliver his findings in dramatic fashion from the stage in the second act. Thus, I fear we must be in attendance, as must Mrs Francis.'

I told her, in all honesty, I had no desire to play along.

'You must, or you will never hear the end of it—and neither will I.' Then she went to fetch Mrs Francis, explaining that the trip would likely be both unpleasant and fruitful, and such was the way of things in cases like these.

Mrs Francis gave in to the proceedings with little comment but asked to go home briefly so that she might dress for the journey. We accompanied her to her rooms, Mary going in with her while I stood by in the downstairs hallway. As I waited, I caught sight of a lemon-faced man of middle years, dressed in a suit that would have looked smart on someone half a foot taller. He regarded me with an unpleasant stare.

'What business you got here?' he spat. I could only assume from the accusatory tone and general air of embittered authority that this was the landlord. I indicated that I was waiting for a friend, giving her privacy as she prepared herself for a train ride to Brighton. This did not appease him.

'No loiterin.' Then, his face puckering in on itself thoughtfully, he added, 'An' no strangers in general. 'ad a break-in last night. Didn't catch 'em, but I saw the face, I did.' And he stared me full in my face, as though looking for any hint of familiarity.

'I assure you, I was at home all night.'

The landlord backed away, apparently satisfied that I was not the culprit after all. 'Was a man broke in, all dressed in black, knockin' about upstairs like 'e owned the place. Not havin' that anymore, not after all the noise here the last few weeks.'

'What noise?'

'Them guests, coming and going, mornin' an' night. I run an honest business. I need an honest night's sleep.'

I recalled what Holmes had told me: barely anyone had come or gone from this building in recent weeks, certainly not enough to account for this level of discontent. But before I could question the landlord about the "intruder" or the newly discovered guests, he had disappeared into his rooms and slammed the door behind him. Mrs Francis returned with Mary not long after, dressed and prepared for the train journey.

'The landlord has just been through,' I said as we made our exit. 'There was a break-in upstairs last night. Was anything missing from your rooms?'

Mrs Francis shook her head, bewildered. 'Everything was just as I left it.'

Holmes and I had left no trace of our visit, save for removing Silas's shirt from beneath Mrs Francis's bed; and she would not have known of that. Had the housebreaker of the night before been just as careful? And if so, why had he come in the first place? Moreover, who were these guests that Mrs Francis had failed to mention?

I briefly considered a light comment—perhaps the fae had returned—but held my tongue.

***

I acquired a newspaper for the train journey to Brighton. While it was mostly for a distraction, I also wanted to look up the play to which Holmes had sent us for the evening. I had never heard of *A Window by Moonlight*, nor had Mrs Francis. Mary recalled it had had a short run recently in London but went largely unnoticed. It received only a small nod in this paper as well, with some polite but not especially exuberant reviews. There was barely mention of the story or performers, leaving me as effectively in the dark after I had read it as before. Whatever this production was, it hardly seemed noteworthy enough to send someone off to in the midst of a kidnapping investigation. It did, however, explain how Holmes had managed to get us three front-row seats so quickly.

The facing page, on the other hand, had a far more enthusiastic article on a play performed in the same theatre once a week. *L'Indiscrétion* was written of in bold, excited prose. A daring, grotesque performance on tour from Paris, shocking audiences with its horrific and realistic effects. Severed limbs, burst eyeballs, and other blood-soaked activities populated the play, if the article was to be believed. Apparently, on the night the reviewer was in attendance, a young lady had fainted and had to be carried out of the theatre. The reviewer, self-described as a "hardened man of much experience" (though he omitted what manner of experience this might be), admitted he had found himself unsettled in the face of such graphic imagery. It was this unsettling nature that had relegated *L'Indiscrétion* to its once-weekly staging, with the rest of its scheduled performances given over to the aforementioned *A Window by Moonlight*.

I would never describe myself as a "hardened man of much experience" (though some might argue I had the right). But despite both my military and medical backgrounds, I had no desire to test my mettle against this Parisian novelty. Moreover, I had even less desire to test the mettle of my wife or a grieving widow with a missing child. I checked the tickets Holmes had given us once again, to ensure that it was in fact the unremarkable play he had shipped us off to see. With the title confirmed, I looked forward, bewildered but at ease, to the undoubtedly dull evening before us.

It was only a short cab ride from the train station to Fortescue Theatre, where posters for both plays were displayed prominently. *L'Indiscrétion* bore a hastily pasted-up addendum concerning its truncated run, along with warnings that "There Will Be Blood" and a quote from the review I had read on the train. The poster for our play remained unadorned.

The interior of the theatre was uncomfortably empty, with patrons scattered far adrift from each other. A small group of college boys sat a few seats to our left in the front row, joking and pointing at the curtained stage— perhaps friends of someone involved with the production. A few lone patrons were dotted about, engrossed in books or staring off at nothing, presumably simply looking for somewhere away from home to bored. A well-dressed elderly man with unruly grey hair and a notebook stared intensely at the proscenium, as though willing the evening's entertainments to start at once. Another critic? Poor man: he had a most unfulfilling night ahead of him.

It may not have been *L'Indiscrétion* but *A Window by Moonlight* had its daggers out for Mrs Francis from the curtain's rise. The story began, as we discovered, with a woman mourning the death of her infant son. I saw Mrs Francis lower her head, tears welling in her eyes. Mary put a gentle hand on our companion's, whispering a suggestion that they step outside. The two rose from their seats and began walking toward the back entrance.

The critic—or at least that is what I presumed him to be—spotted them and began making his way there, beating them to the exit even at his shuffling pace. He placed himself between the two and the door, shaking a finger and whispering something to them. Mary lifted her chin, clearly with words chambered and ready to fire but Mrs Francis shook her head and gestured to our seats again. When the two had rejoined me, the man resumed his seat as well. The altercation had been brief and quiet, not distracting even the bored punters.

'Shall I go have a word with him?' I asked as Mary and Mrs Francis resumed their seats.

'Please don't.' Mrs Francis's voice was tearful, but calm. 'It's very kind of you, Dr Watson, but I would not like to cause any more of a stir than I already have.'

I looked over the stagnant scattering of audience members and considered telling her that a stir might be just what this theatre needed. But Mary shook her head. She was still clearly unhappy, but deferred to our companion, nonetheless.

The play's initial dramatic revelation ended up counting for little. It was soon forgotten as *A Window by Moonlight* focused instead on the fictional grieving mother's sister and her love for a nobleman. I fear I cannot elaborate much more than that. The actors' performances made the awkward text more awkward still, with most of them reciting their lines with all the emotion and enthusiasm of a multiplication table. I fancy myself neither a critic nor a connoisseur of the theatre, but the absence of quality seldom requires an expert's eye.

The only ensemble member to essay any emotion worth nothing was the heroine herself: the romantically entangled sister of the grieving woman (who had now disappeared entirely from the narrative). It would be overstatement to infer that this star shone brightly; but in a firmament otherwise populated entirely by burned-out cinders, any sort of flicker will attract notice. If nothing else, she was certainly the only person on that stage who seemed to want to be there. Her romantic dialogue with the nobleman she loved (or was he a commoner posing as a nobleman? I had stopped listening) was emotionally one-sided, but somewhat amusing.

Mary was less forgiving. 'She's not very good, is she?' she whispered to me. Mrs Francis, though, seemed oddly fixated. Perhaps it was the opportunity to think of anything but her present situation.

I looked over the playbill for the first time since sitting down. The characters' names had passed me by, but I assumed our hero and heroine would be top billed. Edwin Flannery was the actor depicting our leading man, Lord Bartholomew. Edwin, and thus by extension Lord Bartholomew, was shortish and spindly, with a constant grimace that would likely have been visible from the back wall—let alone our front row seats. The ingenue was one Sally Matthews, playing the role of Eleanor Wingate; the longer Miss Matthews's performance went on, the more she seemed to wind herself up. By the final act, she was in the full throes of melodrama. The group of young men to our left were entertaining themselves with mimed impressions of her performance, which I regret to admit amused more readily than the on-stage action.

The curtain descended, bows were taken, and I found I could remember only the most minor of details about the two hours we had just spent. The threadbare audience began its egress—save for the old man with the notepad, who collected his things and shuffled toward the stage door at the same slow, steady pace as before.

'What on earth did he say to you?' I asked, indicating the retreating man.

'That we ought to sit and observe,' Mary answered irritably. 'Some nonsense about actors and insight. He must be their one admirer.'

Mrs Francis remained silent, and I feared the play's unexpected opening scene might still be affecting her. But when I asked if she was well, she simply nodded, a distant look in her eyes. Perhaps she was tired or realised that now she would be forced to return to the real world, where young Silas was still unaccounted for.

As we gathered our things to leave, and as I thought what a waste of time this all had been, another gentleman approached us. He was tall, middle-aged, and unremarkable looking: a bland face that would too easily disappear in a sea of other faces, and that barely made an impression on its own. He was also beaming and holding out a hand, steering toward a handshake that I had not offered.

'You must be John!' His voice was breathless and exuberant, and the handshake happened before I could stop it. 'Alexander Maitland. I've heard you are a staunch supporter of mine.'

'Have you?' I had no idea who he was, by name or by face, and both Mary and Mrs Francis seemed to notice my confusion.

'Yes, yes. Someone at the stage door told me he overheard you earlier, saying you'd love to meet the man responsible.' And here Maitland spread his arms wide. 'So, here I am.'

I was bewildered for a multitude of reasons but felt oddly compelled to weather the conversation regardless. 'Then you're the playwright?'

Somehow, Maitland's smile widened. 'Playwright, director, and sole producer. A few other odd jobs, too. I must thank you for coming so far to see my latest play. Are you local?'

'No, we've come down from London.'

'London! Well, I am flattered. Though I'm surprised—we had a run in London only recently. Did you not see us there?'

'I must have missed it,' I replied, and it was true. Even after Mary mentioned it on the train down to Brighton, I could still muster no memory of it for myself. Now on the other side of the performance, I couldn't say its lukewarm reception in London surprised me.

Fortunately, Maitland seemed unfazed. 'Well, never mind, you've seen it now. I must know—what did you think?'

Mrs Francis surprised me by cutting in. 'Sally Matthews—'

'Oh, a scintillating talent, isn't she? I discovered her three years ago, when she auditioned for my first play. *Romance on the Railways*. You'll have heard of it, of course.' Maitland gave me no time to disagree, continuing his stream of praise. 'She's a natural talent, Miss Matthews. Destined for greater things than my meagre offerings. But of course, I don't need to tell you that. You'll have seen.'

'She's certainly a presence,' Mary offered.

'Yes! A "presence"! A perfect way to describe her! Though I do dread the day her talent is noticed. She deserves only the best, of course. But it would be an unbearable loss to me. Ah. To us, I should say. The Grand Guignol don't know what they've given up but be it on their own heads. There's even been a man here tonight, scouting talent.' His expression was an odd twist of selfish pride and personal dread. 'Though she has always been one to catch eyes.'

It struck me that Alexander Maitland was likely a fine fellow in small doses, but I found myself losing patience with him quickly. Mary's patience was running out more swiftly still, and Mrs Francis remained quiet and distant after her single contribution to the conversation. Eventually Maitland freed us from his presence. Mary wanted to adjourn to our hotel immediately, but Mrs Francis reminded us that we were meant to meet with Holmes afterward.

'Are you sure, Henrietta? Could we not hear whatever Mr Holmes has to say tomorrow, or at home—assuming there is anything to say?'

'He was very particular,' Mrs Francis insisted. 'Please, let me at least do as he asks. That way, I will know I've done all that was asked of me.'

The Seaside Rose was only a few buildings down, a short lamplit walk. It was a small tavern, simply decorated and sparsely attended. I recognised the evening's leading man at the back table, surrounded by the young men with whom we had shared the front row. They flocked around him, lavishing him with praise—a far cry from their mockery of earlier that evening. The wild-haired old man with whom Mary had had an altercation—the one I had believed to be a critic—sat on his own at a table a few feet from us, hunched over his notebook. I feared we might be asked to leave if we did not order something; but the landlord paid us no mind, leaving us to wait for Holmes without so much as a sideways glance.

'That Maitland fellow,' Mary said thoughtfully. 'He's madly in love with Sally Matthews, isn't he?'

'Or if not in love, then certainly charmed,' Mrs Francis added.

How could they possibly know this from such a short conversation? I asked them as much.

Mary smiled at me, and the latter explained. 'His tone. It was quite obvious.'

I didn't want to admit that it hadn't been at all obvious to me. He sounded obsessed, perhaps deluded, but certainly not in love. I began to wonder how much I might give away of my own inner workings without realising it but didn't dare say so.

'Speaking of her,' Mrs Francis began, but soon trailed off. She seemed uncertain whether to broach whatever topic was on her mind. I was about to encourage her to speak it when her eye was caught by something happening across the tavern.

At first, I could not see where she was looking. Her eyes were fixed on someone in the near distance, wide and shocked, and she covered her mouth to stifle an escaping cry. Then, surprising both Mary and myself, she stood from the table and marched across the tavern, where the man we had seen at the theatre now sat across from a dark-haired woman, who must have just recently entered.

I couldn't hear what words passed between Mrs Francis and the woman, but the slap delivered by the former to the latter rang audibly across the mostly empty tavern. The cluster of young men looked up with interest, one whistling shrilly in approval. The dark-haired woman held a hand to her face, eyes and mouth wide. The old man vacated the table quietly, with a much nimbler gait than I'd have thought him capable and approached Mary and myself uninvited.

'Well,' he said, in a voice that was unmistakably Holmes', 'I believe that counts as a positive identification. Don't you, Watson?'

Mary was unsurprised, but not unperturbed. She fixed the disguised Holmes with a sort of ice-chip stare, the kind of which only he could weather the receiving end. I, on the other hand, remained fixated on the scene before me. Mrs Francis had steadied herself, clearly overcome by the situation, but not so much that she couldn't speak:

'Where is Silas?'

Two realisations hit me in the same moment. The first was that, save for the lack of a mole at the corner of her mouth, the dark-haired woman matched Mrs Francis's description of the mysterious Beatrice Spenser precisely. The second, though it took longer to reveal itself to me, was that this woman was also the same Sally Matthews whose performance we had just finished watching.

It was no wonder that Mrs Francis had been oddly entranced throughout the show: she likely saw the similarity but, at a distance and with different hair and make-up, could not quite draw the connection.

Sally Matthews did not answer as she cradled her slapped face delicately in one hand. She looked around—at Mrs Francis, then the unresponsive landlord, then at Holmes standing by our table—and at last leapt from her chair and ran for the door. Holmes tore after her, his speed comical in his disguise, and barred her exit with his person. She backed away, hands clenched at her chest, sizing up her next move.

'Miss Matthews,' Holmes said calmly, 'I believe you have been asked a question. Where is young Silas?'

The young woman cast her gaze back toward the landlord, then toward her fellow cast member at the crowded table further back. None of the gentlemen looked inclined to offer assistance. She raised her head and glared at Holmes, with an imperious look that might have worked well on the stage but did her no good here.

'You stay out of this,' the young woman said coldly. 'I'm getting what's mine, and that's none of your business.'

'In my admittedly minimal knowledge of parenting, I believe the boy belongs to the widow Francis. Not you. She has, after all, put in the majority of the effort.'

Sally Matthews kept her fists clenched by her chest. 'But Archie promised me! He told me we'd have one, too—he promised!'

Holmes raised a hand languidly to the landlord. 'I don't suppose we could get a policeman in here?' In response, the landlord made his one move of the night, nodding curtly and stepping out the back door to oblige.

**

It took some time to get any information of note from Sally Matthews, but we eventually found Silas Francis. He was alive and well, though not especially happy, in a small bedsit a few blocks from the theatre. At the sight of his mother, he scrambled across the cluttered room, clinging to her skirts and weeping. She scooped him up in her arms and dried his tears, holding him close.

We were strongly encouraged to clear the bedsit and leave any further searching to the local authorities. Surprisingly, Holmes obliged. He asked only for a few salient details, which he hoped to relay to his client upon their discovery but was otherwise content with where things stood.

Holmes was nowhere to be seen at the hotel the next day; I assumed he had wasted no time and caught a late train back to London the night before. Mrs Francis and Silas had left early in the morning, likely to return to home and normality as quickly as possible. I, however, opted to spend the early part of the day in Brighton with Mary before returning. We'd been on quite a journey, after all, and both deserved some leisure time.

I met with Holmes the morning after, mostly to satisfy my curiosity concerning the case. He was expecting me.

'It was the blood, wasn't it?' I asked.

'The troupe at the Grand Guignol in Paris is quite secretive about the composition of their special effects.' Holmes still had Silas's shirt, ripped and covered in what I had thought briefly to be real blood. He gestured to it. 'But the presence of glycerine would match the behaviour of their special blend of blood. It is heated and melted before use onstage, and congeals as it cools, much like real blood. It would never fool our friends at Scotland Yard. It most certainly did not fool you.'

I suddenly remembered Mrs Francis's description of her own odd behaviour in Beatrice's presence. 'But for a grieving widow, led to doubt her sanity—'

Holmes nodded. 'She was already unwell from grief and strain. Now her imaginary friend arrives at her door, and she is led to believe she is losing her memory and doing things unconsciously. Her child and the fae friend then disappear—leaving her to fear the worst about her child and herself. We are fortunate she didn't find the shirt. As it is, she was spared the potential anguish, and I received all I needed to begin pulling the pieces together.'

It would require someone close enough to the Grand Guignol to either know the recipe or obtain some of their legendary stage gore. A charming actress in a nearby play might be able to procure such a thing. Mary and Mrs Francis had both seen how Sally Matthews had won over her playwright.'

'But why? What would she want with Silas?'

'She told you herself the other night. Were you not listening?'

I had indeed been listening, but at the time, the information had slipped by. Holmes urged me to wait, as all answers would be forthcoming. And, in short order, they were, as a much calmer Mrs Francis arrived at 221B. Were I not a doctor, I might have declared her fully cured just from a look; even as a medical man, it was clear that much of the strain on her person had been lifted.

'I'm terribly sorry,' Holmes said to his guest as she took a seat. 'I imagine all of this has been an unpleasant surprise for you.'

Mrs Francis shook her head. 'No. Or rather, yes. Some of it has been. But all together, it makes more sense than anything else has so far.'

As the truth of the matter spilled out, I found I was equally, and unhappily, unsurprised. The late Mr Archibald Francis had not been in the company of business partners during his long weeks away, but rather in the decidedly less austere company of Sally Matthews. Mrs Francis recalled that an "associate" by that surname had wired her the news of his death. She had, rather innocently, assumed that it was a colleague.

'As I understand it,' Holmes said, 'Miss Matthews volunteered quite a bit of information to the authorities. She still believes herself to be an innocent party in these proceedings.'

As it happened, what remained of Mr Francis's estate had gone to Sally Matthews in secret. She was well aware of his wife and son at home and grew jealous of her lover's existing family. She claimed—as she had in the tavern—that he had promised to start a second family with her. Of course, with Mr Francis unable to speak for himself, there was no way of knowing if this was true.

'After his death,' Mrs Francis pushed on valiantly, 'she set her sights on Silas. I suppose Archibald must have told her about Beatrice, and how distressed her last words made me. I had told the story to him often enough that he must have known it by heart. I expect it came up in conversation between them; she has those same big, grey eyes. All she had to do was come into my life, then disappear with him in such a way that I would be afraid to tell anyone. She travelled here with a production of her play and found a space she could hide.'

I recalled Mrs Francis's landlord complaining of "visitors" and something in the attic space. 'Surely she didn't take up residence in the attic!' Holmes smiled faintly; I realised he must have been the housebreaker of the other night, confirming that very suspicion for himself.

Mrs Francis nodded. 'She would make herself up in my bathroom mirror before I awoke, with a black wig and a bit of stage makeup. Then she would remove the disguise after I had gone to sleep. Even if she were seen on the stairs, she wouldn't fit the description I had of her.'

'It was a nearly foolproof plan. Had she not decided to bring some of Mr Francis's old letters with her to her little room above Mrs Francis's home—'

I politely pointed out to Holmes that most people don't expect to have their private rooms broken into. He pointed out in return that she shouldn't have squatted in an attic if she wanted privacy. It was a fair point.

'But how on earth did you track her down from my story?' Mrs Francis asked. 'Surely there wasn't enough to work from.'

'Do not discount your assistance so readily, Mrs Francis. You gave me more than enough to work with.' At the lady's look of surprise, Holmes continued. 'I was sent in search of a woman who lived near you, was only out of your sight in the evenings and for a few hours on Sunday, and who had striking grey eyes. I will admit, I had seen the London production of *A Window by Moonlight* not long ago, so Miss Matthews's appearance was fresh in my mind. As was her performance, but the less said about that, the better.'

I still had questions, but Mrs Francis would almost certainly not know the answers. Bar one: where was Silas now?

'With my mother—who is extremely distraught at having inadvertently brought Beatrice—Miss Matthews, I should say—into my life. I will be following him there this afternoon. I may even take her up on her offer to live with her. The city has afforded me quite enough excitement for one lifetime.'

When Mrs Francis had moved along, I felt I could raise my last two questions to Holmes without causing distress. But before I could speak, Holmes had begun to answer one of them.

'You're wondering, I assume, about the murder of Mr Francis.'

I was. 'I cannot help but feel that Sally Matthews may have been directly involved somehow.'

'That remains to be seen. Though I do share a similar concern.' Holmes appeared pensive, but not perturbed. It was simply another puzzle. 'It could be that she simply saw the opportunity after an unfortunate occurrence. Or it could be that she made that opportunity herself. Who knows? Our eager playwright may have grown jealous of the object of his star's affections. But that remains to be discovered by someone else. My role was to find Beatrice Spenser, and thus Silas Francis. My work is done. Even so—'

Even so, he still wanted every answer. But it would be discovered soon enough, and, in the meantime, a family had been reunited. If nothing else, I pointed out, we had discovered that there never was a "Beatrice."

'When did we learn that?' Holmes retorted, though something in what I had said clearly resonated, as I was to discover later.

'You think otherwise?'

'We discovered that Sally Matthews was not Beatrice Spenser—that she created the character from a retelling of Mrs Francis's reminiscences. Whether there truly was a Beatrice in her childhood, or whether she was the creation of a lonely young mind, I fear we may never know. Perhaps she was a neighbour playing pretend, or the daughter of a family forced to live away from society. Perhaps the real Beatrice was just a very sad, very lonely little girl, angry at the thought of losing her one friend.'

'Or perhaps she truly was a fae child.'

Holmes was unamused.

The Woman Who Wasn't: Part Five

'It's quite intolerable,' I grumbled the next morning, barely touching the breakfast laid in front of me. Lifting my head, I found Mary looking at me with a mixture of affection and consternation.

'Is that a statement to which you would like me to respond?' she asked, a mischievous glint in her eye, 'Or has it simply become a habit, like cracking one's knuckles?'

I laughed. I imagine some men might feel wounded by their new bride making jokes at their expense, but I had come to rely on Mary to puncture my occasional black moods and frustrations, a task in which she took great pleasure.

'All right,' I said. 'I take your point.'

'If only you'd take your breakfast.'

I lifted my cup to my lips in a show of truce, but had immediate cause to regret it, the tea having long gone cold. I grimaced, eliciting a generous laugh from Mrs Watson. I shook my head.

'I can see I shall not prevail this morning.'

'I'm sorry, John. I shouldn't laugh. What is wrong? I assume that Mr Sherlock Holmes has something to do with it.'

'What makes you so sure of that? I might be troubled by a difficult case. Or a recalcitrant patient.'

Mary shook her head.

'No, they get an entirely different reaction all together. Much gruffer and more commanding,' said my wife, lowering her voice and adding, in a worryingly accurate impression, 'Bloody fools! If they won't listen, then how I am to be expected to aid them!'

This time, I laughed.

'Ah. And when it concerns, Mr Holmes?'

'No matter how frustrated you are with him, you sound a little worried that he might be right.'

I sighed.

'You are an extremely wise woman, Mary Watson.'

'What is it, this time?'

'I told you of the case surrounding Anastasia Frain?'

'Yes, poor girl. I pray she is soon found.'

'Holmes seems to have hopes.'

'Then what is the issue?'

'Once again, he keeps his own counsel. He has me rooting through old cases, though he won't give me the slightest clue why. It makes me feel quite dim at times.'

'Well, he has you as a confidant, dearest husband. To try out his theories against. Might I not serve the same purpose for you?'

At that moment, I think my love for my wife, never in doubt, reached new heights.

'You might at that,' I said. 'Do you remember the Beatrice Spenser business? Or, rather, the Sally Matthews business?'

'Of course,' Mary replied. 'That dreadful play.' She shivered charmingly at the memory.

'Well, Holmes asked me to look back at my record of it. He's like a headmaster, trying to tease a baffled student towards the solution of a maths problem.'

'Then you must show him your workings out.'

'That's the trouble. I'm not convinced I have any.'

Mary frowned in thought.

'Forget the details, John. In my short acquaintance with Mr Holmes, it won't be something obvious. What was the case truly about?'

'Childhood. Imagination. Trickery.'

'Simpler, I think.'

I slapped the tabletop. Mary's eyes widened.

'Elementary, my dear husband?'

'I think it may well be, Mary. I think it may well be.'

'You're not going to keep me in suspense, are you?'

I smiled, then offered my best impression of my friend, the Great Detective.

'For the moment, Mrs Watson. But all, if I am correct in my deductions, will soon be revealed.'

Mary sighed.

'Very well. But, for goodness' sake, eat some breakfast. You can't possibly be that smug on an empty stomach.'

***

I'll admit freely, as I made my way to Baker Street later that morning, I was feeling somewhat pleased with myself. Yes, it had taken some coaxing from Holmes, but I felt that I had put my finger on the crux of the matter, more or less under my own power.

I had seen *and* observed.

All of those cases, seemingly distinct from one another bar the central disappearance at their heart. That had been Holmes' clue but, true to form, it had not been the line of enquiry he truly wanted me to follow.

For it was not the disappearances that they had in common, but the connivance. False identities, false faces, secrets. These were the common threads at which Holmes was inviting me to pull.

I entered Baker Street straight-backed, gave a more than usually florid greeting to Mrs Hudson and headed straight for our once-shared sitting room.

Throwing the door open, I stepped through and, seeing Holmes in his chair, wreathed in smoke from a newly lit pipe, I exclaimed:

'I have it, Holmes!'

My friend looked up and cocked his head gently to one side. It was hardly the expression of wonderment and awe I hoped for, but it would have to suffice.

'Do you, Watson?'

'I do.'

'I'm very happy for you, but you'll have to excuse me. What is it precisely that you have?'

'Can't you deduce it, Holmes?'

This brought a thin smile to his face.

'If I must, Watson.' He leant forward and his eyes travelled briefly up and down my person.

Then he leant back and, in a sorrowful tone, said:

'I am sorry, Watson.'

'Sorry?'

'I'm afraid your confidence is ill-placed.'

This was too much.

'But you haven't any idea what I'm about to say.'

'Am I correct in assuming you believe that you have solved the mystery surrounding Ms. Anastasia Frain?'

'Why, yes. But that's an easy enough guess. It is the problem that concerns us most at present.'

'True. But I also know that, at my request, you have consulted the case of Henrietta Francis.'

'As you say, at your request.'

'From which you have deduced that my investigations are running along lines of subterfuge, perhaps even of adopted identity. I am right, am I not, Watson?'

'Yes, Holmes. But dammit, I assumed that was what you wanted me to discover.'

'Oh, in that you not mistaken, Watson. It is at the next hurdle I fear you will fall.'

I hesitated.

'I still don't see how you can possibly predict my thinking.'

'My dear Watson, you have the same glint in your eye that I did when I briefly landed on the same solution as you. The realisation that the truth has been staring at you in the face from the off and you have been too distracted to see it.'

'Perhaps I have reached a different conclusion.'

Holmes unfolded himself from his chair and strode to my side. He lay a gentle hand on my arm.

'You are a kind man, Watson. You have dismissed, from the goodness of your heart, the idea that Anastasia Frain has met her end. It does you credit, though no outcome should be disregarded from pure sentimentality. Thankfully, in this case, you are correct. Miss Frain lives.'

'There we are in agreement.'

'Therefore, the question is raised. If she lives, why can she not be found? And why does a young man stalk her lodgings in her place? The common answer, an elopement, does not seem to fit the case. Why the message from our errant maid: "I am not she."?'

I began to grow excited once more.

'Precisely, Holmes. Which led me to my epiphany. Miss Frain is not missing at all. She is—'

'The young man?'

I was immediately crestfallen.

'You came to the same conclusion.'

Holmes was sympathetic.

'Briefly, Watson. Yes. It did seem to fit the facts of the case. A father who would have preferred, it seems, a son. A daughter with a gift for a business, denied the chance to exploit it due to the restrictions on her sex. Perhaps, indeed, something deeper and more profound. It is not unheard of, in London or elsewhere.'

'Blast it, Holmes. I was so sure.'

'Do not berate yourself, Watson. I was equally convinced, until a new fact appeared on the horizon.'

'And what was that?'

Before Holmes could answer, there was a soft knock at the door.

'We shall explore it together,' whispered Holmes, then called out:

'Do come in, Miss Frain.'

***

It was some minutes later, Anastasia Frain having already taken my usual seat opposite Holmes, that my wits truly began to reassemble themselves into something approaching a workable state. It would have been an unexpected turn of events under any circumstances, but to have the theory of which I had convinced myself overturned, with such force, sent my mind reeling.

In truth, I remained standing for fear that if I made my way to the couch, I might not be able to leave it. Instead, I paced, waiting for the young woman to tell her almost certainly fascinating tale.

As for Anastasia Frain herself, she seemed in perfect health, if somewhat pale and thin. There was something of her father about her, the set of the mouth perhaps, a glint of steel in the eyes, but one could only assume the remainder of her open, gentle countenance came courtesy of her mother.

'Mr Holmes,' she began.

But, in another surprise, my friend threw up a hand.

'My apologies, Miss Frain but I must beg your patience. I am eager, as I know Doctor Watson must also be, to hear your story, but I feel I must pay for the pleasure with one of my own.'

Miss Frain looked perplexed and her face matched my feeling.

'Watson?'

'Yes?'

'There is a bundle of paper on my worktable. No doubt you will recognise it as the work of your own hand.'

I made my way over to the table and picked up the untidily stacked manuscript. Glancing at the first page, I gave a start.

'Holmes? You can't possibly be thinking of relating this to Miss Frain.'

'Can I not? I feel she would find it most instructive.'

'Dash it, Holmes,' I protested. 'She's an innocent young woman.'

'Yes, Watson. And I would very much like to keep her in that state for as long as is possible. Virtue is not tainted by knowledge but by the lack of it. We must acknowledge the dark to know when to light our lamp.'

Miss Frain gave a small but deliberate cough.

'Mr Holmes. Dr Watson,' she began, in a firm, yet somehow lyrical voice. 'I am no shrinking violet. However, when you have heard my tale, neither am I sure that you will see me as an innocent. But if Mr Holmes believes that this story of yours will help me navigate the treacherous waters in which I find myself, then I am happy to risk my delicate nature.'

Holmes gave me a glance and gestured for me to hand over the papers.

I shook my head.

'I set the foul deeds to paper. If there is good to come from them, then I shall do the telling,' I acquiesced.

My friend inclined his head in gratitude.

I took one last look at the anxious but determined Miss Frain and began to read.

The Lady and the Craft

J.P. McCourt

One darkly overcast morning that year we received, amongst the usual bills of service and other excessively capitalised solicitations of lunatics, a ray of tropical sunshine in the form of a picture postcard from, of all places, Patagonia.

It was addressed simply to "The Gentlemen Detectives, Baker Street, London, England."

Marvelling, not for the first time, at the endeavour and perspicacity of those fine men of the General Post Office, I turned the card over in my hand to determine its provenance.

On the reverse of the postcard I encountered a rather delightful lithograph of some particularly picturesque peaks and a message which read, 'Greetings from Y Wladfa. Best wishes, M.'

I allowed myself a nod and a wry smile before passing this communication to my friend, seated opposite me at the breakfast table.

Arching one eyebrow questioningly, he set aside his Times and accepted the proffered card.

He read its brief message, turned it over to examine its various exotic stamps and postmarks in his usual minute detail, then finally raised it to his legendary proboscis and inhaled deeply.

The slightest of smiles played across his lips as he gently laid the postcard, picture side up, upon the table.

Lifting the newspaper once more, he opened it with a snap and resumed reading.

From behind this paper carapace came one word:

'Good.'

***

In September of the previous year, having no more taxing demands on our time than that all-too-familiar staving off of the all-engulfing mittens of ennui, Holmes and I were to be found in the sitting-room of our shared lodgings at 221B Baker Street, engaged in nothing more strenuous than periodicals and tea-drinking.

'Ha!'—a derisory snort from Holmes as he read something he clearly found amusing and, most likely, very stupid. I set aside my *Sporting Life* and cocked my head expectantly in his direction, sure that he would expound further upon the damnably foolish passage which he had just read. Strongly suspecting that I myself was the damned fool responsible, I was all too keenly aware of the utter futility of trying to continue reading whilst awaiting the dropping of the other shoe, so to speak.

Getting to the bottom of why the White Hart Friendly Society had suddenly called it a day after eighty-five years would just have to wait, I supposed.

That other shoe dropped soon enough.

'I can see why you kept this to yourself for so long, Watson.'

And here we go, I thought to myself.

'I mean, your excruciating prose style aside, you have the facts of the case all wrong! I suppose I can allow a certain leeway, given that it relates to one from your early days of observing my methods in the field, if I may borrow from your military vernacular, but even so.'

Knowing that the Great Literary Critic was only warming up, I sighed and reached for my pipe and ship's. I surmised that Holmes' dissection of my writing prowess was likely to take some time, so I might as well make myself as comfortable as practicable during the impending slicing and dicing. To borrow from my own medical vernacular.

'And the title! My God, Watson! Such sensationalism may well play to the penny seats, but for a man of your education, it's a very poor show.'

He looked with some distaste at the magazine in his lap.

'It might also have been an idea not to include our address in your little tale; that is bound to come back and slap us around the chops at some point—'

I struck a match and held it to the bowl of my pipe, hoping the motion would hide the flush I felt rise in my cheek. I doubted, however, that it would.

Holmes shook his head, more in disappointment than distaste.

'Look here, my good fellow,' he said, his tone mellowing somewhat. 'If you were short of funds, you should have said something. Come to me first before prostituting us both to this, this dead cook.'

He brandished the offending magazine with something between despair and disgust as I inadvertently snorted plumes of smoke from both nostrils.

'What? No, I—', I spluttered through tearing eyes.

But Holmes continued: 'I mean, technically, it is her dead husband's periodical, I suppose, but that is entirely beside the point. I understand that your Army stipend may not stretch as far as you would wish but—'

Mercifully, Holmes' literary and fiduciary criticism was stayed at this point by a knock on the sitting-room door, followed, as it invariably was, by the entrance of Mrs Hudson, our landlady-cum-housekeeper.

'You have a visitor, Mr Holmes: a Mr Auric, I believe he said his name was. He wishes to engage your services in a matter of some delicacy, as he put it.'

'Don't they always, Mrs Hudson, don't they always?' Holmes sighed. 'Very well, please show Mr Auric and his delicates in.'

'Mr Holmes!' she all but shrieked, a reaction belied by her sly smile and raise of one eyebrow towards myself.

A soon as Mrs Hudson had left the room to retrieve our visitor, Holmes turned his attention back to me.

'Ten shillings says it's another blessed missing heiress.'

'A guinea on simple burglary,' I puffed in reply.

We shook hands on the wager.

Mr Roland Auric, for as such he had introduced himself on entering the room, was a peculiarly average man. The sort of man of whom a dozen people would have given a dozen different descriptions.

The only feature of note which I could remember about the gentleman later was his weak chin, a feature he sought to disguise under a marginally less weak beard. This he stroked nervously when discomfited, which he seemed to be often.

Holmes strode towards our guest, hand extended for the shaking thereof.

'At your service, Mr G—. I am Sherlock Holmes, and this is my associate, Doctor John Watson.'

I snuck a glance at Holmes: had I heard him correctly?

Auric's free hand had veritably flown to his chin as he started to splutter: 'Wh— why I, I don't, whatever do you, what?'

'Come now, sir. You clearly are aware of how I earn my daily bread. Why should you be surprised that I am aware of your true identity?'

Auric could only stare disbelievingly in reply.

'Holmes,' I enquired. 'Have you skipped ahead several chapters again, leaving the rest of us still reading the preface? What, precisely, is going on here?'

'All in due course, Watson, all in due course.'

He turned to the slowly recovering Auric.

'Please, Mr G—, take a seat. May I offer you a sherry?'

Auric, lowering himself into the proffered armchair, replied, 'Well, it's a little early—'

'Poppycock, man, it's long gone five in Shanghai!'

A visible start from Auric, followed by more beard stroking.

'You served there under Staveley, I believe?', asked Holmes, in that manner which I had come to recognise as indicating that the question was entirely rhetorical and was in fact designed purely to unsettle his interlocutor.

I should know, the bugger had done it to me often enough.

'I did, yes,' confirmed Auric.

'Then all's well!'

So saying, he handed the bemused and compliant gentleman a snifter of sherry.

Holmes winked knowingly at me as we took our seats. Why knowingly, I cannot imagine; I was quite baffled by this exchange with our guest.

'And how may I be of help to the widow's son?' asked Holmes.

Auric peered at Holmes over the top of his glass, before placing it on the occasional table beside his chair.

Still regarding Holmes, he asked, 'How do you put up with him, Doctor Watson?'

'Partly morbid curiosity, partly a keen appreciation of the absurd,' I replied. 'But mostly because he pays half the rent; lodgings in London can be frightfully expensive.'

'Ha! Indeed, sir, indeed. Well, Mr Holmes, to business.'

'To business!' replied Holmes and drained his glass. The Great Detective, it is fair to say, was no stranger to day drinking.

I rose from my chair to fetch the decanter and top up his and Auric's glasses. A nod of thanks from the latter, nothing from the former as he focused those gimlet eyes on our guest.

'I understand from my housekeeper that you have a matter you wish to discuss with me,' Holmes began.

'Yes, a somewhat delicate matter,' Auric replied, indicating myself with what he presumably thought of as a subtle tilt of his head.

'She said that too, yes.'

'No, I mean—'

Holmes' eyes narrowed in that way that they sometimes do.

'I know exactly what you mean, G—,' he brusquely interrupted our visitor. 'However, the good Doctor here is not merely my associate—whatever you take that nebulous term to mean—he is my confidante, my friend and—may the Good Lord save us all—my biographer. So you may speak freely in front of Watson. His discretion can be assured.'

'Indubitably,' I chipped in. 'One of the most important lessons I learned during my military service was when to keep my mouth shut.'

'You were in the military too, eh? Where did you serve if I may ask?' Auric inquired.

Our guest's attention having thus been focused upon myself, Holmes reached for the decanter I had placed on the table beside him, and in so doing judiciously managed to knock the copy of the periodical he had been reading earlier from the table and down behind his chair. For discretionary reasons, you understand.

'Afghanistan,' I answered Auric. 'Army medic. I was invalided out after catching a bit of shrapnel in the old pin here.' I rubbed the offending limb, grimacing and generally laying it on a bit thick.

'A rum do and no mistake,' said Auric, nodding in sympathy.

'No doubt,' Holmes interjected. 'And now that we have established Watson's bona fides, perhaps you'd be so kind as to intimate the reason for your visit here today?'

'But of course.'

Auric visibly composed himself before beginning.

'I don't know how much you know about The Craft, Doctor Watson?'

'Freemasonry?' I replied. 'Enough to recognise the charm on your watch chain as one of its totems—'

I nodded towards the square and be-compassed fob on the chain dangling from Auric's waistcoat pocket.

'—and the peculiar but very specific handshake Holmes gave you earlier, which you reciprocated.'

'Good work, Watson!' Holmes ejaculated.

'And?' prompted Auric.

'And what?' I replied.

'*Omne trium perfectum,* my dear chap. The rule of three?' he prompted again.

'No, that's the lot; those are the only two things I know about Masons.'

This seemed to disappoint our guest somewhat.

'Oh, I see. Never mind, it's not important,' he said, his face belying his words.

'In any event,' he continued manfully, 'it does not affect matters one whit, other than that I may have to explain certain elements to you as we proceed.'

'That would be most helpful, sir, thank you,' I replied.

Auric turned to Holmes.

'I'm so sorry, Mr Holmes, how presumptuous of me not to direct the same question to yourself. Given your reputation—and, indeed, the grip you proffered earlier—I had believed you to be quite well versed in The Craft. Is that indeed the case?'

'I know slightly less of Freemasonry than I do of apiculture,' replied Holmes.

'And he does know an awful lot about bees,' I confirmed.

'So please, if you will, why are you here?'

'Very well. We are being blackmailed. Or perhaps being held to ransom is a more accurate way of putting it.'

'*We* being?' I asked.

'The Freemasons. Specifically my own Lodge, the *Quatuor Coronati*. A certain item has been stolen from our premises on Great Queen Street, and the thief has threatened to destroy it unless his demands are met.'

'Have you contacted the police?' I asked. 'Inspector Lestrade, our contact at Scotland Yard, is a pretty decent sort.'

A snort from Holmes.

'No, he isn't.'

He addressed Auric.

'Tell me, G—, in plain terms, what was stolen, and exactly what demands have been made?'

Auric, or G—, as I suppose I should call him, looked at his expensively-derby'd feet, embarrassed.

'I would rather not disclose the demands for now, Mr Holmes.'

'Damn it all, man, you cannot handicap me before we even begin! Those demands could well give us the motive for the theft, and thus narrow our field of suspects!'

'I appreciate that, Mr Holmes, but it is rather outwith my control. You see, this is a much larger issue than mere burglary. In fact, I do not believe that I would be overstating the case by describing it as one of national security. In further fact—'

'No, don't say it,' interjected Holmes.

'—I was referred to you by a member of Her Majesty's Government.'

'For the love of all that you hold holy—'

'Your brother Mycroft.'

Holmes' head collapsed forward into his chest, where he let it rest for a moment.

G— and I exchanged concerned glances before turning back to Holmes.

He let out a great sigh then raised his head to regard each of us in turn.

'You know,' he began, a somewhat manic smile beginning to spread across his face, 'This may turn out to be quite good fun after all.'

'So tell us. What was stolen?', continued Holmes. 'Nothing of great financial value, I'd wager; perhaps one of your arcane trinkets? Solomon's fez or the like?'

'Well, this is rather embarrassing actually,' began our visitor.

'Not at all, my dear chap, you're amongst friends here! Or at least amongst people who wish you no harm.'

'Thank you, I—'

'Not actively, at any rate.'

'Quite so—'

'Yet, anyway.'

'Ah, yes, I, uh—'

'Holmes is just pulling your leg,' I intervened.

'Please, continue.'

'Ah, right, I see.'

He cast a nervous glance at Holmes and I before continuing.

'So. Have either of you gentlemen heard of a document called the *Regius Poem*?'

I looked blankly at G— and then to Holmes.

'I am aware of it, yes,' the detective responded. 'Sort of a Holy Writ for you chaps, is it not?'

'It is what one might call a significant document in the history of The Craft, yes. It is the oldest of the Old Charges, the earliest known document of its type. In the same way as the Old Testament is thought of as the very foundation of Christianity, so the *Regis Poem* is the foundation of what we now call Freemasonry. It consists of an epic poem in rhyming couplets, inscribed on sixty-four pages of vellum.'

'My God, that sounds awful. And the vellum? Calfskin, I presume?', asked Holmes.

'The exact source of the vellum is... uncertain.'

'Ah.'

'Quite so. It is thought to date from at least the fourteenth century, a time when they were a little less fussy about where they sourced their writing materials.'

He paused to let that one sink in for a bit.

'In any event, that it is a document of… reverence is not quite the *mot juste*, but it is of particular interest and importance to my own Lodge, given that our name is taken from it. Specifically from the section concerning the legend of the Four Holy Crowned Ones.'

'Severus and so forth, yes,' interjected Holmes.

G— looked to him, impressed at the detective's familiarity with the subject.

'Yes, indeed.'

'I had understood that this document was held at the British Museum,' said Holmes. 'I take it that you managed to convince them to loan it to you for your research?'

'Correct, Mr Holmes.'

G— turned to me.

'The Quatuor Coronati Lodge is unique in The Craft in that it is entirely devoted to the research of our history. We seek, in our own small way, to cut through the myths that surround Freemasonry. As such, we study ancient tracts such as the *Regius* to mine them, so to speak, for the facts contained therein. For the actual verifiable history. We believe that only by studying the past can we build for the future.'

'A noble aim indeed, G—,' Holmes commented. 'And one that would surely be made infinitely simpler if you did not lose your holy poem.'

'With respect, Mr Holmes, we did not lose it; it was stolen from us.'

'Semantics, sir. And possibly sophistry.'

G— spluttered in protest.

'How dare you—'

'Your part in this theft may be purely that of victim—albeit the document was not in fact yours in the first place, but again semantics—but without knowledge of the demands made by the purported thief, I am unable at this time to speculate on the motive for the theft, and thus also unable to rule you yourself out as a suspect.'

'But I came here seeking your help—'

'Which may well be sophistry on your part; did I not just explain that?'

Red-faced and seething, G— rose from his chair and stood over Holmes.

'Why you smug little—'

Holmes, being Holmes, merely grinned at the agitated man.

I rose from my own seat to intercede and attempt to defuse the situation.

'Now Mr G—, Holmes is merely playing devil's advocate,' I began in my best bedside manner. 'It is simply logic at work on his part, without evidence to the contrary—and, of course, we have yet to gather evidence of any sort. We cannot possibly at this stage rule out anyone from our enquiries.'

'But to accuse me in that manner, I mean, this is my life's work!'

'I understand, and perhaps my friend could have expressed himself better, but he is who he is. Please, sit down, take a little sherry to calm your heart.'

I all but shoved G— back into his armchair before turning to retrieve the decanter on the table by the detective's elbow.

Holmes received my best basilisk stare before I turned to our guest and topped up his glass with Spain's second-finest export.

Returning to my own seat, I addressed the other men:

'May I suggest in the first instance that we return to the scene of the crime?'

***

The Freemason's Tavern, home of *inter alia* Quatuor Coronati Lodge No. 2076, was on Great Queen Street, in the West End of the city between Holborn and Covent Garden.

The administrative offices were towards the back of the building, in what a century ago had been a separate house from the original Tavern. The Great Hall separating the two had been built on the garden which had formerly lain between the two old properties.

G— escorted Holmes and I through the building to his office, from whence the *Regius* had been stolen.

'And this door is kept locked when unoccupied?' Holmes asked.

'It is, yes,' replied G—.

'And where is the key kept?' I asked.

'Here on my watch chain.'

G— pulled the chain in question from his waistcoat pocket: at its terminus were three keys, but no watch.

'What are the other keys for?' I asked.

'The front door to my town house, and my gun cabinet,' he replied, fingering each key in turn.

'Duplicates?'

'Only one, in my study drawer at home.'

'Who has access to that drawer?'

'Only myself. The key to that drawer is locked in my gun cabinet, hidden under a small satin pillow which bears an original Philadelphia Deringer. This is the only key to the gun cabinet.'

'I see, thank you. Now if we may, Doctor Watson and I would like to examine the crime scene in more forensic detail.'

'By all means.'

The three of us stood there for a moment before the penny dropped.

'Oh, you mean—'

'Yes, I do.'

'Right, right. I'll leave you to it then.'

'Thank you, most kind.'

G— left.

Holmes and I shared a wry smile before turning to contemplate the office door.

I tried the handle; it was locked.

'What do you think?', asked Holmes.

'Thirty seconds, twenty-five if I was in a hurry?' I replied.

'Off you go then.'

Retrieving a stout safety pin from the reverse of my jacket lapel, I squatted down until my eyes were level with the door's lock and paused.

Holmes fished out his pocket watch and flipped it open.

'And in 3, 2, 1—go!'

Less than a minute later we were standing in G—'s formerly locked office as Holmes tucked away his watch.

'Thirty-six seconds. Losing your touch, old man.'

'Those lunchtime sherries do eventually take their toll, you know.'

'Pfft,' Holmes replied.

Grinning, we went to work.

***

Back at Baker Street, we compared notes.

'So, what do we have?' began Holmes.

'Four long red hairs, a dozen or so fish scales, and some white clay mud,' I replied.

'So we're looking for—?'

'An Irish mermaid.'

'Ha! The game's a-fluke, Watson!'

116

A confession: I took an almost childlike pleasure in making my friend laugh. And an adult-like sense of accomplishment, too: it was not an easy task.

He, on the other hand, could make me laugh seemingly whenever the mood took him.

But I digress.

We surveyed our evidence in silence for a moment, then:

'Is it just me—?' he began.

'—or is this too easy?' I finished.

We thought about it for a moment, looked at each other and simultaneously said:

'Occam's Razor.'

Shrugging, we made for the pantry to see what Mrs Hudson had left out for our supper.

Over said victuals—the remains of a very fine pork pie and some of Mrs Hudson's excellent homemade pickle— Holmes reached into his waistcoat pocket to pull out a coin, which he flipped across the table in my direction.

Catching it in mid-air, I beamed smugly in acknowledgement before tucking the guinea into my pocket.

***

The following day, after some perfectly ordinary investigating on our part, Holmes and I found ourselves standing outside a distinctly scabrous house front in Miller's Court, Whitechapel.

'Shall I—?' I asked Holmes.

He nodded his assent and I knocked on the decrepit door of No. 13.

No answer.

We looked at each other; Holmes indicated with another nod that I should knock again.

So again I knocked, louder this time.

Again, no response from within.

Gesturing me to stand aside, Holmes raised his silver-pommelled cane to rap on the door.

The door opened on his downswing and he narrowly missed braining the semi-naked man who had answered it.

'Oi! Mind 'ow you go!'

At this remove in time, I find it hard to recall whether it was the man's filthy genitals or the fetid overall stench of fish, sweat and gin emanating from him which caused us to recoil. Either way, there was definite recoiling on our part.

'Joseph Barnett?' I enquired.

'Oo's ah-skin'?'

'I am Doctor John Watson and this is Mr Sherlock Holmes. Perhaps you've heard of us?'

'No.'

'Really? Oh, all right. Er, may we speak to the lady of the house?'

'Which one?'

'How do you mean?'

'Oi mean as 'ow apparently there's two ladies of the house most days recent-like, and which one do youse two want?'

'The red-haired one?', I proffered.

'MARY!', he screamed without turning around, causing a second recoil from Holmes and me.

A brief pause then a cry of 'WHAT?' from within.

'THERE'S TWO TOFFS 'ERE LOOKIN' FOR A SHAG!' Barnett replied.

'No, we—', I attempted to explain.

'BUGGER!' came the reply.

'POSSIBLY! THEY WEREN'T SPECIFIC!' he replied, tutting and rolling his eyes at us. Not literally, thank the Lord.

Various grunts, curses and one loud crash later, a red-haired woman aged anywhere between eighteen and fifty-two appeared in the doorway, pulling a thin shawl over her shoulders.

She shooed Barnett away before addressing us.

'Well?' she asked.

'Well, indeed,' replied Holmes.

She ran a practiced eye up and down Holmes before dismissing him, probably due to that bloody hat of his, and addressed herself to me.

'You're from them then?' she asked, in a pronounced brogue.

'In a manner of speaking, yes', I replied. 'I am Doctor John Watson and this is Mr Sherlock Holmes. We are private consulting detectives and we'd like the document back, please.'

'He's been sorted out first, aye?'

'Who's been sorted out?' asked Holmes.

'Don't you be playin' the innocent now, I know what youse lot are like.'

'What lot, Mary?' I asked.

She looked me dead in the eye, cocked her head to one side. Then, apparently having made her mind up about something, she looked up and down the street before replying.

'Youse don't know what this is about, do ye?'

'We know that you stole a very old document from an office in the West End, and we've been asked to get it back,' I replied. 'Why, is there something else we should know?'

'Sure I could fill Vicky Docks with what you don't know, posh boy—'

Another quick look up and down the street.

'But not here, all right? Let me get dressed and we'll meet in Mrs McLatchie's down the road there.'

I looked at Holmes, who had kept quiet throughout. He nodded.

'Off you bugger then,' Mary prompted. 'I'll see you in ten minutes.'

***

Holmes and I sat in uncomfortable silence in Mrs McLatchie's Coffee Shop, both silently convinced that Mary had fled while we sat there waiting for her like the good little posh boys that we were.

She arrived a full half hour late, having clearly used the extra twenty minutes to spruce herself up for respectable company.

The effect was not entirely successful but bless her for the effort.

'Sorry, gents, had to set Julia on her way and see to Joe first. Buy us a coffee and a cream bun, would ye?'

Holmes and I looked at each other. Unusually he blinked first, rose and went to the counter for refreshments.

'She's an old Proddy hoor but not a bad sort really,' said Mary, to break the silence.

'Who is what now?' I replied, confused.

'Mrs McLatchie, her what runs this place. All right when ye get t'know her like.'

'Ah, right, I see.'

She smiled, and I returned that smile.

Now that I had a better view of Mary, I realised that she couldn't have been more than twenty-three or four. She was attractive in a homely way, albeit with a little more décolletage than perhaps I was used to seeing in polite society. Her eyes were a piercing Arctic blue, unusual in a redhead.

'So, Mary,' I began as Holmes rejoined us. 'Do you have the document with you?'

'Do youse think I came up the Thames in a banana boat? No chance, show me yours first.'

'My, uh, what?' I replied, having no clue what she meant.

'Has he been arrested yet?', she asked.

'Has who been arrested yet?'

'That murderin' bastard Eddy, of course!'

***

To this day, I have no idea what Mycroft Holmes did for a living. Of course I was aware that he worked for the Government in some capacity, but I could not tell you what that capacity was. I doubt even Holmes knew precisely.

He did have an awfully nice office though.

Seeking to avoid the seasonal rain, Holmes and I took a hansom cab to the unfashionable bit of Whitehall where Mycroft was nominally based, in a large but somehow unprepossessing Georgian grey stone building.

Once inside, we were ushered into some sort of anteroom containing a few green leather armchairs and a great deal of oak panelling and asked to wait.

We were given no indication of how long that wait would be, which I found vaguely troubling.

Holmes did not seem so troubled as I; he lay down on a very inviting-looking chaise longue and appeared to immediately fall asleep.

The sleep of the just, I suppose. Just what though, I could not say.

I sat for what felt like several hours but was in all likelihood probably about twenty minutes, riffling through an almost complete back catalogue of Punch magazine spanning the years 1853 to 1872. Typical waiting room fare to this day, I should imagine.

Finally, a very thin young man sporting pince-nez and an entirely unreasonable cravat popped his head through a doorway I had up until that point thought to be mere wall and beckoned us to enter.

Holmes immediately sprang to his feet and strode towards the hole in the wall.

***

The office we entered was massive, about the size of a small provincial ballroom. The curtain-less south-facing windows spanning the length of one wall should have made the place light and airy, but instead it felt like an abandoned library. This impression may have been inspired by the empty bookshelves which took up the entirety of the wall opposite those windows, in combination with the thick carpet which reduced our footsteps to silence as we crossed the room.

A large disapproving portrait of Queen Victoria dominated the wall at the far end. Under that portrait, behind a large teak desk whose surface was bare save for a pencil, a pen and a very large ledger, sat Mycroft Holmes.

In his facial features one could easily discern the familial resemblance—the clear, sharp eyes; the furrow of the brow; that unmistakable aquiline nose—but below that nose the resemblance ended.

Mycroft seemed to have gained even more weight since I had last set eyes on him and was now roughly the size of four of the younger Holmes strapped together.

He did not rise as we approached his desk, which I noticed lacked even a single visitor's chair. It seemed that Holmes Major did not encourage long meetings.

'Doctor Watson, Sherlock.' He nodded at each of us in turn, by way of greeting.

'Good afternoon, Mr Holmes,' I replied, managing to overcome a strong urge to bow.

'Hello, brother dear,' said Holmes, perching himself on the edge of the desk. 'Good lunch, then? Was the mustard and garlic roast goose at the Diogenes to your satisfaction?'

Mycroft's eyes flicked briefly down then back to his brother, a slight nod acknowledging the yellowish stain on his tie.

'It was agreeable enough. Why are you here, Sherlock?' he asked. 'I understood that you rarely venture from Victoria Street and Lady Morphia's sweet embrace these days.'

'Ha! Good one, my sebaceous sibling,' Holmes replied.

Mycroft drew him a dangerous look, which Holmes ignored.

'No, we're here to inquire about the health of your Captain Eddy, dear chap.'

He flicked his head up and behind Mycroft, indicating the portrait hanging there.

'I understand that he is quite well, a touch of gleet notwithstanding,' Mycroft replied.

'He'd hardly be the first of his line to suffer that malady, would he now? Isn't that right, Watson?'

'I'm sure I haven't the faintest idea what you're talking about, Holmes,' I replied.

Was that paraffin I smelled? Were we being recorded?

'Of course you don't, old boy, of course you don't. My butyraceous brother on the other hand certainly does, don't you, Mycroft? Quite the past master at sweeping these little *affaires d'État* under the Axminster, *n'est-ce pas*?'

'Is there a point at the end of this stream of quasi-treasonous effluvia, Sherlock? Or are you just here to air your cocaine-inflamed gums at me? Because if it is the latter, you can bugger off now or I'll have you shot.'

'No you won't,' replied Holmes.

'You seem awfully certain of that, little brother. Best not to test me though, eh?'

Mycroft leaned back in his chair, his fingers steepled over his ponderous paunch.

'What do you want, Sherlock?'

'I want him off the streets, Mycroft. Find him a war to play with, throw him in the Tower, disappear him; do what you have to do. Just keep him off the streets of my city, else I shall deal with him myself.'

Mycroft pondered this request for a moment, looked at Holmes and I in turn before speaking.

'Tell me what you know. Then tell me what you can prove.'

So we told him about the murders.

We told him about the first one, the frenzied one, the one with almost forty stab wounds.

We told him about the second one, more deliberate at its outset, the throat slit once, twice—then the angry thrusts of the knife as she lay whimpering on her side, bleeding out into the filth by the stable gate, before he pushed her on to her back and tore open her gut with his bare hands.

And the third one, finally finding his voice: the woman lying in the street, the throat again cut twice, but this time more, her entrails torn from her and thrown over her shoulders, and part of her womb sliced out.

Then we told Mycroft about how we found the thief, the thief his friend with the weak chin and the false name had hired us to find on his recommendation, about finding the red hairs and the fish scales and the distinctive Whitechapel mud, and a perfect imprint of a decayed ladies heel from a boot that was never fashionable in London but was in Galway some ten years ago, and how those clues had led us to the door of the red-haired woman.

And we told him about the red-haired woman, the one who had crossed the Irish Sea three years ago to tell her half-sister about her parents, the red-haired woman's father and his sister, how they had been found in bed together by the priest and how the townsfolk, good Catholics all, had burned them in that same bed.

And how the half-sister was the second one, the one with her gut torn open, and how the red-headed woman refused to believe it until she was in the morgue with the policemen all laughing around her, and how she broke after seeing her sister laid there naked and white with no blood left in her.

Mycroft vomited then, into his wastepaper basket. It seemed that the garlic and mustard roasted goose was not so agreeable after all.

Two swigs from his hip flask, and he nodded for us to continue.

We told him about an earlier theft from Masonic Lodge No. 2076, a theft where the culprit was uncovered but no charges brought.

We told him what had been stolen—a dozen watch chain fobs, miniature squares and compasses, just like the one G— wore on his waistcoat—and we told him who the thief was.

Mycroft nodded at that part, as though this was knowledge he already had. Which obviously he did; he was The Government, after all.

Nor did he show any surprise when we told him that three of the fobs had been recovered, one each in the mouths of the first one, the red-haired woman's half-sister and the third one.

This information was not of course made known to the general public, but the red-haired woman knew about the fobs because she had been questioned about the one shoved down her half-sister's throat.

We told him about how the red-haired woman had been a frequent guest at Lodge No. 2076, introduced there by her half-sister, and how she had become popular with the members, and how, after the murder of her half-sister, she had become very popular with one weak-chinned member in particular.

'Bit of a pillow-talker apparently, old G—,' imparted Holmes. 'And something of a name-dropper too.'

That surprised Mycroft all right.

'So this Irish whore stole the Ark of the Covenant,' he began.

'The *Regius Poem*,' I corrected.

'Whatever. She stole it. Because her incest-begotten whore sister—'

'Half-sister,' I again interjected.

'Damn it, man! Do not interrupt me! It does not bloody matter if she was the Pope's granddaughter!'

'No more than it matters who those poor murdered women in Spitalfields were?' I countered. 'Or who their assassin was?'

Mycroft glared at me with a ferocity that no doubt had reduced subordinates and superiors alike to smoking ash.

I returned his gaze with a steady eye born of a calm rage unlike any I had before experienced.

'We are beyond the point of exchanging parchment for justice, Mycroft. Both John and I are now invested in the case, for want of a better term, and it is a very different case to the one which G— hired us to investigate at your behest; this case is actually important, for one thing. And I guarantee you this, dear brother—I will see justice done for those women even if I have to bring down your incest-begotten monarchy to do so!'

Mycroft recoiled from his younger brother's outburst as though he had been slapped.

Inhaling deeply then exhaling sharply to settle himself, Mycroft eyed each of us in turn.

'What do you want?' he asked.

'Just as I said earlier—get him off the streets.'

'And how do you propose I do that, Sherlock? I am not as omniscient as you seem to believe.'

'Yes, you are.'

Mycroft stared at the closed ledger on his desk for a moment.

'I will deal with it,' he eventually responded.

∗

In the days following our meeting with his brother, Holmes drastically upped his cocaine intake, to the extent that I was driven to broach the verboten subject with him.

He laughed off my concerns, of course.

'I'm just bored, Watson, that's all. We haven't had a case since the thing with the Masons, and I have to entertain myself somehow.'

Almost immediately thereafter, Mary Morstan walked into our lives, and we were suddenly too busy with the dwarf and his wooden-legged master to be bored.

But that story you already know.

At the end of that month, we read in the morning papers of how two Whitechapel prostitutes had been murdered within an hour of each other the day before, and of how their bodies had been mutilated.

We sat there for some time, I frozen in shock while Holmes' expression grew darker with rage at every tick of the clock.

Finally he rose without a word and went to his room. Dazed as I was by the news, I sat alone for perhaps ten minutes before I realised that Holmes had not returned.

Fearing I knew not what, I ran to his door and rapped my knuckles raw, begging him to open it.

Growing afraid of the silence from within, I tried the handle. Locked.

I charged the door with my shoulder, and then again. On the third charge the lock gave way and I stumbled over the threshold into an empty room.

A discarded cocaine vial lay on the nightstand, the window was open to the elements, and both Holmes and his revolver were gone.

Pausing only long enough to collect my own pistol and my hat, I ran from the flat in pursuit, sure of his destination and his target.

***

There apparently being no hansom cabs to be had within a ten-mile radius of Baker Street, I ran the two miles to Whitehall, arriving in front of Mycroft's building red-faced and gasping some thirty minutes later.

I found Holmes sitting on the edge of the pavement opposite, dishevelled and with a bloodied nose. There was no sign of his revolver.

'What happened?' I asked as soon as I had recovered sufficient breath to do so.

'His secretary, Haynes. Disarmed me and broke my nose, I think.'

He tentatively took his nose between index finger and thumb and winced.

'Yes, that does seem broken. I don't suppose you have any morphine on you do you, old man?'

'Because that is exactly what you need on top of however much cocaine you've taken this morning, isn't it?' I retorted.

'Might balance me out a bit?'

'Or make your heart explode. One of those. Come on, let's find a cab and get you home. Here, take my handkerchief.'

***

Once we were safely ensconced in a cab and headed back home, I ventured to ask Holmes what in the name of the Bishop of Ely he had thought he was doing charging after Mycroft like that.

'For once in my life, I don't think there was a single thought attached to my actions, Watson,' he replied. 'It was pure instinct, and anger. Anger at the stupid pointless waste of life, anger at my fat, arrogant brother, but mostly fury at this archaic feudal system that guarantees he will not pay for his actions.'

'Who, Mycroft?'

'Him? No, he's just a large, well-greased cog in the machine. I mean the Idiot Prince.'

He sniffed, grimaced, wiped some blood from his upper lip.

'He's supposed to leave today, you know. Eddy, I mean. Off on a cruise round the colonies.'

'So what was last night, his last hurrah?'

'Certainly seems that way, doesn't it?'

He turned and looked out of the cab window at the city waking up to another dull Monday, at all the people for whom the worst that would happen today would be a torn hem or stepping in a puddle.

'I wish I could get my hands on the little swine—'

'You and I both, Holmes. You and I both—'

***

I spent the next week dividing my time between keeping Holmes' mind engaged and becoming engaged myself, to Miss Mary Morstan.

Life at Baker Street returned to what passed for normal for Holmes and me, with a couple of mildly interesting cases, enough to keep him from reaching for the needle.

One such case involved a Californian gold prospector who claimed to have been unable to remain in touch with his wife due to having been captured by Apaches. At the denouement of that case, Holmes wondered aloud, in that way that he has, as to why members of the Apache Nation were to be found so far West.

I took this to be a sure sign of his depression lifting, and consequently left him to his own devices for longer and longer periods while I spent time with Miss Morstan.

And then one afternoon in November of that year, I was informed that Mary Jane Kelly had been found dead in her room at 13 Miller's Court, Spitalfields, in Whitechapel.

***

I received the news by telegram from Inspector Lestrade, who had heard it from a colleague who had been seconded to the Whitechapel Murders investigatory team after the fifth victim had been discovered within the London Metropolitan Police's jurisdiction.

We did not in those days receive many telegrams so I knew it would be impossible to keep its arrival and contents from Holmes. So rather than even attempt subterfuge, I immediately apprised him of the missive's contents, and we agreed to travel by cab to the police morgue in order to pay our last respects to our red-haired woman.

After we had done that, well, we would see.

***

We arrived at the police station at a little after 3 p.m., elbowed our way through the usual crowd of newsmen and lollygaggers, and introduced ourselves to Lestrade's man Richardson, who was expecting us.

We were ushered through the station to the morgue, where Mary Kelly lay under a white sheet, stained browny-red where it lay on her wounds.

'You're not likely to recognise her, gents,' advised Richardson. 'The bastard cut her face up something rotten.'

We nodded our understanding.

Holmes gestured to Richardson to lower the sheet.

Almost reverentially and seeking to preserve what little modesty the poor girl had left, the constable lifted the sheet, folding it in such a manner that only her face and shoulders were revealed.

She was indeed unrecognisable as our red-headed woman, her face so badly mutilated that it could barely be said to still be a face at all.

Also her hair was dark brown.

***

After taking our leave of Richardson and the dead woman, Holmes and I did not speak until we were in our cab and on our way back to Baker Street.

I broke the silence first.

'That wasn't Mary Kelly, was it?'

'I do not believe so, no,' Holmes replied. 'The woman we just saw was taller, had differently shaped earlobes—'

'And judging by the roots of her hair and what I could make of her complexion, was a natural brunette. Whereas our Mary—'

'Was a redhead, yes.'

'So who was that woman in the morgue?'

'If you were to press a revolver to my temple in order to force me to guess, I should say it was Julia. The woman whom Mary mentioned that morning in September, and presumably whom Barnett meant when he said that apparently there were two ladies of the house recently.'

'I remember, yes. The poor woman.'

We lapsed into silence, each staring out of the cab's windows.

'So is that an end to it, do you think?' I eventually enquired.

'Do you know, I think that it might be. Once Captain Eddy was brought to heel, Mycroft's superiors would have seen Mary as a loose end and acted accordingly. The good lady did not strike me as an idiot and may have already come to the same conclusion and left London; if not, word of Julia's fate will likely have reached her by now and she will surely have bolted.'

'But where could she go? They have eyes and ears the length and breadth of the Empire, she may never be safe from the bastards.'

'Scandinavia, perhaps. Or the Americas. Somewhere the Empire never rose or else has long since set'

Another moment passed in silence.

'What about Julia? Shouldn't we do something about her murder?'

'Why, what good would it serve if we raised a stink about the wrong woman being silenced? Her death was made to look like the work of the same man as before, a feat they would no doubt repeat if word of Mary's continued existence reached them. No, pursuing the matter would only place Mary back in danger. It is unfortunate, but you see what we are up against.'

'I suppose so,' I replied.

We rode the rest of the way back to Baker Street in silence, lost in our own thoughts about the case, and about Mary.

***

Holmes made no move to exit the cab when we arrived back at 221B.

I opened the door on my side, closest to the pavement, and stepped out.

'Come on, we're home,' I said, thinking him to be lost in thought and unaware that we had reached our destination.

'You go on in, Watson. I'll be home in a day or so'

'Holmes—' I protested feebly.

But I knew it was no use.

'Victoria Street, driver!' Holmes cried. 'To Ah Sing's, as swiftly as you can!'

As I stood on the pavement watching the cab race away, I felt a familiar hand grasp my own and squeeze it tight.

I turned to see my own sweet Mary beside me, her brow furrowed in concern. I smiled wanly, squeezed her hand in return.

'Will he be all right?' she asked pensively.

I looked back up the street, the cab now too far gone to reach, and found myself unable to answer her question.

The Woman Who Wasn't: Part Six

Holmes placed his index finger to his lips and let out an almost imperceptible sigh. The tale, it seemed, had taken more of a toll on him than I would have imagined.

Do not mistake me, my friend was a man of deep passions. I had seen him ebullient, despondent, pained and fired with righteous indignation. I do not think, until that moment, I had ever seen him quite so weary.

I found myself growing frustrated once more. What in the Devil was Holmes playing at? It was one thing to send me on these missions into the past. As to why he would choose to confront this poor, troubled creature with one of the most sordid, the most *wicked,* cases that it had been our misfortune to encounter, well, I was entirely at a loss.

'A foul business.'

Holmes' tone was that of someone who had just been read an unpleasant telegram, rather a man recalling a misadventure of his own.

'Is that all you have to say, Holmes?' I asked, a trifle curtly, glancing up for the first time to see what damage had been wrought on the equilibrium of our guest.

Anastasia Frain sat stone-faced, gazing at a point somewhere over Holmes' shoulder. There were no signs of tears upon her cheeks and the lace handkerchief tucked unobtrusively into her sleeve had not been disturbed.

She turned and caught my gaze.

'You think it strange, Doctor Watson,' she asked, 'that I should seem so unmoved?'

'Not at all,' I replied courteously. 'We all manage shock, horror, even grief in our own ways. I have seen men in battle laugh as their comrades fell around them.'

'You veer closer to the truth than you imagine,' offered Holmes. And with that, he leant forward and with a conjuror's speed and grace, retrieved the very handkerchief whose disuse I had been pondering only moments before.

Then he retrieved a second from his own pocket, the one we had stumbled upon while pursuing the mysterious young man who remained at the heart of the mystery.

He leapt to his feet and held them both before me.

'What do you see, Watson?'

'They appear to be very like each other.'

'Indeed. A pair, I should think. Cut, quite literally, from the same cloth.'

'Both embroidered with—' I stopped short.

'Yes, Watson.'

'But—'

'Quite.'

I turned to Miss Frain.

'Your handkerchief is embroidered with an "S" rather than an "A."'

Miss Frain nodded.

'Yes.' She turned towards Holmes. 'I am beginning to think that Mr Holmes knows rather more about my situation than he is letting on.'

'That,' I said, 'is something to which one becomes accustomed. But why "S"?'

'I was known as 'Stasia as a child.'

'Then "A" belongs to?'

'My brother.'

'Your brother?'

'Alistair. My twin.'

'Your father mentioned no brother,' said Holmes. 'Does that surprise you?'

'Not in the least.'

'He spoke very much,' I added, 'as a man who has no son. No one to pass his business down to.'

Miss Frain laughed bitterly.

'He would pass it to me, his lowly daughter, before he would place it in Alistair's hands.'

'They are estranged,' offered Holmes.

'Alistair is dead to my father. And with good reason. My brother was a cruel and wicked child. And he has grown to be a cruel and wicked man. But—'

This proved to be the limit of Miss Frain's stoicism and tears formed in her eyes.

'A cruel child treated cruelly,' I speculated.

'Yes, Dr Watson,' nodded Miss Frain. 'My father believed he could beat the Devil from my brother. I rather think he beat it more deeply into him.'

'You, on the other hand,' said Holmes, beginning a slow circuit of the room, 'loved your brother despite his faults.'

'God help me, yes. He is my twin. A part of me.'

'You tried to help him.'

'Yes.'

'Your father mentioned that, were it not for your sex, *you* might have inherited the business. You had, he said, a talent for it.'

Miss Frain tipped her head modestly.

'I took an interest as a child. Observed my father carefully. I imagine I thought it would cause him to take an interest in me. But that is not the fate of daughters.'

Suddenly, I thought I began to see the outline of Holmes' reasoning.

'You thought instead that you might become a proxy. For your brother. Steer him into business and perhaps towards a reconciliation with your father.'

'Excellent, Watson,' cried Holmes. 'My thoughts, exactly.'

'It was a foolish idea, but I was at a loss. The brother I loved was lost to me. My father grew more distant and brutish by the day. Of course, I couldn't tell my father my plans.'

'What of your sister?'

'Doctor Watson, my sister and I are different in many ways. We love one another, but we have never been truly *simpatico*. Perhaps she resented the closeness between Alistair and myself. I couldn't take the chance. She might have felt honour-bound to inform my father. Or, once you and Mr Holmes became involved, to confide in you.'

'But *you* came to us yourself?'

'Ah,' said Holmes, 'there we were mistaken. Until today, Miss Frain had no intention of contacting us.'

'The message was from Alistair Frain?'

'Signed with an "A",' Holmes reminded me. 'I am not she.'

'Whatever does it mean?' I asked. 'Apart from the obvious fact that he is not Anastasia Frain.'

Miss Frain was quick to reply.

'I have mentioned the closeness of our bond,' she said with great sadness. 'It is something I have always treasured, despite the pain it has brought me. My brother does not feel as I do. To him, it is a burden. A millstone around

131

his neck. He ran away to escape it, burning every bridge along his route. But I would not allow it. I sought him out. Tried to find a way to bring him home.'

'He resented this.'

'More than resented, Doctor Watson.'

'What do you mean?'

'I said my brother was a wicked man. That he had done wicked things. Until recently, I did not realise how deeply his soul had been corrupted.'

Holmes stopped pacing.

'He has killed.'

'Yes, Mr Holmes,' said Miss Frain. 'I knew you had the measure of it from the tale you had Doctor Watson relate. You wanted me to know that you have previously encountered such darkness. That level of depravity.'

Holmes nodded.

'And yet,' she continued, 'to my shame, I still had no intention of turning my brother in.'

'You thought he still might be saved?' I asked.

'No. He is lost. But he is still my brother.'

'Then why?'

Holmes supplied the answer.

'Because it is no longer enough for Alistair Frain to avoid his other half. He intends to destroy it once and for all.'

'Yes,' said Miss Frain. 'My brother means for me to be his latest victim.'

***

Some hours later, after Miss Frain had been handed over to the temporary care of Mrs Hudson and I, once more, sent word to my ever patient wife that I would not be home that evening, Holmes took me further into his confidence.

'This is a dark business, Watson,' he said, leaning back in his chair and drawing on a fresh pipe. 'And it will take our best efforts to bring it to a satisfactory conclusion. As satisfactory a conclusion as is possible, in the light of the blood already spilt.'

'How long have you known that Miss Frain was not the sender of the message?'

Holmes smiled gently.

'You expect me to say I knew from the moment it arrived and that I have led you a merry dance for my amusement?'

'The thought did occur.'

'Then you may put your mind at rest,' said Holmes. 'I was, for some time, as bewildered by the entire enterprise as you. I was not dissembling when I said I had considered, as did you, that Miss Frain and the young man were one and the same. Though I abandoned that line before you, it was only by a hair's breadth.'

'What changed your mind?'

'I returned home and found a calling card from Miss Anastasia Frain, stating her intention to visit at my earliest convenience.'

I smiled.

'The handwriting was different from that of the message.'

'Indeed. I favour deduction, Watson, as you know, but I cannot entirely dismiss the benefits of good fortune.'

'So,' I said, reaching for the large tumbler of whisky at my side. 'How are we to proceed?'

Holmes frowned. The next statement did not come easily.

'I don't know, Watson. Or rather I don't know yet. This is a delicate matter. Miss Frain has a strong attachment to young Master Frain. We cannot entirely trust her to act judiciously. And yet, she must be protected.'

'If she has broken faith with her brother, he may already be on her trail.'

'And more than likely obscured his own. We will not find him at their previous lodgings.'

'Then how *will* we find him?'

'As I say, Watson, I have no answer as yet. I must give the matter careful consideration.'

My eyes darted guiltily towards the violin case on Holmes' workbench. If Holmes was ill at ease, I suspected we would be treated to the more atonal end of his repertoire.

'Do you remember,' I asked quickly, heading off any musical notions he might be forming, 'our trip to Paris last year?'

Holmes eyed me suspiciously. I suspect he found my attempted subterfuge more than a little transparent.

'Geoffrey Welford-Cattermole,' he mused.

'That's right,' I said.

'An interesting case, Watson. Now let me guess beneath what garish title it flounders in your collection of penny dreadfuls. The Case of the Copious Captains? The Adventure at the Palais Garnier?'

'The Missing Husbands,' I said, with a grin. Holmes looked almost disappointed.

'A rather restrained title for you, Watson. But if you feel it will be instructive, please do lay out the facts of the case as you remember them.'

The Missing Husbands

Tim Gambrell

It was a blessedly quiet Autumn afternoon at 221B Baker Street. Holmes and I had spent the best part of week traversing the length and breadth of the country in search a particularly troublesome quarry and it had quite sapped our energies. We had thus decided, in lieu of immediate resolution, that rest and recuperation might do almost as well. I had asked my usual locum to cover my practice and my then new bride was not expecting me home for another two days at least. I sent word, of course, but she too saw the sense in Holmes and myself taking a collective breath in one another's company.

It was, then, with some resignation that we accepted a visit from Mrs Maltravers, a young lady not of our acquaintance, when she called. At Holmes' beckoning, Mrs Hudson showed the lady in and hurried off to prepare some tea.

'Mrs Maltravers, you are most welcome,' I said, offering her the chair nearest the hearth, more out of habit than necessity.

She inclined her head politely and took the seat. Holmes was standing as usual, like a sentinel at the fireplace. He cut immediately to the chase.

'To what do we owe this visit, dear lady? Are you in need of assistance?'

Mrs Maltravers smiled coyly. 'Thank you, gentlemen, for deigning to see me without prior notice. And I am, as you suggest, Mr Holmes, in need of some assistance on a matter regarding my husband.'

The woman paused and held a handkerchief to her nose and mouth. She mentioned her husband as if he was closely acquainted with either myself or Holmes, but I was not familiar with the name. I wondered, instead, if embarrassment had caused her to pause, suggesting, perhaps, a matter of infidelity. Holmes had been approached with such cases previously and more often than not declined to become involved. 'Crimes of passion,' he told me once, 'I can countenance. Crimes of boredom, I cannot.'

However, when the lady continued it turned out to be nothing of the kind. In fact, it was clear that the delay in her speech was due to her being undecided in her own mind whether anger or heartbreak should lead the dance.

'My husband, gentlemen, is Captain Jefferson Maltravers. I am seeking your assistance because… because he has vanished.' Here she paused again, and I detected the shaking of her pearl white hand.

Holmes needlessly indicated that I should pour the lady a drink; I was already of a similar mind. As I handed her a small brandy, I caught a flash of anger behind the tears welling in her eyes. This was quickly replaced by gratitude and she took a moment to compose herself.

'You wish us to locate him?' Holmes asked. A little abruptly, I felt.

'Why, yes, Mr Holmes—' the lady began.

I was certain that this would now be a very short interview, and as I expected, Holmes briskly cut her off.

'Then I fear you have had a wasted journey, Mrs Maltravers. The police, or an advert in the press, would serve you far better in trying to trace news of your husband than a consulting detective.'

Her face dropped and I couldn't avoid a pang of guilt at my friend's somewhat brusque dismissal of her predicament. I looked sternly at Holmes and he rolled his eyes as if telling me to do what I wished.

'Please, Mrs Maltravers,' I began, in as comforting a voice as I could muster. 'If you would, perhaps, expand on the particulars surrounding the Captain's, your husband's, disappearance, we can at least advise you on your best course of action. That way you won't have had a completely wasted journey.'

Her shoulders shuddered with pent-up emotion. This was a woman much in need of relief. She took another sip of brandy and indicated her acceptance.

'We met about three months ago, in Paris. I was there with my mother, visiting an aunt. The Captain was there for some brief seasonal diversion, he said, away from his regiment. I don't think it would be untrue to say that he fairly swept me off my feet. We fell so very much in love, and I agreed to be his wife upon our return to England. With my father's blessing, we were married at the end of last month. We had a blissfully happy week after. One day, nearly two weeks ago now, I waved him off at the door on a matter of business. I've not seen him since. I feared him dead, at first. Yet, this morning, I discovered he has taken my fortune. That was when I set upon my plan to seek your assistance.'

Holmes was next to us in a trice. 'My dear Mrs Maltravers,' he gushed. 'Why didn't you say so immediately? That puts a very different slant on the matter.'

Her eyes brightened. 'It does?'

'Where was he going that day, madam?' I asked. 'Or rather, what had he told you he was up to?'

'To his Club on Beak Street. The Grosvenor. That's where he usually conducted his business, advising on international trade. It's a sideline to his military career.'

My friend frowned. 'There is no Grosvenor Club on Beak Street, or anywhere around those environs, to the best of my knowledge.'

Mrs Maltravers told us she had discovered as much upon her initial enquiries.

'Could he have been urgently recalled to his regiment?' I asked. 'Unusual though it may be for a husband not to inform his wife of such.'

'Again, Doctor Watson, I considered this,' the lady confirmed.

'Don't tell us,' cried Holmes, rising to his feet and turning sharply on his heel. 'The regiment to which you believed him commissioned does not exist.'

Mrs Maltravers nodded once again. 'You must think me an utter fool.'

This I denied, very much pained for the lady.

'Quite so,' confirmed Holmes, I assumed in agreement with my denial rather than the lady's self-assessment. 'In matters of the heart,' he continued, 'we are not wont to mistrust information freely given. As Doctor Watson here will surely confirm, suspicion and insecurity are not conducive to falling in love. I fear, Mrs Maltravers, you are the victim of a heartless swindler, a jackanapes who has stolen your poor innocent heart and robbed you of your fortune.'

At the detective's request, the lady provided us with the particulars of her errant husband. I silently observed that her description easily fell into the classification of "generic" for a handsome young army officer. Despite her obvious poor usage, Mrs Maltravers laced her words with tender and appreciative metaphors, showing how very much in love with the rogue she remained. I noted down as much as I thought appropriate.

'And what of his family?' Holmes asked.

'His father and mother died on the continent when he was a boy. He told me he grew up with a harsh maternal aunt in Dorset. There was no love lost between them.'

'Convenient,' I muttered.

Holmes growled his agreement.

'I have the aunt's address. Naturally, I wrote to her, expressing my worries. This is what I received back.'

Mrs Maltravers produced a letter from her bag. Holmes cast his eye over it before passing it to me to note down the salient details.

'It's in keeping with everything else, then,' Holmes confirmed. 'A fabrication.'

I looked at the letter, on formal notepaper. 'A guest house?'

The lady nodded. 'But not according to the address I was given by the Captain.'

The top of the letter read Sandhaven Guest House, Swanage. It was signed by a Mrs Finch, the proprietress, who stated that she knew not of a Captain Maltravers, nor had she any nephews. Furthermore, she thanked the correspondent not to write to her again.

My friend continued: 'Although, we must be careful not to overlook the possibility that the landlady is also in on the scam.'

Something of the specifics of Mrs Maltravers' tragedy had a ring of familiarity about it, and just now my memory sparked to the connection. This must have been evident in my facial expression, as I found myself immediately questioned by the great detective.

'Sorry, Holmes,' I said, a little flustered. 'I'm sure it has no bearing on Mrs Maltravers, here, but I suddenly recalled discussing a similar situation to this at my Club, some months back. I'd seen a plea in the Times seeking information regarding the whereabouts of another missing husband. A captain, also, as I recall.'

'No bearing?' burst Holmes, jubilantly. 'My dear Watson, it's quite possible you are a genius!'

I felt my cheeks flush and raised my brows modestly at our guest.

Holmes dashed to his bureau and immediately began flicking through a drawer of indexed cards. With a sharp gesture he removed one and proceeded to inform Mrs Maltravers and I that he had been keeping a note over the past few years of any missing persons reported in the *Times* for which there was no publicised resolution.

'With a few odd exceptions, something of this nature has, roughly, occurred once every six months, for the past three years. Another has been due for some time.'

'Are you suggesting this has all been orchestrated?' I asked.

Mrs Maltravers gave a sharp intake of breath.

'I'm not suggesting anything yet, Watson. But there is a detectable pattern, you must agree, and I, for one, am keen to find an explanation for that.' He turned to address our guest. 'Mrs Maltravers, I shall take your case.'

She beamed. 'Thank you, Mr Holmes.'

'One thing further, dear lady,' he continued. 'Where in Paris did you first meet the Captain, your husband?'

'At the Palais Garnier. I was there at the opera, with my mother and a chaperone when I caught his eye.'

'No doubt you did,' he replied, complimenting her. 'Thank you. We shall be in touch again in due course.'

Knowing that this had brought the interview to an end, I showed Mrs Maltravers back down to the street.

***

Holmes was already donning his hat and coat by the time I returned to the sitting room.

'Come, Watson,' he said, clapping his palms together with eager excitement. 'I believe we can still make plentiful use of the afternoon on this case. Strike while the iron's hot, as the saying goes.'

A few minutes later found us out on Baker Street hailing a cab. Holmes gave the address to the driver as we sprang aboard. I recognised where we were headed from the infrequent visits we had already made there during our time working together.

'What business do we have at the editorial offices of the *Times*?' I asked.

He glanced at me and held up the index card. 'We have some letters to write. But first, we need to gather some addresses.'

'The other missing persons?'

'Precisely. Also, it will do no harm to double check that the originators have not since received unpublished closure to their enquiries. No sense in wasting our time.'

***

We entered into something of a trade-off at the *Times*. The information requested was provided, but on the proviso that their reporter had sole and immediate access to the details of the case upon completion. Holmes acquiesced, but only if the reporter agreed not to overly sensationalise events. The sub-editor who had agreed to meet us looked aghast at this accusation—with which I sympathised, having been the recipient of it myself—until Holmes produced four clear instances, from memory, where admittedly dramatic events had borne the weight of especially purple prose. To give the sub-editor his due, he accepted this, and the conversation quickly moved on.

I was glad not to linger longer than necessary amongst the hustle and bustle of the newspaper offices. Once back at Baker Street, we had nine letters to write between us, before the last postal collection of the day. One of Holmes' Baker Street Irregulars waited patiently to one side, ready to run our completed missives to the post office. The lad would also be checking, over the next few days, for any telegrammed responses. He had been promised a handsome reward for his patience. Where possible, on important affairs such as this, Holmes preferred to rely on his local agents, rather than the establishment. For one thing his agents provided much faster results.

***

The following morning was grey and overcast. The persistent spring drizzle that accompanied our cab ride to Waterloo Railway Station was more than enough to dampen our spirits. One never likes to travel in sodden clothes, after all. We took a London & South Western Railway train to Dorset. By the time we arrived at our coastal destination, our spirits had lifted with the clouds. The train pulled into the old spa town of Swanage in a haze of pleasant sunshine.

A brief enquiry at the ticket office was enough to furnish us with directions to the Sandhaven Guest House, which was situated a short walk away, in a prime location adjacent to the seafront promenade. A middle-aged lady rushed to attend us as we entered. We offered her the compliments of the day.

'Can I get you gentlemen rooms?' she asked, with a gap-toothed smile.

'My friend and I are only visiting for the day,' said Holmes. 'We wish to speak with the proprietress.'

'Well, you're looking at her,' Mrs Finch replied, tartly, her smile vanishing. 'And what might two gentlemen such as yourselves want with an honest landlady like me? Careful, now. I'll be having no sauce.'

I gave a harrumph, but Holmes didn't rise to the provocation.

'My name is Sherlock Holmes. This is my accomplice, Doctor Watson.'

She looked me up and down. 'Accomplice, is it?'

'Do you have a secluded parlour,' Holmes continued, 'or somewhere else where we can speak in confidence?'

Mrs Finch wiped her hands on her apron, sniffed and said 'Follow me' before leading us into a vacant dining room. She took a seat for herself at a table by the window, and we eased ourselves into the chairs opposite. I studied the gingham tablecloth and decided to keep my hands in my lap.

The lady spoke immediately. 'Come on then, let's have it out. London gents, by the looks of you. What's all this to do with? I got a place to run, here. Can't be sitting around all day, jabbering.'

'Mrs Finch, I believe?'

'What of it?'

'Watson and I are here-'

Mrs Finch cut him off. 'I know why you're here. You think you're the first to roll up in posh togs and start laying down the law? Well, I'll tell you what I've told all the others. I don't know him. Don't know any of them. Reckon it must be some prank they all came up with, dupe young girls into marriage, give out my address and then skulk away never to be heard of again.'

Holmes paused, his mind clearly processing the information.

'Does it happen regularly?' I asked.

'Regular enough, that's for sure. New ones from time to time, then there's all the follow-up queries. I ask them every time not to contact me again, but they don't take my word for it. Must reckon I've got something to hide. Letters, telegrams, legal whatnot.' She held up her hand with her thumb and forefinger barely parted. 'I'll tell you, gentlemen, I'm this close to packing up and moving elsewhere.'

'You have a list of all the names?' Holmes asked.

There was a pause, then the lady began to reel them off.

'Captain Maltravers, Captain Bowyer, Lieutenant Caldicot, Major Frankham, Major Douglas and Lieutenant Colonel Derbyshire. I don't know their families. Never had any of them staying here to the best of my knowledge—unless they came under an assumed name. Happens from time to time, although, Lord bless me, I don't encourage it. Never done anyone any harm, me, neither. Why folks should ever want to involve me in such things, I've no idea.'

Holmes checked his index card. 'The names all match, Watson. Thank you, Mrs Finch. You've not encountered anyone by the name of McLaughlin, Sharpe, or Simpson?'

'As sure as I'm sat here,' Mrs Finch replied, 'I've never been approached about anyone with those names. Although there's a milliner hereabouts by the name of Sharpe, if that helps?'

'Thank you, it doesn't,' Holmes confirmed. 'And you mentioned in your letter to poor Mrs Maltravers that you have no nephew, is that correct?'

'Nieces, nephews, none. Nor have I a son. Or husband anymore—much good he did me when he was alive.'

'I am sorry to hear that,' I said with genuine feeling.

'He gave me a daughter, Gladys, but that was about all, except a few debts. She worked the rooms for me, here.' Mrs Finch's voice caught slightly, and she paused a moment. 'Gladys may as well be dead now too, for all I know of her.'

'It can't be easy running a place like this all by yourself,' I noted.

'I do all right. Got a girl from the village who pops in and does the beds for me. And there's always someone staying, to help me make ends meet. My Gladys was a useless wench, anyway,' she added, bitterly. 'Got airs and graces and ran off with some rogue.'

'Recently?' asked Holmes, butting in.

Mrs Finch appeared slightly taken aback at being interrupted in her narrative. 'Er, no, back before all this started.'

I took 'this' to mean all the letters and callers about missing husbands.

Holmes nodded. 'Thank you. Please, do continue. The rogue?'

Mrs Finch licked her dry lips and picked up her train of thought. 'Yes, rogue's the word, Mr Holmes. Never liked the look of him myself, but he had a way about him, and I could see how he might turn an innocent girl's head. If she's still alive, she'll come back in time. When he's had enough of her, no doubt. It's always the way with posh folk.'

'What was his name?' Holmes asked.

'Can't see how that's any business of yours,' she replied, abruptly.

'Doctor Watson and I are well-connected. Perchance we may have heard of him or his whereabouts and can give you some comfort as to the situation regarding your daughter.'

'Oh, I see, well—' Mrs Finch grew uncharacteristically flustered. 'Geoffrey, that was his name.'

'With a gee or a jay, Mrs Finch?'

'Gee.'

Holmes noted this down. 'And the surname?' he asked. 'That's most important.'

For my part I had assumed that Geoffrey was the surname. Mrs Finch licked her lips again. 'Oh, yes, that,' she replied, and gave a light, mirthless chuckle. 'Fancy one, it was. Welford-Cattermole.'

'Geoffrey Welford-Cattermole,' Holmes repeated as he wrote.

'Yeah. Not from around here. Dorchester, he said. But I can't say as I ever believed anything that came out of his mouth.'

'Mean anything to you, Watson?'

I shook my head. 'Never come across anyone by that name, I must admit.'

Holmes nodded. 'Nor have I. But thank you, Mrs Finch. We'll keep our ear to the ground and let you know if we unearth anything.'

She gave another gap-toothed grin. 'Oh, thank you, Mr Holmes. Much obliged, I'm sure.'

'It's the least we can do for the help you've given us.' Holmes then suggested we make it worth the lady's time by taking some lunch there. I was in full agreement, so we partook of a little smoked fish. Mrs Finch's mood continued to improve. Ours declined, as the repast was not a particularly enjoyable one. The fish was past its best, and no amount of seasoning could conceal the fact.

Despite her frosty attitude, I couldn't help feeling sorry for Mrs Finch. This whole situation appeared to be nothing more than a game at her expense and she was as much the victim as any of the poor girls who'd contacted her in the hope of finding their missing husbands. I said as much to Holmes as we toyed with our lunch.

'Presumably the originator of the scam had known of Mrs Finch, perhaps taken offense at her demeanour, or some such,' I observed.

Holmes appeared to agree. 'Most likely,' he replied, before pushing his plate to one side, half his fish remaining. He nodded a salutation and I turned to find that two of the other tables were now occupied, one by a miserable-looking, aged gentleman and another by a lady, also sitting alone. Of her age or demeanour, I could tell little, as she had turned away from us in response to Holmes' gentlemanly salute.

We then took our leave of Mrs Finch and Swanage. The return journey to London was less than comfortable, despite the restorative mixture I carried with me, of which we both partook. We were relieved when we finally arrived back at Baker Street and were able to take to our beds.

***

A pair telegrams awaited us upon our return from Swanage, but it was the following morning before we were able to read the responses to our letters of enquiry. By the time we rose the following day, thankfully quite restored, three further telegrams had been deposited by our faithful Irregular. Holmes sifted through them. He retained four of them and passed one to me. In quick succession, he opened and cast his eye over each telegram. They all confirmed a negative response to the enquiries about their husbands, and each gave the same Swanage address as the only known information about their husband's origins.

I was exasperated. 'What is it with these girls, I wonder?'

He indicated the fifth telegram, which I was still holding unopened. The author of this one thanked us for our enquiry and advised that she had found her missing husband, whom she had originally met at the Louvre gallery. It was not clear from the wording if his discovery was a good or bad result for the lady in question. Holmes checked the names and confirmed he had suspected that this lady's case would have a different result, as the dating was out of sequence.

Mrs Hudson appeared and advised us that Mrs Maltravers was downstairs, enquiring if we would see her. Knowing the fragile state in which we'd both arrived home the previous day, our venerable housekeeper thought it best to check first. Holmes wasted no time in permitting the visit and our good lady client was shown in and offered a little mid-morning tea.

'I appreciate that it is barely two days since I was last here, gentlemen,' Mrs Maltravers told us, 'but I have such hopes pinned upon you that I could barely stay away.'

'I fully understand the strain you must be under,' I replied.

'Indeed,' confirmed Holmes. 'And we have not been idle in that time, I can assure you. We have visited the formidable Mrs Finch, in Swanage, and received several replies from other distressed ladies in similar situations to yourself.'

'I am grateful.'

'And by calling on us today, your timing is capital. Our next move has to be tomorrow. Mrs Maltravers, I wonder if you would do Watson and I the honour of accompanying us to Paris?'

I confess my eyes boggled at this suggestion, not having been party to it previously.

Mrs Maltravers looked somewhat taken aback at the suggestion, also. 'Why, on Earth would I wish to do that, Mr Holmes?'

'To find your missing husband, of course.'

She gave a giggle. 'What makes you think he'll be there?'

'I have reason to believe that is his base of operation.'

The lady was dismissive. 'He was there on holiday at the time we met, the same as I.'

'He said,' Holmes replied, darkly.

Mrs Maltravers looked suddenly unsure. The detective continued.

'And would you otherwise have considered returning to the place where you first met the captain?'

'Certainly not,' the lady confirmed. But the answer faded on her lips and the colour drained from her face as realisation dawned on her.

I reached for my bag, never far from my chair, and immediately administered a restorative to the lady. However, it was sometime later before she felt able to face the journey home. We agreed to call for her on the morrow, having arranged to take the train to Dover and from there the crossing to Calais the following lunchtime.

***

'Paris is somewhat akin to London,' I said after Mrs Maltravers had left. 'How long are you intending for us to stay there to search for this scoundrel?'

Holmes had immediately lit a pipe. He peered at me through the smoke. 'You have other pressing duties?'

I smiled at him, warmly. 'A wife and patients, as you well know. But for the moment I am simply wondering what I need in my portmanteau.'

'Pack to dress for the opera, Watson,' he told me. 'That much is a necessity. A new Saint-Saëns opens tomorrow.'

'And are we going for a week? A month? How does one go about finding a solitary man in such a place?'

Holmes mused. 'Oh, I suspect one or two nights will be sufficient for us to achieve what we need. You may inform the esteemed Mrs Watson that I will return you to her tender ministrations within the week.'

It suddenly occurred to me. 'You believe you know where he is, don't you, Holmes?'

My friend gave a smile as he sucked on his pipe and held up the four telegrams that he had earlier perused.

'The evidence placed before me thus far strongly suggests that, not only will Captain Maltravers be in Paris, but that he and the other swindlers operate out of the Palais Garnier. But I do not wish to take that for granted, so we shall see what we find when we get there.'

***

The following afternoon, we stepped from the railway carriage at Gare du Nord, in Paris. There was a bohemian air about the place, which always hit me on such occasions. A mixture of fragrant tobacco and strong coffee. Wafts of ancient revolution in the forthright voices on the breeze. We left the station and hailed a cab.

'Hôtel Regina, s'il vous plaît,' Holmes politely instructed the driver. Mrs Maltravers had advised that this was where she stayed previously. The hotel was known to Holmes also, and it was generally agreed between us that familiarity would benefit us all in a foreign city.

Adorned in travelling clothes suitable for a sea crossing, Holmes and I had collected Mrs Maltravers earlier that morning, then travelled to Victoria Station for the Dover train. A pleasantly uneventful journey passed, and once at Dover we were able to secure places on the next crossing to Calais. Again, this leg of the journey passed without incident—not that we expected otherwise.

It was a particular pleasure, for me, to see how happy Mrs Maltravers was whilst out on deck. The day was fine, and so she and I spent the majority of the short crossing out on the top deck, walking up and down and appreciating the bracing sea air. I commented on how refreshing it was.

'Nature's freedom, Doctor Watson,' she replied with glee, whilst tightening the ribbon of her bonnet beneath her chin. 'This is how the air ought to be, not the murky soup that we breathe in London.'

She was right, of course. But for all its murky soup, I dearly loved London. As we walked, we talked. Mrs Maltravers spoke freely about her youth, the love her parents had invested in her and the hopes she had for her married life. This latter was tinged with sadness, of course, and it was a relief to the both of us, I'm sure, when the port of Calais hove into view.

When we moored, we found Holmes brooding in a smoky corner inside. He had clearly been mulling over details in his head. We disembarked and took the train to Paris Gare du Nord. I will freely admit, I found this final leg of the journey rather tiresome, but I believe that was down to a combination of travel fatigue and still being slightly out of sorts from our Swanage escapade. I was grateful when the cab driver dropped us at the Regina, on the Rue de Rivoli, not far from the Seine, and I was able to settle both my feet and stomach.

Upon arrival, Holmes asked to see the manager. Mrs Maltravers and I stood to one side as the attendant scuttled off. This seemed a very bold move from my friend. However, we all found ourselves welcomed warmly when the manager appeared. It seemed there was some history, there, with Holmes, who was welcomed like a returning hero. I made a note to enquire further into that at some point. But for now, we were each given rather extravagant rooms to ourselves and it was clear that nothing would be too much trouble.

I enjoyed a settling glass of burgundy on the balcony and spent some time absorbing the life and spirit of Paris before I took a bath to refresh my weary limbs. It was a while later before I saw either Holmes or Mrs Maltravers again, when we were called to dinner. Mrs Maltravers looked exquisite, which made it all the more painful that she had fallen foul of some roguish wretch. As we were seated, the maître d'hôtel approached and handed my friend an envelope. Upon opening it, Holmes produced three tickets for the Saint-Saëns opera he had mentioned previously, opening at the Palais Garnier that evening.

'Perfect,' he said. 'I take it neither of you object to a curtailed dinner?'

We did not, and with the taste of mussels in a white wine sauce still fresh on my tongue, we boarded our cab.

There had clearly been some discussion between Holmes and Mrs Maltravers earlier, while I had been resting, as they were both of a mind as to how we should proceed when inside the opera house. All around us was finery and extrovert wealth. People came here to see the opera but mainly to be seen themselves. More so on opening night. I was in equal measure enchanted and appalled at the heedless, monied decadence on display. As I followed my colleagues through the crowded foyer and bar area, I noted how Mrs Maltravers suddenly gave a sigh, stopped and pointed with one hand whilst the other flew to her mouth. I immediately stepped up behind the lady in case emotion overcame her.

'Please,' hissed Holmes, insistently. 'Steel yourself, Mrs Maltravers. If you have spotted your husband, assist us by confronting him.'

She had indeed spotted her husband, the self-proclaimed Captain Jefferson Maltravers. I followed her gaze across the room and matched him, roughly, with her colourful description. The scoundrel was conversing with a pretty young lady in a group—most likely, I thought, a vulnerable ingenue. Mrs Maltravers showed her mettle, stepping forward firmly and approaching him through the crowd. Holmes and I held back. Either through the focused determination of her approach or some unlucky stroke, the captain saw his advancing wife and quickly attempted evasion. Holmes and I spotted his potential escape routes and ensured he was outflanked and unable to avoid the confrontation without resorting to cries or calls for assistance. Neither of which would have met with approval in such an environment.

We detained him in a corner, where he began to complain loudly about impolite usage. Though he grew pale and silent as Mrs Maltravers caught us up.

'I believe the lady wishes to speak with you,' Holmes told him, levelly.

'Jefferson,' she cried, angrily. 'Just what is the meaning of this?' Tears were evident in her eyes and her voice began to falter. 'What have I done to deserve such treatment? We were so happy, my darling. We had such plans. And now… you have ruined me.'

Heads turned in our direction. Conversations stalled as glances lingered—not least because voices had been raised in English and not the native French.

'You must be mistaken.' The man gave a nervous laugh and looked between Holmes and me. 'Please, I've never seen this woman before in my life.'

'Then why did you try to run away?' I asked, earning an approving nod from my friend.

'You are Captain Jefferson Maltravers,' insisted Mrs Maltravers. 'My husband. I have the papers here to prove it.' She held up her bag as if that were evidence enough.

'I'm sorry to say, but you're wrong.' This new voice came from another lady, approaching from within the dense crowd. She stepped into our group and insinuated herself between me and the man I'd assumed was Captain Maltravers.

Mrs Maltravers looked dumbstruck.

'Why do you say that, madam?' asked Holmes.

'Because he's my husband,' said the new lady. 'We've been married for some years. And I also have the paperwork to prove it.' She glanced pointedly at Mrs Maltravers.

This was not the young woman we saw him talking to when he'd first been spotted. I looked at our client, but her anger wasn't abating. Clearly, she felt she was not mistaken.

'Who are you?' she demanded.

'I don't see how or why that's any business of yours, quite frankly,' came the curt reply. 'My husband and I were just out to enjoy the opera and you start hurling accusations around. I've a good mind to have the management throw you out and be done with it.'

'I don't believe that would be appropriate, Gladys,' said Holmes.

The lady looked at Holmes as if he'd just shot her.

'Gladys Welford-Cattermole, née Finch. From sunny Swanage. Am I right?'

She was clearly shaken by this revelation. Her husband moved forward and took her in his arms, leading her to a nearby chair.

'We've been speaking to your dear mother,' Holmes continued.

'I don't know what you mean,' the lady said, holding a palm to her forehead as she sat.

Holmes indicated the lady's husband—the husband of both ladies, allegedly. 'And I'm afraid, Mrs Maltravers, that this is not Captain Jefferson Maltravers. Captain Jefferson Maltravers does not exist. Nor has he ever. Neither, my dear Watson, have Captain Bowyer, Lieutenant Caldicot, Major Frankham, Major Douglas. Nor Lieutenant Colonel Derbyshire, much to the disappointment, I'm sure, of all the other married ladies on our list. They were all the same man. This man. Geoffrey Welford-Cattermole. Serial scoundrel and bigamist extraordinaire.'

'By Jove,' I gasped, appalled, before my thoughts returned to Mrs Maltravers. I quickly fetched her a chair, for which she was clearly grateful. There was a hushed awe all around us, and I realised the entire assembly was hanging on every word Holmes uttered. Welford-Cattermole seated himself beside Gladys and hung his head. She roughly removed her arm from his grip and shoved him away in anger.

A number of Palais Garnier stewards appeared and began to shepherd the crowd away.

Holmes glared down at the man, Welford-Cattermole. 'Tell me, what pseudonym had you given your latest attempted conquest, with whom we just saw you?'

'Lieutenant Major Bradshaw,' he muttered.

'To be married in about three months, upon your return to England, I assume?'

The scoundrel did not respond.

'Upon which you will defraud her of her fortune, or as much as you can get your hands on, disappear suddenly and transfer the money to your legitimate wife, Gladys, here, to use to maintain your profligate life here in Paris.'

Mrs Maltravers gave a muted cry, and I placed a comforting hand on her shoulder. Holmes continued, unabated.

'You must have amassed quite a fortune by now.'

'Spent, you mean,' spat Gladys, looking up with a wicked sneer. 'Good living costs a lot around here.' She prodded her husband in the ribs. 'Pull yourself together, Geoff. He ain't the law.'

Holmes raised a hand—clearly a signal to someone across the room. He must have pre-arranged for a number of gendarmes to be on hand, because uniformed officers suddenly appeared through the thinning crowd and not a moment too soon. The wicked couple had sprung to their feet and, knocking us from ours, tried to make a run for it. As we picked ourselves up, we found they had thankfully been restrained.

Poor Mrs Maltravers, however, had fallen into a swoon.

I quickly attended her, but it was evident that the new Saint-Saëns opera would have to wait for another occasion. However, we had achieved what we set out to do.

And all in a single evening, as Holmes had suggested.

***

We spent a few, pleasant days in Paris, all told, although Mrs Maltravers never felt up to returning to the Palais Garnier, so we had to forego any operatic pleasures. We returned to London once Inspector Lestrade had arrived with a band of Metropolitan police officers to collect the Welford-Cattermoles, which Holmes skilfully negotiated with the Parisian authorities. Mrs Maltravers was of the hope that some of her fortune, at least, could be rescued. We assured her that we would do our best, although whatever could be retrieved would no doubt have to be shared amongst all of the wronged women. For her part, she advised us that she would be returning to live with her parents, and that they would endeavour to have the marriage annulled. She would revert to her maiden name, Miss Cunningham.

When we parted, at Victoria Station, I heartily wished that she would be able to put this whole sorry business behind her and start her life anew. She was a bright and beautiful young woman, and I was certain that she would find little trouble in gaining a husband far superior in every respect to the rogue, Welford-Cattermole.

Holmes thanked the lady once again for providing him with an endearing case which showed how narrowly-focused the criminal mind could be. He had relished being able to set his trap without the villain's awareness, and then spring it perfectly.

***

I had held back on voicing my queries and concerns around the resolution to this case until Holmes and I were once again alone. As we clattered through the grey London streets in the cab to Baker Street, I found I could contain myself no longer. Holmes gave a sly grin and admitted he expected as much from me, which made me feel less like I was imposing an interrogation upon him.

'I take it all of Welford-Cattermole's victims separately confirmed they had first met him at the Palais Garnier?' I asked.

'The responses I received all did, yes. It seemed a safe assumption that this would have been the case for all of them. It was this detail that convinced me we were dealing with one man and not a gang.'

I shook my head. 'But why would he be foolish enough to always work out of the one venue?'

'My dear Watson, it is simplicity itself,' he chided, 'and Mrs Maltravers was a fine example. Each girl thought they were the first and only love of his life. Even if any of them had returned to Paris after the scoundrel had vanished from their lives, surely the last place they'd want to visit whilst there would be the venue that held such painful or shameful memories for them?'

'Maybe, but I still think it was foolish.'

Holmes gave a sharp bark of a laugh. 'That's because you are not a scoundrel, my friend. Had the fiend spread his net wider, and taken in more of Parisian society, he would have run a higher risk of detection. As it was, he kept his true wife close by in case of accidental discovery and confrontation—carrying her marriage certificate with her, too, just in case. Quite ridiculous.'

'And that's another point,' I said. 'How or when did you work out that Mrs Finch and her daughter were involved?'

'I'll confess I wasn't absolutely certain until the confrontation at the opera house. But it struck me as odd, while we were in Swanage, that Mrs Finch's daughter had been through something similar to Mrs Maltravers and the other girls, only she'd actually run away with her husband. I'd mulled, at length, on the idea of that being the progenitor to the wicked scheme, somehow. Mrs Finch's sob story was well-rehearsed, but clearly an act all the same. You may recall she became flustered when I interrupted her and asked for specific details. I daresay she had told the story many times before and the audience had accepted it and walked away afterwards—feeling sorry for her without thinking to question her further.'

I confessed that much of our experience at the Sandhaven Guest House had been superseded, at the time, by our discomfort on the journey home. I continued. 'Surely there was a risk that she had made up the details, though?'

'I considered the possibility, but I don't believe Mrs Finch was quick-witted enough to falsify anything on the spot. She tried, of course, by telling us the fiend's name was Geoffrey. One of Lestrade's Yard boys would no doubt have walked away looking for a Mr Geoffrey. But Geoffrey and Jefferson are not too far removed from each other. So, I played it as if there was no doubt it was the rogue's Christian name. Cornered in this way, Mrs Finch gave up the rest of the details. I'd wager, too, that all of Welford-Cattermole's pseudonyms had the first name Geoffrey, Jeffrey or Jefferson. I doubt any of those in on the scam had the wit to vary their details much.'

I nodded.

Holmes continued. 'Mrs Finch was there to check progress on the various marriages and to make sure any enquiries reached a dead end. I'm sorry if that disappoints you. I could see at the time that the story of her personal struggle had moved you.'

This was true. But I was grasped, now, by anger. Such crimes they'd committed, and on that scale, ruining young girls' lives for their own hedonistic pleasures. Did the perpetrators not think that they were bound to be discovered in the end?

Holmes agreed. 'It is partly a thrill for them, I believe. A challenge. A sense of superiority, using others in such a fashion. And it is self-perpetuating; the more they do it, the more they want to do it.'

I shook my head. 'Such a waste. If they applied their drive and efforts to legitimate means they would likely succeed in life anyway, rather than trying to do so through bringing heartache and ruination to others.'

The cab pulled up at Baker Street and the driver retrieved Holmes' portmanteau. Holmes looked at me and replied. 'As I have said often enough, my friend, you cannot comprehend undertaking such activities because you yourself are such a good and moral man.'

I was still smiling from the compliment as I walked through the door of my house, a while later, and into the waiting arms of Mary.

***

A few days later I was back at Baker Street when Inspector Lestrade called upon us. I could tell, by the slant of his brows, that he bore bad news even before he opened his mouth. He apologised and informed us that when he had arrived at the gendarmerie, to collect the felons, they found Geoffrey Welford-Cattermole had taken his own life in the cell.

'I don't know how frequently our continental counterparts were checking on the pair, but it was just as much of a surprise to them to find him hanging there as it was a disappointment to us.'

'Disappointing, indeed,' murmured Holmes. 'His trouser belt, or shoelaces, I presume?'

'Laces,' confirmed Lestrade. 'Judging from the wife's reaction, hiding away in the corner, he'd done it against her wishes, too.'

'A coward's way out,' I spat.

'Somewhat ironic, then, that Gladys is now like all the other poor women,' Holmes observed. 'Left behind alone to pick up the pieces.'

'Not for long, I suspect,' added Lestrade. 'She'll do her time. Her and that mother of hers.'

Holmes beamed. 'You've met the redoubtable Mrs Finch then?'

'You mean the screaming harpy. She's winning no friends. Gave my officers a few scratches, as well as an earful, when they collected her.'

'As long as they didn't let her cook for them,' I added, with a gentle pat of the stomach. That was one aspect of this case that would be lingering in my memory for some time yet.

The Woman Who Wasn't: Part Seven

Holmes had shown the good taste to chuckle politely throughout my tale, though he did interrupt more than once to point out certain faults in my reporting, not to mention engaging in an on-going dialogue regarding the florid nature of my prose.

As I reached the conclusion, however, he did me the great honour of leaping to his feet, seemingly energised by the tale.

'Watson,' he exclaimed. 'Once more you have proven yourself invaluable.'

'Have I?'

But Holmes was on the cusp of an epiphany and was not to be interrupted. 'I've been a fool!'

I wasted no energy on a reply.

'Don't you see, Watson? It is simplicity itself. I know exactly where to find Alistair Frain and how to bring him to justice.'

He stood rooted to the spot, his expression blazing with purpose.

'Would you care to enlighten me, Holmes? Or do I sense another "Not just yet, Watson" on the horizon.'

'On the contrary, Watson. We have much to discuss. So as not to keep you in suspense, I shall lay out the key facts now, but after that, I think you should return home to Mrs Watson. Sleep if you can. For tomorrow, we are men of serious purpose.'

***

Not for the first time, as Holmes took me through his reasoning and his plan of action, I felt a familiar, creeping sense of my own foolishness. As explained by my friend, it *did* seem the very essence of simplicity. Every piece of the puzzle connected to every other, fitting snugly and revealing a portrait hitherto obscured.

At the same time, I was made aware once more of the true breadth of my friend's gifts. It was not in the power of ordinary men to make those connections, to see the picture in spite of the pieces.

What happened next would be dangerous. It might even prove tragic. Yet, somehow, it was not fear that I felt. It was a peculiar, particular sense of duty, unlike any I experienced in any other sphere of my life. I had served Queen and Country, but I still felt fear when the bullets flew. In the service of Sherlock Holmes, my only misgiving was the concern that I might fail our greater cause and contribute somehow to a miscarriage of justice. I could imagine no greater failure.

I returned home, as Holmes suggested, though I knew Mary and the rest of the household would be abed. I poured myself a final glass of whisky and took to my study.

There was one more story pressing insistently upon my consciousness, a final piece of the *other* puzzle. The one Holmes had set me at the beginning of this case.

I fumbled through my papers for half an hour before I found what I was looking for. It took me a further quarter hour to steel myself what I knew I was about to read.

The Lambeth Devil

Paul Birch

The manuscript with which I settled into my chair was a long forgotten one. Although, perhaps it would be more correct to say that I had put the case from my mind, for it was an affair of a most unsettling nature and re-reading it, I remained disturbed by the outcome of that singular and troubled day. I am a man for whom the past usually proves instructive, but our dark encounter with the Lambeth Devil returns nothing to me but a shiver of fear. Nevertheless, it falls to me, as an honest chronicler, to remedy its absence from the record. Perhaps, in confronting it afresh, I might discover something to mitigate its terrors.

The year, according to the near unreadable scrawl atop the first page, had been 1886. My happiness had not yet been made complete, having not met my beloved Mary, but even so, I remembered being content in my work and those adventures I shared with my friend. I was ill-prepared for such an inauspicious day, in which the very world seemed to cease its merry spin and the sun to shroud itself in black. I woke before six having had the most curious dreams: bloody remembrances of Maiwand nightmarishly entwined with a desperate run through the cramped alleyways of London, pursued by a creature of such dread that my newly conscious mind immediately dismissed its image from my memory. It left, however, in its wake, anxiety and shortness of breath.

Further sleep seeming neither possible nor desirable, I washed and moved quietly to our sitting room. Holmes, I noticed, had not returned from his most recent investigation. A fresh clue had recently presented itself in a knotty and he had wasted no time in procuring the services of that magnificent bloodhound which had been so invaluable to us in resolving the puzzle of the Sign of Four. A hunt in the dark for a woman in black seemed to me to be a fool's errand. I could not understand why he had not waited for the light of day, until I realised there was to be no light of day. A thick fog had descended across the city. Yet, this fuliginous event was most peculiar in its aspect. You may, if you were in the Capital at the time, recall the day when the fog abandoned its usual greys and yellows for a most unnatural green. The colour alarmed me as if it were an infection in a wound. Had I been a doctor to the climate I would have proclaimed it very sick indeed. The cure, however, was beyond me.

My musings were abruptly interrupted, the door flying open with such force that I leapt from my seat, ready to set upon any intruder, and found myself face to face with a wild-eyed Holmes.

'It will not do, Watson!' he cried, his nostrils flaring as if he were a hound aroused in the fury and frustration of a hunt. 'This simply cannot be allowed to continue.'

I opened my mouth to speak but soon realised that his turbulent state, expressing itself in a wild ritual of kicking off his shoes and flinging his heavy woollen coat across the table, left him in no mood to listen. 'How is it that even the very weather contends against me? Is it not enough that I must strive against villainy and vagabonds? Am I also to be continually confounded by the English elements?' At this he picked up his Persian slipper and, instead of reaching for his usual relief, hurled the entire object at the window. 'Damnable weather!' He shouted with such vehemence that I wondered if our upcoming shared breakfast would consist entirely of my consoling him.

Then came Mrs Hudson's deliberate knock. No doubt she, fearing for her windows, had come to try and distract us both with tea, eggs, and toast. 'Mr Holmes,' she said opening the door, 'You have a visitor.' She stepped back and revealed a formidable figure in an expensive morning coat, scrutinising the chaos of our small sitting room with undisguised contempt. Mrs Hudson made quick her exit.

'I have come early and I make no apology,' said the gentleman, removing his gloves and flexing his thick fingers, as if warming for a bare-knuckle brawl. 'I note your woman did not trouble to introduce me properly.' Holmes eyes narrowed at the remark, and I watched as his long limbs, which had been wildly sprawled across the settee, rearrange themselves into a more formal pose. He then turned his remorseless attention entirely upon our uninvited guest.

'You need no introduction, Lord Meiros, for you are as painfully obvious as the ingrowing toenail on your left foot. I am surprised, however, to see you so mindful of courtesies when you have no intention of staying more than a few minutes. Indeed, I am truly sorry that your stay at the Langham proved to be so unsatisfactory; although I am sure you will be able to catch up on your rest once you have taken your carriage on the eight o'clock train to Cardiff. You have lost both time and sleep and you take out your loss upon the very people from whom you require assistance. Does it not then strike you as absurd that, given your situation, you freely abandon courtesy whilst at the same time demanding it from your fellows?'

I could not help but allow a half-smile to creep across my face at seeing Holmes unsettle the confidence of this noble giant. Lord Meiros struggled to regain his composure but eventually stuttered, 'You, sirs, are not my fellows!'

***

'Indeed, we are not,' replied Holmes. 'And we wish you good day.'

Lord Meiros' expression was caught somewhere between fury and bewilderment. Had this been the Dark Ages, I have no doubt that the Lord would have sent immediately for pyre and kindling, intending to twice-burn Holmes at the stake: once for witchcraft and once for insolence. The latter being the greater crime. He moved towards the door and then turned back towards us.

'Gentlemen, you would do well to reconsider your treatment of me. I am a man of considerable influence and, as such, my affairs are not my own. An intrusion 'pon my business does not merely inconvenience me, it inconveniences high men of industry and it would not be too much to say, the Crown itself. You would do well to listen, for a successful outcome in this case may well prove to be most profitable for you both.'

Holmes smiled thinly. 'I am otherwise engaged, Lord Meiros. If a crime has been committed, I suggest you avail yourself of the police force.'

'Damn your eyes! How am I to do that when no crime has been committed? My man is missing, sir. Missing! And I need you to find him. I will pay you anything you require. D'you hear me? Anything.'

'Money does not interest me,' replied Holmes, 'and if your need is so very great then perhaps you might reconsider coming into a person's place of business and barking orders as if it were your own.'

Meiros' hands gripped hard the silver head of his walking cane as he sought to suppress his anger. 'You are right, Mr Holmes. Forgive me. I would be most obliged if you would simply hear my predicament. I will pay you for your time and then you are at liberty, of course, to offer further assistance if you so please.'

'Excellent!' cried Holmes. 'Pray, my Lord, take a seat and furnish us with the details.'

Lord Meiros looked with some scepticism at the untidy chair to which Holmes was now pointing. It was covered in papers and contained a veterinary's fleam, a broken electrical coil and several etching needles. Our visitor looked to me, clearly suggesting I should address the matter, and I found myself, under the fearsome man's gaze, obliging him. Holmes rolled his eyes and our guest sat down.

'I have a man,' he began. 'My Chief Steward, Foley. Ivor Foley. He is not an educated man, being born in the valleys and raised in the coal field, but he is an extraordinarily capable one. Never sit down at Whist with my Mr Foley, Gentlemen, for he memorises every dealt card with extraordinary ease. He has the remarkable ability to retain information and juggle figures in his mind without ever once setting them down on paper. I suspect that it is this mental gift which has prevented him from learning to read and write, for his very genius has removed the need of it.'

Holmes' eyes began to light up with interest and he leaned forward. 'Do you mean to say, Lord Meiros, that the chief steward who manages your affairs has neither written nor read a single letter?'

'Indeed, that is the case, Mr Holmes. You understand that my business is the excavation of coal. The life blood of the British Empire. The day-to-day running of the enterprise is largely conducted via word of mouth. Foley has excellent relationships with the various pit-bosses and miners for he comes from the same stock. When I send him here to London to negotiate the selling of my coal, something he does, par excellence, he simply uses my seal to sign the necessary documentation.'

'But,' I interrupted, 'is it not a hazard that he might place your seal on a document which might compromise or cheat you?'

'It has never been a concern,' replied Lord Meiros, 'for I supply coal to Her Majesty's Government and not the common jack-in-trades. The Government is reliant upon my continual supply. Were they to cheat me, why then, I would use my influence within the community and the mine would be shut. The mine is a fruitful one and even a day's interruption would cause a good deal of chaos. No, it is not fear for my business that has brought me here. It is that my extraordinary employee came to London and has disappeared.'

'How long has he been gone?' asked Holmes.

'Since the twelfth of last month,' replied our visitor.

'And yet, your business has not been inconvenienced?' continued my friend, with a mysterious smile on his face.

'Not in the least. The coal is arranged and shipped as if nothing was wrong and yet no one has heard or seen of Ivor Foley in over five weeks.'

'But that is not quite the whole truth is it, Lord Meiros?' provoked Holmes, his smile now verging on mockery. I saw Lord Meiros shift uncomfortably in his seat.

'Whatever do you mean?' he said in severe tone.

'You receive copies of the documents upon which Mr Foley affixes your mark.'

'I do. From his person or by the post or by other courier depending on the matter at hand.'

'And whilst the coal is still being shipped some of the documents have ceased to arrive, am I not correct?' pursued Holmes.

Lord Meiros puffed out his cheeks in exasperation. He appeared to want to bellow his frustration but settled instead for a warning. 'You are, Mr Holmes, but you must not speak of this! To anyone! D'you hear me! If it were to come out that my operation were in even the slightest jeopardy then I would surely lose valuable contracts which have been in place since the mine first opened, over seventy-five years ago. Yes, the documents have stopped but they did not stop when Foley first went missing.'

'No, in fact, they came to an end in the past few days,' said Holmes quietly.

'How in the Devil's name d'you know that?' He leant forward and snarled. 'You have been spying on me—for you know my name before I gave it, the train on which I intend to travel and even my medical complaints! This will not stand!' Suddenly, the peer was on his feet, his cheeks crimson with fury.

Holmes chuckled at the extraordinary display. 'It is perfectly clear, Lord Meiros, from the way that you entered the room that your left foot was causing you pain. You could put full weight on it and so it was not a fracture or a sprain. The irritation was uncomfortable but not pressing and so I deduced an ingrowing toenail. A bad blister might account for the matter but as your shoes are clearly over six months old, I discounted that possibility. That you were Lord Meiros is clear from the emblem on your ring; indeed, it is the very signature ring with which you make your own mark. I have made it my business to acquaint myself with the rings of all the noble houses of Europe. No doubt your Mr Foley has its twin.'

Lord Meiros huffed and puffed, reluctant to acknowledge Holmes' perspicacity. 'He does. The only other one of its kind. But what of my hotel and the train? How come you to know my arrangements?'

'I have not gained a practice as a consulting detective without being able to tell whether or not a man has had sufficient sleep. You are a practical man, of some importance in the business world. A man of your station would most likely stay at the Langham; it is the most conveniently placed for the Cardiff train whilst also the only one suitable for his Lordship's undoubtedly high standards. The morning papers mention a rather riotous party held there, last night, by the young Lord Gilbey on the occasion of his eighteenth birthday—the consequences of which are marked under his Lordship's eyes. Having arrived here at this early hour proves that you wish to waste no further time and, as your travelling bag appears behind you, you are clearly bound for the next train home, which, according to my Bradshaw is the 8.00.'

'And the documents?' spluttered our guest. 'How on earth did you know they had ceased to arrive?'

'Your key lieutenant has been gone for weeks and you have done nothing,' said Holmes sharply. Lord Meiros moved to protest but was silenced by a flick of my friend's hand. 'You say the coal has moved in normal fashion and so the engines turned. It is only now you have come to me. Why? Because something new has occurred or rather something old has ceased to occur. The documents have failed to arrive and so you rushed to me.'

***

There was a silence in the room as Holmes presented his theory. 'It is the very truth, Mr Holmes. Will you assist me in this matter?'

'No,' said Holmes. 'I'm afraid I am not in the least bit interested in ensuring the supply of his Lordship's contracts.'

'But, Holmes,' I said. 'What of the man, Foley? What if he is in danger?'

'Present me the evidence of such a hazard and I might consider it. In the meantime, I wish your Lordship a very pleasant journey home.' Holmes waved the man away as if he were a wasp at a picnic.

'Damn your eyes!' shouted the noble, turning on his heel and exiting in an entitled apoplexy. His rage could be still heard as he reached the street, neatly matched to the strange weather.

'Oh, don't look at me like that, Watson. The fellow was insufferably rude. It is his own mess, let him clear up. He has, after all, considerable resources. The case is of no interest to me.'

I was about to respond when a second clamour was to be heard: a tremendous barking from outside. As I was nearest the window I looked down upon the fog-bound street to see Mr Sherman, owner of that fine bloodhound, Toby, in the process of tying an assorted menagerie of creatures to our railing. 'It's Mr Sherman, Holmes,' I said, 'and it seems he's brought his household with him. No doubt you are taking Toby out in the further pursuit of your prey?'

'As usual, your observations, whilst logical, are incorrect, Watson. I made no such arrangement with—'

My friend's words were obscured by the opening of the front door and a cacophonous array of barking, squeals and clucks from the assorted dogs, badgers, pigs and fowl with which Mr Sherman constantly surrounded himself. The pained lament of Mrs Hudson at the embarrassing assemblage before her added to the din. Within moments, Mr Sherman himself was before us, white as a sheet.

'Mr Holmes,' he cried. 'Forgive me for the chaos. But I have brought my animals to you with good reason. I fear grave danger may come upon them were I to leave them at home.'

'How so?' replied Holmes gently, concerned at the man's distress. My friend could play at being imperious when roused, but his care for those in his circle was fierce.

Mr Sherman was shaking as he spoke, 'The Devil, Mr Holmes. The devil is walking Lambeth!'

**

I am by no means of a superstitious inclination but stepping out into that peculiar and unsettling fog was not for the faint of heart. Mr Sherman had given us a neighbouring address to visit and we had procured a Hansom cab to take us there. The driver took one look at Mr Sherman and feared for the interior of his vehicle, but our curious "Noah" had no desire to head back to his Lambeth dwelling, preferring instead to take his beloved creatures to the safety of his sister's home in Stockwell. We left the terrified man in Baker Street surrounded by the caterwauling of his remarkable flock and, as our carriage moved, the strange company soon disappeared into the mists.

**

The journey was like no other. We proceeded slowly for neither horse nor groom could see very far ahead. Indeed, it was a wonder that the cabbie was out at all. The air felt thick with gloom and I noticed my own spirits sink into a sadness and a dread for which I could not account.

Holmes, for his part, did not seem to pay the bizarre weather any attention and settled his mind on a small pocket manual of physiology which he had chosen to carry with him. I, on the other hand, stared out into the strange green mists with more than a little unease. I was just beginning to settle into the practice of attempting to determine our location by deciphering the dark shapes of the mysterious buildings which occasionally penetrated the mist when, all of a sudden, our carriage came to a sharp halt. Our terrified horse whinnied at a high pitch having been surprised by something on the road.

Holmes and I were soon equally surprised, as we caught sight of a wild and deranged figure staring into our carriage from the street. He was an older gentleman and in professional attire. I had him marked as some kind of clerk or legal secretary. His manner, however, was far from contained and his hysteria was utterly at odds with his respectable garb.

'You must return, gentlemen! Do not go this way for Hell itself has opened its doors!' And, at this, he began to hammer on our door.

'Please, calm yourself,' I said, from the safety of our vehicle.

The stranger, however, refused to quiet and though he was close enough to whisper, his voice was loud and strained. 'Calm myself? When I have seen the fiery furnace and white angels turn black? There is no peace to be found here. I am marked. Sulphur and brimstone! Repent and turn back your carriage, gentlemen, before it's too late'

'Get out of it!' came the hoarse cry of our cabbie; with a crack of the whip, he urged our horse on, leaving the curious prophet behind on the pavement, issuing cries of further warning. Soon, he too, was dissolved into the unfathomable mists.

'What on earth do you make of that, Holmes?' I asked my companion.

'I make nothing of it except to say that in once respect the fellow is telling the truth.'

'The truth?' I said in disbelief.

'There was indeed the distinct smell of sulphur upon his person.'

'You don't mean to say you believe him?' I cried, incredulously.

'If folktales are to be believed,' replied my friend with an enigmatic smile, 'we are surely hot on the trail of our Lambeth Devil.' Upon which note, he returned to the study of his book as if nothing unusual had occurred at all. Of all the mysteries I have encountered since I first lodged at Baker Street, I have often had cause to believe that the strangest was Sherlock Holmes himself.

**

At a quarter to the hour, our lengthy journey came to an end; we finally found ourselves at the address which Mr Sherman had pressed into our hand. It was the residence of one Mrs Holly, a neighbour of Mr Sherman.

Mrs Holly's yard was filled with blood.

An unusually large hog lay on her back, quartered from head to hind by some butchery. The damp of the fog seemed to keep the discharged fluid moist, as if something wanted to maintain the freshness of the gore. Yet it was clear that the creature had met its end for a purpose other than to put food on someone's table—the only further work that had been done upon the unfortunate creature was that its innards had been removed and scattered about its corpse. Heart and liver on one side, kidneys and split stomach upon the other.

It put me in mind of the sort of dark ritual that one might find in the Americas or the pages of a penny dreadful. There seemed no rational reason as to why the giant sow had been gutted in this way. I could see why Mr Sherman had fled, fearing for the creatures under his care.

'We came down to this,' said Mrs Holly evenly. 'A sight to see, ain't it? And heaven only knows what the neighbours make of it. Happened in the night, Mr Holly reckons, for he is what tends to the pig since we got it. He mucked it out late and we hears it snuffling well into the night so it can't have happened but in the queer hours of the morning when he was woke.'

Holmes was poking around the creature, taking several hairs from its back. 'It's an unusual breed, I think, Mrs Holly. I suspect not the tenderest meat and not young enough to rear offspring. Why, may I ask, did you purchase this particular specimen?'

'Only to stretch our pennies, Mr Holmes. Beggars can't be choosers and when the police wanted rid of them at auction, I thought we could turn a small shilling on it come winter,' replied Mrs Holly. 'Not that it's worth much now,' she added with a pained look upon her weathered face.

'I am sure you can put this in the hand of a capable man and make some profit yet,' remarked Holmes.

'Oh, you think so, do you? After it's been got by the fiend? There's not a soul round here would put that on their fork, even if we was giving it away. No. No good will come of this. No good at all.'

'What's this, Mrs Holly?' came a nervous voice from the doorway to the yard. 'Who are these gentlemen and what are they doing in my yard?' The husband, it transpired, had been watching us for some time.

'These are friends of Mr Sherman, Oliver. He said as to how they might get to the bottom of what happened' replied the wife, clearly worried about the whole affair. 'This is Mr Holmes and Doctor Watson.'

'We don't need detectives and medics. We need a minister of the church. There's devilry here, Mr Holmes, and all your cleverness can't put it to rights. I can tell you straight who did this. It was Satan himself!' He stared us both directly in the eye, as if daring us to contradict him.

'And how can you be sure of that, Mr Holly?' I asked as respectfully as I could manage.

'Because I seen him. I seen him myself, up there.' At this the husband pointed to an upstairs window overlooking the yard. 'I heard a rattling of my windows in the night. Woke me up it did. So I got up, for Mrs Holly don't wake when she don't have to. I thought it must have been her what left them open.'

'I did not leave 'em open and you know it, Oliver,' protested the woman.

'I know it now, Mary! Don't I know that to my own cost, now?' answered the husband. 'For on entering the room I see its windows wide and there, God help my soul, I see the Devil. Flying in the air. It's face looking right at me. Arms clawing at the desk. Now you might think me mad, Mr Holmes, or a liar, and it makes no difference to me if you do, for I seen it and I can't unsee it, not for as long as I live.'

'Why, I don't see any reason to doubt you, Mr Holly,' said Holmes, who had finished his examination of the pig. 'Can I ask you what the upstairs room is for?'

'Why it ain't for anything, Mr Holmes,' answered Mrs Holly. We used to rent it but have not had a lodger there for over a year, so we keeps our odds and sods in there. Mr Holly do hate to throw anything away for he knows it might come in handy.'

'And you mentioned a desk. Next to the window, I assume. Tell me, does it contain anything of value?' enquired Holmes, fixing his gaze upon the husband.

'Why, do you think we have anything of value in this house, Mr Holmes? We are not as prosperous as all that,' replied Mrs Holly. Mr Holly remained still and silent.

'So, nothing was taken?' asked Holmes refusing to shift his gaze from Mr Holly.

'Nothing at all, Mr Holmes, not that it's any business of yours. Now I can't say as I like the way you're looking at me,' said Mr Holly, clearly affronted by the interrogation. 'I say I seen the devil and you're asking questions about a blessed desk? Why, if you don't believe me, you can see his prints and if that isn't proof of the matter, I don't know what is.' At this, Mr Holly pointed to a part of the yard I hadn't noticed. There, plain as day, were the small prints of cloven hooves. With the distraction of the massacred sow, I had failed to notice them.

'I have already observed them, Mr Holly,' replied Holmes. 'Evidently, this Lambeth Devil walked into your yard before he flew to your window. And you saw him fly?'

'He was there, all right, hovering at the window. I sees him and turns on the lamp saying the Lord's prayer and he vanishes from sight. It takes me a moment but eventually I get the pluck to come direct to the window but then see nor hide nor hair of him. Gone,' replied the man with a deep conviction in his voice.

'And there was no ladder?' I ventured.

'A ladder? What use has Lucifer of a ladder? Besides, it's a small yard, not Hampton Court. I only took but a minute to recover myself and I tell you that when I got there, there was no devil and no ladder. Just an open window and the pig as you see it now.'

'Could he have climbed the ivy?' I ventured, for there was a strong crop of it growing up the sides of the house.

'Excellent, Watson!' triumphed Holmes, grabbing a handful of the vine and giving it a tug. 'But hardly enough to support the weight of a grown man.'

'A child, then?' I offered.

'T'weren't no child. I tell you. This creature had an ancient face. Weathered and worn,' protested Mr Holly.

'There you are, Watson. You have your riddle. No ladder, no handhold save the ivy, which will not bear a man's weight and yet the creature had a mature face. And so we have the explanation that the thing flew to the window. Capital! And to think we almost spent ourselves in the pursuit of a missing administrator! I think this a much more galvanising chase.'

'Well, I'm glad someone is enjoying hisself,' said Mrs Holly sourly, 'for I don't find this a bright matter. Not in the least.'

'Mrs Holly!' said Holmes warmly. 'Forgive me! I do not intend to make light of your distress. Though can I recommend you report this matter to the constabulary, for I am sure they will be interested in the criminal damage you have suffered.'

'Out! Out of it!' cried Mr Holly, suddenly. 'We've had enough bother without the police coming in and making a fuss. Why, if it weren't for buying this cursed pig from them in the first place p'raps we wouldn't have seen any of this devilry!' The enraged husband then picked up a nearby spade, which he no doubt used in the sty, and began to brandish it in our direction.

'Come along, Watson,' whispered Holmes in my ear. 'I believe it is time we caused some trouble elsewhere.'

***

Our Hansom, now retained by Holmes for the day at the expense of a half-sovereign, deposited us outside Brixton Police station. Our arrival immediately attracted a miserable flurry of beggars, those who dared to ply their trade directly beneath the eyes of the law. These poor unfortunates came swiftly out of the mists with various cries of appeal. 'Gis' a farthing!' cried one in a thick Scottish brogue, already pawing at my pockets. His breath was as heavy as his accent, equal parts gin and cheap tobacco. I brushed him aside only to find two more of his like coming on fast behind. Holmes, meanwhile, was using his exceptional stride to outpace another.

'Move yerselves!' came a commanding cry from somewhere in the fog. Almost immediately, the mendicants scattered, and I expected to see a member of the local constabulary. Instead came the sorrowful sight of a crippled man, emerging from the dark. 'Out of it, now, before the coppers catches ya!'

A more harrowing sight it was hard to imagine. The fellow, dressed in little more than scraps, pushed himself along on what looks to be a child's wooden trolley. A wracking cough shook a fragile frame that was limbless from the waist down. It called to mind the many amputees from my days in Afghanistan and I could not refuse his outstretched hand. How many legs had I been called to remove to preserve a life? Too many in that bloody conflict. I found my own hands shaking at the bitter memory.

'God bless you, for your noble deed, sir,' the man said, before rolling himself slowly on. I had only just donated to that soul when two identical children with shocks of bright red hair began tugging at my trouser leg. It took me a moment to realise that both were blind; milk-white cataracts stretched across their eyes and the cruelties of this present age began to further weigh on my soul. I pressed a few pennies into their tiny hands and wondered what other sadnesses might suddenly appear when Holmes' voice boomed out through the fog: 'Come Watson! We have work to do.' I moved up the steps, following his voice, and soon found myself inside the offices of the Lambeth police.

***

'The area's thick with them,' said Constable Rowe. 'They says beggars can't be choosers but they chose Lambeth alright. We lock 'em up from time to time but it don't do no good. Besides, what's the good of giving them a roof and a square meal at our expense? Only encourages 'em. No, Mr Holmes, let winter claim 'em and be done.' The constable was preening his moustache as he talked. He was clearly a man of great pride—if little charity—for the brass of his uniform was brightly polished; I fancied he must pay regular attention to his mirror.

'You recently auctioned off some rather large pigs—a Tamworth among them?' asked Holmes.

'Pigs? We did as it happens, three of them, what of it?' responded the Constable.

'I was wondering how the police came by them?'

'Come down in the world, 'aven't you, Mr Holmes?' laughed Rowe. 'Oh, they're always talking you up round 'ere. How you do your own kind of policin' for royalty and the like and yet here you are asking poor old constable Rowe about pigs. Times must be hard for the amateur "detective." Oh yes, oh yes, indeed!'

'I am simply curious,' replied Holmes, ignoring the constable's scornful manner.

'Curious is the word. No sooner do they leave here than two of the creatures end up dead and I don't mean on the butcher's hook neither.'

'Two?' I cried.

'Didn't I just say so, Doctor? One went to the Westalls on Lower Fore Street and t'other to Salamanca, can't remember the name now—but a low couple if you ask me. Anyway, in a matter of days someone's had a pop at both porkies. Course, the Westalls come back asking for us to find that what did it but as I told them then, Her Majesty's Constabulary have got better things to do than spend our valuable time looking into prankery.'

'Prankery!' I protested, but Holmes stopped me with a sharp look.

'A nuisance indeed, Constable,' said my friend, 'for we have come from a third house where the final pig was similarly dispatched last night.'

Constable Rowe raised an eyebrow before easing back into another self-satisfied smile, 'Is that so? Well, it's a good job you're on the case, Mr Holmes. This sort of work sounds much more along your lines. Credit where it's due, Mr Holmes, for it seems you do have your uses. I'll leave the twopenny-ha'penny matter in your hands'

'Quite so,' said Holmes, 'this need not draw you from your very important duties. Though I would be grateful if you could tell me when the two pigs met their end.'

'Yesterday and the day before yesterday,' sniffed Rowe.

'And the pigs themselves? How came they into your hands?'

Constable Rowe puffed himself up, 'Well, now, that were some real policing. Broke up a nasty ring of roughs working out of the Lambeth Coke ovens. A brute by the name of Orton Blythe was conducting all manner of trouble under the guise of that place. High stakes gambling was the least of it but there was other darker business which I shan't go into. Not before it's come to trial. Anyways, we had our eye on the place, but we couldn't get near enough without rousing suspicion. Besides it was respectable on the outside—coke there going straight to the army itself, with Whitehall approval, so we daren't move too boldly, not without evidence. We'd not set eyes on Blythe, the foreman, but word was getting out that although he never seemed to leave the ovens, he was maintaining a rather large felonious enterprise. Behind all the noise and heat of the coking yard, other quiet deeds were being done by him and his gang. Long story short we collared a poor beggar by the name of Lazarus. Lazarus used to work the mines before losing his legs and had somehow squared an occasional nightwatchman job through some of his old collier friends. When we pulled him one day for possessing stolen goods, he agreed to turn on Blythe and his cronies. So last week, he tips us the wink and we bring the whole lot down.'

'Remarkable,' said Holmes. 'So you have Blythe in custody?'

'Ah, well, he absconded but we were able to collar many of the gang and recovered a good deal of money and stolen property. A significant blow to the criminal underworld and I was proud to play my part. It's not on the level of pig-hunting, Mr Holmes, but I'm pleased to say justice was done.'

'Congratulations, Constable. Dare I wonder where your Mr Lazarus is now?' enquired Holmes with a curiously delighted expression on his face.

'One good turn deserves another. After his assistance we procured him the role of assistant foreman back at the coke ovens.' Rowe laughed again. 'Perhaps you can pay him a visit and he can help you with your confusion over the pigs.'

***

'Well, Watson,' cried Holmes, 'I fear I must go against my better judgement and assist Lord Meiros, after all.'

'What ever do you mean, Holmes?' I spluttered; we had arrived at the Lambeth Ovens and between the fog and the stinking sulphuric smoke from the large yard, I was finding it hard to draw breath.

'Why the answer to the mystery of the missing Steward, of course. I believe the solution to the puzzle lies in this very place. See, look here.' Holmes swung his walking cane towards a blackened wagon, upon which was stamped a curious emblem. 'You recognise the mark?'

I shook my head. 'Oh, come, Watson it is the very same emblem as on the ring of our obnoxious visitor,' scolded Holmes. 'It was before you this very morning. Surely, you can do better than that?'

'That is Lord Meiros' wagon?' I said in surprise.

'That it is,' came a rasping voice from somewhere in the smoke. We turned and heard the sound of strange rolling wheels as the legless beggar we had seen outside the police station emerged slowly from the murk. Despite having the foreman job, he clearly had not left his former occupation entirely behind him. 'What can I do for you, gentlemen? Lost, are you?' At this he gave a sharp smile. 'Treacherous fog today sirs, and more than one stray soul has stumbled into the ovens here today. Nothing but muck and marks in a place like this. Tread here, gentlemen, with those fine shoes of yours, and you'll be leaving a coal trail 'cross your carpets for months. Happy to show you to the gate and gets you back safely on your way.'

We looked down at the seemingly pathetic figure of Constable Rowe's informant, Lazarus the beggar. On closer inspection, he was not quite as frail as he had previously seemed; his arms had considerable musculature and his wracking cough had vanished. His clothes too were not as worn as I remembered. They were simply stained with coal dust—in the fog and chaos of our earlier encounter, I had mistaken this for holes and tears. A leather pouch hung from a cord around his neck and from his belt, both cosh and knife. I began to wish I had brought my revolver, for there was something ill about the man: a quiet menace which, though not displayed directly, seemed to hang about him like the curious green fog which surrounded and infused the city.

'I wish to speak with the new assistant foreman,' asked Holmes coldly. 'Would that be you?'

'Tis today,' replied Lazarus, 'though who knows tomorrow? We've had trouble and the men is quite upset. Work is hard at the best of times. Can't say any of us likes it at the worst.'

'You're talking of Orton Blythe.' I said. No sooner had the name left my lips than Lazarus spat angrily at the ground.

'I curse him. I curse him, sirs, for twas him what turned an honest day's work into darkness. The ovens are greedy and burn both day and night. A man who wants to lose his soul past midnight can always find our doors open. The law don't peek here because the place is respectable. But also too dirty for men with crisp cuffs to venture into. I mourn it. I weep that this place became a place where Blythe and men of worse character still could come and drink and gamble and store what they had taken from the pockets of others. I thank God that the police came when they did.'

Holmes raised an eyebrow. The man's impassioned speech had clearly failed to move him. I, on the other hand, wanted to shake the fellow's hand.

'You have a sty there,' mentioned Holmes, pointing in the direction of a makeshift pigpen. 'Is it not unusual to keep animals in a Government coking yard?'

Lazarus shifted uncomfortably, 'None of my doing,' he said coldly.

'And yet you have procured fresh hogs?' pursued Holmes. 'Tamworths, if I'm not mistaken?'

'Nothing fresh about them. Them's full-grown,' said Lazarus. His tone was rapidly gaining steel.

Holmes chuckled.

'Forgive me. I merely meant that the pigs were recently bought.'

'Says who?' countered the assistant foreman.

'I do. Blythe's pigs were sold after the raid. The police put you in charge and one of your first tasks appears to have been to purchase new livestock. Rather than, as might be expected, the production of coke.'

'My concerns are my own. Now I've flapped my mouth out of respect to you gentlemen but I've work to be done, so I'll thank you now for leaving. Gate's behind you.'

At this, the fellow sprung with surprising agility from his trolley and, producing a set of weathered crutches, raised himself to meet our gaze. It was an unsettling sight for his eyes were piercing and he suspended himself with astonishing poise, worthy of a circus acrobat. After a final stare of warning, he turned his muscular back and made his way towards the dome shaped coke ovens, where men shovelled in the intense heat.

'Do you note it, Watson?' whispered Holmes. 'His workers at the ovens?'

'What of them?' I answered.

'They are turning black,' he replied.

'From the coke and smoke,' I replied. It seemed the most obvious occurrence to me, but I had grown accustomed to Holmes drawing revelation from less.

'No matter how much you wipe your shoes you cannot get rid of the coal.' Holmes was staring at the figure of the foreman moving swiftly towards the ovens and grinning with childish delight.

'Holmes, I really don't see—'

'The marks, Watson. On the ground! Look at his prints!'

And I looked and saw the truth before me. The prints from the crutches were the same as those from Mr Holly's yard.

***

'The age of the wood has caused the feet of the crutches to split. Giving the impression of a small cloven hoof.'

'How extraordinary!'

Holmes frowned and tutted. 'You use that word so often, Watson, that it can no longer bear any meaning. Deception is perhaps the most commonplace thing in all of Christendom. And Mr Holly's senses have been thoroughly deceived.'

'Lazarus is the Lambeth Devil,' I cried.

'Indeed. An agile man, deprived of his full weight, would surely be able to climb to that window. And given the darkness, the fog and Mr Holly's less than complete wakefulness, such a man might even be mistaken for a creature in flight.'

I narrowed my eyes in Holmes' direction.

'How long have you known?'

Holmes waved a hand dismissively.

'Oh, from the moment we saw him outside the police station, of course. A devil, he may be, Watson, but of a decidedly earthly bent. And I rather think it is time that he paid the price for his earthly crimes.'

'The killing of a pig?' I said in surprise.

'The killing of a man,' replied Holmes, his delight making way for solemnity. 'For now I have the proof, we are finally free to act. Come!'

Holmes moved quickly to where Lazarus was giving instructions to one of his men. His stride was so long and fast that I had to half-jog to keep up.

'You! I told you to sling yer hook!' called out Lazarus on our approach. Gone now was his mock-subservient demeanour. Gone too was the feigned sorrow for his lot at the criminal hands of Blythe. His face seemed cruel and ancient, and lined with contempt. The venal and selfish devil of Mr Holly's nightmares, in the flesh. I wondered that I had not seen it before.

'I will go,' cried Holmes with an urgent charge to his voice. 'When I have what I came for.'

'And what is that?'

'The ring. The seal of Lord Meiros.'

Lazarus sneered. 'So that's it. The boss sent you snooping. Well, you tell him it's with his man.' At that point the assistant foreman laughed, with a callousness that convinced me that some men are truly without soul. 'If you can find him.'

'Oh,' replied Holmes, 'you need not concern yourself on that score. I know where he and the ring are to be found.'

Lazarus, for the first time, looked afraid, but quickly rallied. 'Then, what are you asking me for?'

'Because you have kept it close to your black heart!' With lightning speed, Holmes snatched the leather pouch and ripped it from the man's neck. Lazarus gave a cry of alarm and spinning, used his crutch to topple Holmes towards the oven. The factory-man, his vest and skin blackened by his work, stumbled backwards in surprise.

'Watson!' cried Holmes, throwing the pouch towards me. It was no sooner in my fist than I found Lazarus upon me. He had abandoned his crutches and had flung himself in my direction, forcing me onto the ground. A knife was in one hand, the other was feverishly reaching for the pouch. The blade was almost at my throat when Holmes appeared, the avenging angel, my revolver in his hand, cocked, and trained on my assailant.

I was astonished, for he had taken it without my knowledge.

'That will be quite enough of that.' said Holmes evenly. Lazarus rolled from me, dropped his knife and smiled up at my companion. 'The cosh too.' Lazarus shrugged and pulled the weapon from his belt.

'What now?' said he.

'The police,' said I, furious for having been taken off-guard.

'A beggar often finds himself in possession of discarded trinkets. No crime in that.'

'No crime?' said Holmes. 'Ivor Foley wore the ring as part of his essential duties, overseeing the shipments of coal to this yard. Unbeknownst to him, however, the yard was in the control of a criminal gang run by Orton Blythe. Blythe, in turn, knew that with Meiros' seal he could control and manipulate the supply of coal to anywhere and anyone he wished. He had Foley killed and got rid of the body.'

'And you have the body, do you?' snorted Lazarus. 'The police raided this yard and they didn't find anything. All you got is words.'

'I have much more than that. Your surety that I cannot be in possession of the body accuses you. You know I cannot. Because it has been destroyed. Or should I say consumed.' At this Holmes cast his glance towards the recently welcomed pigs. 'Tamworth's. A breed not fit for the table but perfectly suited to the consumption of others. Foley was murdered and fed to the hogs. Blythe had others do it, it would seem, for a man clever enough to disguise his identity and escape from the police would have known to remove the ring first. The ring joined its owner in the belly of a pig. The beasts were then taken to police auction and sold. In desperation, you attempted to recover them, but came up empty-handed.'

I was staring at Holmes incredulously. Once more, I marvelled at his ability to weave a tale from the slenderest of threads.

Lazarus proved an ungrateful audience.

'You can't prove a damned thing!' He was grinning from ear to ear. Although clearly soundly beaten by Holmes, he had the countenance of a man celebrating a great victory.

My friend was undeterred.

'We have you at Mr Holly's yard. We have prints and a witness. The ring was in a desk by a window. You will recall, Watson, the man's uneasiness when we talked of calling the police? No doubt the creature had expelled the thing and Mr Holly discovered it when cleaning out the sty. He kept it, surely intending to sell it on quietly. Unfortunately for you, Lazarus, having killed the pig and vainly searched its empty stomach, you assumed the same narrative and climbed to the open window, intending to burglarise the house. Your luck changed, however, in an instant. For on the table by the same window, lay the prize. Upon the sudden entrance of Mr Holly you then fled.'

Lazarus' face fell. The fellow's bravado disappeared and he began to shuffle away from us awkwardly, almost as if truly ashamed. 'You speak the truth. I went to the yard and took the ring. But it was Orton who had Foley killed. I swear it.'

'He's lying, Holmes,' I murmured to my friend.

'Sherlock Holmes?' breathed Lazarus, his eyes widening in surprise.

'No, Watson. This time he's telling the absolute truth. It was Orton Blythe who murdered the man.'

'I will swear to it, Mr Holmes.' said the pitiful fellow, his hands were shaking in terror. 'I will swear to it in Court, if you have mercy upon me.'

'It takes a perverse courage to condemn oneself,' said Holmes. 'For there is no doubt in my mind that you are Orton Blythe. That you were, and have always been, in charge of this enterprise. That you used your disguise as a police informant to spread misinformation and to grant yourself a cloak of safety should any officer come too close. Believing matters to have reached a crisis, you had them raid the yard and then quickly reinstated the business knowing well that the eyes of the law were now focused elsewhere. Why else would you buy more swine if not to continue in your wickedness?'

Holmes was interrupted by a sudden flurry of hot coals. For, quick as a fox, Blythe had seized the nearby coke shovel and flung its contents at his accuser.

'Look out, Holmes!' I said, pushing him out of the path. The thick coat I had worn as protection against the damp found itself afire and I was forced to shake it from me and stamp it out upon the ground. When I looked up again both Holmes and Blythe had completely vanished into in the terrible fog.

***

An hour hence, we made our way back to Baker Street in the cab that had waited so patiently. Even Holmes' deductive powers had been of little use when it came to tracking Blythe in the dark and fog. It was a bitter victory. Blythe ought to have swung for his dreadful crimes. Instead, we were forced to take comfort that he had been discomfited and displaced.

Holmes rarely spoke of him; although, on a later occasion, he once inferred that Blythe was to rise through the ranks to become one of Moriarty's chief lieutenants. Whether this is so, I do not know, but the rogue was certainly wise enough to stay out of Holmes' path in the years that followed.

The matter was explained at Brixton Police station, forcing Constable Rowe to eat a healthy portion of humble pie. He was later, however, awarded a commendation for a second raid on the coke ovens—where other, more recent bodies were found. We informed Lord Meiros of the death of his steward and though he went through the motions of sorrow, the return of his ring was clearly uppermost in his mind. An amount was charged for Holmes' services and it is fair to say, it was one of the largest that I can recall. Chiefly, I think to offset his Lordship's callousness with a pain he would mark. Certainly, Holmes himself gained no satisfaction from the affair.

'The death of that unfortunate man, Watson,' he said, gloomily poking the fire in our lodgings, 'weighs heavily upon me.'

'But Foley was killed before you were even involved, Holmes.' I tried to reason with him for although the fog of London had lifted there was another in the heart and mind of my friend.

***

'You will recall the distressed man in the street. He stopped our carriage.'

'The lunatic?' I said.

'An unkind word, Watson, and ill applied. A man, afraid of the wickedness of his time. The fog descended and, no doubt, he stumbled into that den of murderers and thieves. He smelled the sulphur and saw the flames and wondered if, truly, he had not fallen into hell itself. I am not a man who often dwells on the worlds beyond, but I am not entirely convinced that he was wrong.'

At this Holmes withdrew into himself and spent the next several days in silence. I silently cursed the weather for obstructing immediate justice. Indeed, it is my constant hope that there might be a final justice, above the actions of the courts, which would be a true remedy. Although, in my darker moments, it is hard not to imagine that the devil himself leant Blythe a hand, first in seeding such wickedness in his heart and then procuring his escape.

Holmes and I were eventually distracted by further cases, further chances to impose some sense of justice on the shadows surrounding us, but I found it hard to shake a dark image in my mind. The fog eventually lifted but my terrible dreams continued for some months. They were always the same. I lay on the floor of a pigsty with Lazarus's ancient face hovering above me, laughing at the cruelties of men and our constant failure to stop them.

The Woman Who Wasn't: Part Eight

Those final lines resounded in my head. *The cruelties of men and our constant failure to stop them.* A powerful phrase, driven by an even more potent sensation, impossible to articulate complete.

Those nightmares of Lazarus, of the "Lambeth Devil" had eventually faded, but I knew that, in all the cases that had followed in their wake, I had shut down many of my finer feelings, preserved them for home and hearth. I felt for those whose fates were placed in our hands and, as I said, I was faithful to my duty. But though Holmes and I had faced down evildoers since, I had refused to let the evil touch me in the same way it had done once. It was something to be fought, not something to take to heart.

Holmes knew this. A man as observant as he could not have failed to do so. But he never rebuked me for it. Nor, indeed, did he congratulate me on finding the emotional restraint in which he took what I could only assume to be comfort.

But he also knew, from the moment Sir Harrison Frain stepped into the rooms at Baker Street that we were careening towards an encounter with an evil as ferocious as any we had faced before.

And so he put me on a path. He forced me to confront our recent history, not as a documentarian but as a detective. As a surgeon. He pointed me, so subtly, towards cases that would prepare me for what I was looking at now. Cases about loss and identity, and the great chasm into which the human creature can descend without the succour of his peers.

We reached the club where we had arranged to meet Sir Harrison Frain, ten minutes before the time we had given the frustrated knight of the realm. The morning after Miss Frain's arrival, Holmes had sent word for him to meet us at Baker Street, as soon as was convenient.

In that meeting, he informed Sir Harrison that his daughter had been located, was in good health and would be returned to him as soon as it was safe to do so.

Before that, however, there was the matter of the mysterious young man. Our investigations, said Holmes, had led us to the conclusion that we were dealing with a dangerous, violent ruffian who would continue to bedevil the Frain family unless stopped.

We were close, Holmes insisted, to tracking him down and delivering him to the good officers of Scotland Yard, but we required one final piece of information. A piece of information that only one person could provide.

The man that Sir Harrison had employed to first track his daughter.

Might we be permitted to speak to him?

There had been some disagreement over the wisdom of this course, but eventually Sir Harrison was prevailed upon to contact the man he had hired and deliver him to us, to answer our questions, this afternoon, at his club.

My hand curled around the pistol in my pocket.

'Quick, Watson!'

A cab was moving slowly up the road towards the club entrance. Holmes dragged me by the elbow to the corner of the building, where we watched, hidden, as Sir Harrison and his cut-price detective disembarked.

The man was tall, though slight, and heavily bearded. He wore a pair of dark spectacles that all but obscured his eyes. Beneath his heavy cap, what little of his hair protruded appeared thick with grease.

And yet, it seemed almost impossible that Sir Harrison Frain would not recognise his own son.

'Now, Watson!'

Holmes sprang into action, throwing himself directly into the path of Sir Harrison and Alistair Frain. I followed, my pistol drawn.

'Mr Holmes!' cried the elder man, clutching his chest with one hand, startled into near apoplexy.

'Sir Harrison,' replied Holmes calmly.

'Was there any need for you to leap from the shadows in that manner?'

'A great need, Sir Harrison,' I replied, cocking the gun. 'The preservation of your daughter's life and liberty.'

Sir Harrison did not appear to have the words to protest this new affront and simply stumbled backwards.

He stopped as his back met the point of his son's knife.

'Very clever, Mr Holmes,' said Alistair Frain, clearly shedding whatever false voice he had been employing with his father. Sir Harrison began to turn, but his son increased the pressure of the blade.

'Alistair!'

'I don't know whether to feel proud of my disguise or disgust at your inattention,' seethed the younger man. 'Yes, *Father*. The prodigal son has returned. Only not for the first time. I have returned over and over again since you first cast me into the wilderness.'

A pall fell over Sir Harrison's face. He was beginning to draw his own conclusions as to the true nature of what had and was about to happen.

'Anastasia!' he spat accusingly. 'Holmes, you said she was well. She was safe.'

'She is and she will be. But not while your son walks the streets.'

'All those times she disappeared. She has been with *him*?'

I tried to pity Sir Harrison but found it difficult.

'She, unlike her father,' I said, as levelly as I could manage, 'could not discard a family member with such ease.'

'Ease!' exploded Sir Harrison. 'There was no ease about it. My only son. My heir. Who I loved above all others—'

Alistair Frain snorted with derision.

'Your love is measured in pounds, shillings and pence, Father. I should know. You paid me handsomely, in my current guise, to find my beloved sister. My angelic other half. I don't suppose you ever employed anyone to keep tabs on my whereabouts, did you? Out of sight, out of mind.'

'I would have given you everything,' the elder Frain shot back. 'I sheltered you. I hid your sins. To keep you with me.'

'His sins?' I asked.

'Young Master Frain,' said Holmes with contained fury, 'did not begin his murderous career when he was cast from the paternal bosom. It was already well underway. Isn't that right, Sir Harrison? I made enquiries about your family, as I always do on taking a case. How many servants have left your employ mysteriously over the years, never to be seen again?'

Sir Harrison had the decency to look stricken but seemed to demonstrate insufficient sincerity for Holmes.

'Please, Sir Harrison,' said the detective, 'spare me the speech about a father's devotion. You didn't report your son when he strangled a scullery maid or savaged a gardener because they *didn't* matter, not because he *did*. But then you saw his attention turn towards his sisters. In particular, his twin.'

'My twin, as you call her, is as much like me as you are, Mr Holmes. Whatever she chooses to believe. I was a twisted, broken mirror of her *decency* and her *kindness*.' The younger Frain spat these last words like curses. 'But she refused to see it. She believed that her love could bring me around. That if she just stayed with me, she could fix everything. I did not care to be fixed. And I knew I would be forever burdened by her attempts if I didn't do something about it.'

'You planned to murder her,' said Holmes.

'If it came to it. At first, I simply wished to see her corrupted. Perhaps she might have been bearable, brought down a peg or two. Ruined, like her brother. So I let her believe that I was willing to learn about Father's business, to try and impress the old man, to come home and be a good, dutiful son. I convinced her to stay with me longer each time, telling her how much I benefited from her presence and her counsel.

Of course, the idea that Father would be beside himself with worry also appealed. And then, I heard it go round that a Sir Harrison Frain was seeking a man, capable of travelling in low circles, to track his errant daughter. It was too delicious an opportunity to pass up.'

'And the letter to Holmes and myself?' I asked.

'Ah, you're missing an important part of the story, Doctor Watson.'

'Your sister discovered your secret,' said Holmes.

Alistair grimaced.

'Such a little busybody. I had been enjoying myself. Pulling the wool over Father's eyes. Feeding little 'Stasia's delusions about her poor, beleaguered brother. It was exquisite. One night, I decided to celebrate my successes with a lady of the evening. Only she'd followed me, hadn't she? Caught me with my blade at the tart's throat. I had to keep her under lock and key for a while, until I figured out what to do for the best.'

I could feel my finger tightening on the trigger of my pistol. The glee with which this damaged young man described his exploits was finding its way inexorably through my defences.

'Then I conceived of my masterstroke,' crowed Alistair Frain, now too pleased with his own ingeniousness to hide the truth. 'Disguised as the eager little detective making his report, I sent a message to you, Mr Holmes. Taking care to discard a "earlier" draft amongst the ashes of the hearth. I knew it would draw Father to you, and he would lead you to me. Anastasia is my sister, after all. I had to give her a fighting chance.'

A sliver of sorrow worked its way into my breast. This was a broken boy and it was all too clear who had broken him most violently.

'I was fair though. I signed it with my own initial. But my loving Father had forgotten me too thoroughly to make the connection.'

'You had your sister, who you wished to destroy, at your mercy,' I interjected. 'Why involve us? Why risk your liberty? Your life?'

Alistair Frain's eyes hardened. It was the coldest gaze I had ever met.

'I wanted to see what would happen,' he said. 'It was all beginning to get a little… dull.'

'I am led to understand that killing does,' said Holmes. 'Eventually.'

'I suppose we'll soon find out. You know, it's better this way. Anastasia is a sickeningly sweet creature, but I know in my heart she meant me no ill. Our father, however, he meant every bruise.'

Sir Harrison's mouth began to open, some justification lurking on his tongue. But then a great weariness seemed to overcome him and he remained silent.

'Nothing to say to that?' Alistair pressed him.

'I will be there.'

'What?'

'Alistair. You are my son. And I will be there. When you stand in the dock and when they lead you to the gallows. I will be there with you until the end.'

A horrible, choking laughter erupted from the younger Frain.

'If I chose to let you go, Father, there would be no gallows for me. For all of Mr Holmes' skill, there is no evidence of my crimes. And the only witness is dear sweet sister who will, on hearing of my mercy, believe even more strongly in my capacity for change.'

'I am aware of all of that, Alistair. Terribly aware.'

Then Sir Harrison turned with great force and before Holmes and I could react had thrown himself and his son bodily to the ground. The knife between them plunged into the older man's chest and he let out a soul-chilling groan.

Holmes and I rushed to the men, heaving Sir Harrison free of both blade and heir.

I knelt beside the body, but it was painfully clear that there was nothing to be done.

Wide-eyed, Alistair stumbled to his feet, covered in the blood of the Frains. He made no attempt to flee, simply stood over his father's body and began to weep.

Epilogue

Some weeks later, Holmes made an unexpected call at my home. He was carrying a mangled newspaper and was, for reasons he did not immediately choose to explain, disguised as a village priest.

Mary, to her great credit, simply greeted him with a kiss on the cheek and invited him to sit down.

Holmes seemed to be in fine fettle, making a great show of the Cornish accent he had affected as part of his latest investigation. He took tea with us and told us of his adventures, amusing my wife greatly with tales of the characters he had encountered while in disguise.

After an hour or so, Mary made some domestic excuse and left us to our pipes and our whisky.

'I've not seen much of you since the Frain affair,' I said lightly.

'Which I have yet to see in print, Watson,' he chided me, in his own voice. 'Was it not sufficiently bloodthirsty for the readers of the *Strand*?'

'I received a letter from Miss Anastasia Frain requesting that I delay publication of her family's story. Until it is somewhat less painful.'

'I wonder then if it will ever find its public.'

He placed the newspaper on the table and opened it. He indicated a column towards the bottom of one of the pages. It was a report on the execution of Alistair Frain for the murder of his father.

'I take no delight in it,' I said, surprising myself as the words left my mouth.

Holmes looked shocked.

'Watson, if the day comes when you *do* take delight in the waste of a young life, we shall part company for good.'

'But I thought that's what you were trying to do,' I said, rubbing my brow with one hand. Between the whisky, the pipe smoke and the newspaper, I suddenly felt all of a fog.

'What was I trying to do?' Holmes seemed genuinely perplexed.

'Having me go through all of those old cases. You've all the details you need locked away in that steel-trap mind of yours. You didn't need me to find connections to the Frain case for you. So I imagined you were trying to reengage me in… the fight, I suppose.'

'Had you left it?'

I shrugged.

'Ah,' said Holmes, 'you feared that it had become dull. As killing had for Alistair Frain. You felt you had become numb to the evil that men do.'

'Yes, that's it, precisely.'

Holmes leant forward.

'My dear Watson. You mistook me entirely. I know that, since your marriage, since the renewed growth of your practice, that our adventures, as you are pleased to call them, have left you feeling torn. You have a home, a wife, a profession, yet you still feel compelled to join me on errands that often put your life on the line.'

He paused.

'I'm not making myself clear at all, am I?'

'It might be the whisky.'

Holmes chuckled.

'What did you deem the common denominator between the Frain case and all the other cases you revisited?'

'Missing women?'

'Ah, Watson. Sometimes I think you do it deliberately. No, not missing women. Not at their heart. They were all matters concerning *identity*.'

I tried to assemble my features in a way that suggested this had answered all of my questions. I failed miserably. Thankfully, Holmes was now in full flight and needed no further assistance.

'Who we are. Who we are to other people. Who we *wish* to be. Those questions were at the root of every case you studied. In one form or another, at the root of every case we have ever encountered. Alistair Frain met his end because he didn't care for who he was—a twin, tied to a kind, forgiving sister—and cared even less for who others wanted him to be. He was so incensed at the idea of the woman he wasn't, he never explored the man he could be. Instead, he gave into every dark urge, believing that to be rebellion.'

'And the lesson to me?'

'You assume I would be so bold as to suggest a lesson to the fearless Doctor Watson.'

'Holmes—'

'If there was a lesson, friend Watson, it was this. Married or single. Medical man or partner in fighting injustice. You are John Watson. Kind-hearted, brave and graced with a depth of feeling that I should be very sorry to see you lose.'

I was moved beyond words by this uncommon outburst from my friend but knew better than to express it.

'And you?'

Holmes took a deep draw on his pipe.

'I am an animal of a different stripe.'

I laughed at the elegance of his understatement and raised my glass to us both.

www.ingramcontent.com/pod-product-compliance
Lightning Source LLC
Chambersburg PA
CBHW021008180626
46814CB00003B/1197